THE
STEP
DAUGHTER'S
LIE

BOOKS BY TERI TERRY

The Patient

THE
STEP
DAUGHTER'S
LIE

TERI TERRY

bookouture

Published by Bookouture in 2024

An imprint of Storyfire Ltd.
Carmelite House
50 Victoria Embankment
London EC4Y 0DZ

www.bookouture.com

ISBN: 978-1-83525-642-8
eBook ISBN: 978-1-83525-641-1

For Auntie Seija
Sorry I missed your 90th;
looking forward to your 100th!

PROLOGUE

I throw myself at the door. Pound with my fists, scream for help. Claw the smooth surface until fingernails are torn and bloody. I'm bruised, battered, but the drive to escape pushes me beyond reason, until exhausted, dizzy, I slowly sink to the floor. Lean against the door, panting.

He can't do this, just lock the door and leave me here in the dark. Can he?

He already has.

He's angry. He'll calm down, see reason. Let me out. Or maybe someone heard me scream and help is on the way.

No one comes.

I'm thirsty, parched, throat sore from screaming. My head aches, a dull insistent drumbeat inside my skull.

Is he out there, listening?

I swallow, find my voice. Try for calm, reasonable.

'Let me out and we'll talk this through. I won't tell anyone, I swear it.'

No answer.

'*Please.* I'll do whatever you say if you just let me out.' The last words are broken, cut by gasping sobs.

No answer. There is nothing in the silence but my breathing, shallow and fast.

My thoughts are sliding – slipping – spinning from one moment to another that led to me being thrown in here, looking for the point when I could have got away, saved myself.

But it's too late.

I push it all away.

One perfect face, I hold in my mind:

Be brave, my darling.

ONE

ROWAN

Nobody knows me. They think they do, but they don't. Sometimes even I forget that so much of what I do and say is contrived. Beyond method acting, I've become what I portray. But not always.

My secrets wait in the shadows, between light and dark. Before and after. Life and death. Even the transition from asleep to awake, where there should be a single point when one becomes the other. Instead, confusion and fear have me balanced on the edge of a knife. I don't know where I am. When I am. Even, *who* I am. Without knowing these things, how can I risk waking up? But the very act of thinking this pushes me over the threshold.

I open my eyes. My racing heart stills. I'm safe. I'm well. No one can hurt me, not who I am now. I strip away the fear and school my face to calm, composed, like a well-worn uniform.

I'm a lyrebird, a perfect mimic. Years of practice have made me so.

Play the part.

. . .

They are both at the breakfast bar when I come downstairs. I slip an arm around Theo's shoulders, kiss his cheek.

'How does it feel to be fifty?'

'About a day older than yesterday.' He pulls me closer. 'Do I look it?'

I shake my head and it isn't just a nod to his ego; he really doesn't. He's tall, imposing – our eyes are level with him sitting on the stool and me standing. His dark hair is just silvering and it somehow makes him more attractive.

I kiss him, on the lips this time.

'Ugh,' Ellie says. 'Do you mind? I'm trying to eat my breakfast.'

I pull away, reach for the kettle. 'Birthday breakfast – eggs, pancakes, whatever you fancy?'

'Sorry, darling,' Theo says. 'I've got to get going.'

'You won't be late tonight, will you?' Ellie says. 'We're making you a special dinner.'

'How could I forget anything as momentous as that?' he says, managing the words without a touch of irony. For his daughter and me to collaborate on anything, let alone in the kitchen, is ridiculously hard to imagine. She should have come up with a better cover story because he'll certainly be wondering what is actually going on. 'I promise you that my memory hasn't deteriorated that much just yet,' he adds. 'I'll be home by eight at the latest, as per instructions.'

Ellie has her phone out, tapping at the screen. 'Are you sure about the memory thing? Because you've been alive now for... eighteen thousand, two hundred and fifty days.'

'Then I better leave before I forget where I'm going.'

Ellie gets up when he does. 'Happy birthday, Daddy.' She kisses him on the cheek, then heads to her room.

I can't resist working out how many days I've been alive. At forty-two and change it comes to just under fifteen and a half thousand. And at over five years of marriage plus a few hundred days when we were dating, I've spent over two thousand of them with Theo.

I hesitate, then do more sums. The days *before*, so long ago that all I have is a hazy picture, reality and supposition mixed up, probably more than I know. The days *after*, when I became someone new. That, at least, is clear, defined. But what lies between? Fragments. Pieces of me torn apart and reassembled in a different order.

Snap out of it or I'm going to be late. I head to the loo. When I come back, Ellie is in the kitchen, putting her mug in the dishwasher.

'I'm off,' she says.

'Can you try to be on time tonight?' I say.

'Well, sure. I could *try*,' she says, with all the disdain a seventeen-year-old can muster in her eyes when she glances at me.

'It's not for me, Ellie. You know that.'

Her eyes narrow. 'Don't you *dare* imply that I wouldn't be here for my dad. Letting him down is your specialty.'

'That is uncalled for. Just be on time, all right?'

Later, on the Tube from Richmond, I'm trying to stop thinking about birthdays and days and to start thinking about the presentation my team has got to deliver this morning – it's a huge deal, a client with a big advertising budget that we've been after for months – but my mind keeps wandering. I study my reflection in the door windows where I stand, unsmiling. Recently I've had to start adding highlights to my long, dark hair to disguise the grey sneaking in. It's not a pleasing silver, like Theo's, and it's an annoying double standard that it's fine for him to be a silver fox, but I've never heard anyone refer to a silver vixen. Theo at fifty is every bit as attractive as he was when we met – in some ways, more so. Perhaps I can persuade myself that I don't look forty-two or even forty; but is thirty-eight or thirty-nine really any better?

Besides, I feel every bit of my age. I sigh. Lately I've been so tired, distracted. Thinking too much about things I'd rather not think about. As if time is going backwards instead of in the usual direction, things I've mostly forgotten – that I've worked so hard to put behind me – come back at unexpected moments. I've been on edge, too, a lot of the time, without having a reason to point to. I mean, I can guess, but it's something else on the trying-not-to-think-about-it list.

I'm too young for that. I'm not ready to go on to the next stage of my life, whatever it may hold. Joyful things like, say, hot flushes, maybe a long course of stroke-enhancing HRT. I'm in denial and hanging on to it as long as I can.

I need to focus, be who I am supposed to be. The stakes are too high to risk falling apart now.

TWO

When I finally rush through the doors of Fisher & Whyte, I'm late and flustered with it. We'd been held for ages outside Blackfriars, no explanation given. Once we finally pulled in, I half ran along the platform and up the escalators, dodging grumpy commuters, impatiently waiting to go through a ticket gate. As I got up to street level, insistent messages vibrated on my phone but I was nearly there and ignored them, knowing I'd be faster if I didn't stop to answer.

I make it to the conference room with just minutes to spare. Relief is all over Alex's face when he sees me.

'I'm so sorry. Transport for London were doing their level best to sabotage things.'

'No problem,' he says. 'We're all set up. Take a few deep breaths. You made it.'

His eyes hold mine, radiating calm even though I know he's faking it. He's keyed up over this one. We're a good team – the creative side mostly mine; the tech and visuals, Alex. We've been working together long enough to know how to make best use of each other's strengths.

'All right?' he says.

'Yes.' I'm good at faking calm, too. He reaches across, straightens my hair, as our assistant, Hannah, peeks through the door.

'They're here,' she says.

'Ready?' Alex says.

'Ready.'

Adrenalin gets me through the morning. We've drilled this presentation for days, so, despite my poor focus earlier and the last-minute rush, once I begin the pitch it all comes back. Alex does his part well and, between us, we nail it. There is a sense of both relief and euphoria when we are done. The clients are all smiles, shaking our hands and saying they'll get back to us later today. All we can do now is wait.

We head back to our desks; I slump in my seat. Now that it's over, my energy is gone.

'Sugar or caffeine?' Alex says.

'Best to cover all the bases.'

'Start with these.' A box of chocolate chip cookies materialises from Alex's desk drawer, crumbly and all shapes and sizes.

'Home-made?'

'Nothing but the finest. Olly and Jack helped make them. I supervised so they're perfectly safe.'

'Sure. I believe you.' They're good, and I inhale a few of them, suddenly ravenous.

I go to check messages on my phone but when I swipe up, I get a surprise. It's not in English. I sigh, remembering now that I left my phone on the breakfast bar this morning; Ellie was there when I came back. She must have got to it before the screen locked. This time I can't even recognise the language.

I roll my eyes, hand it to Alex. 'Pranked again. Can you fix it?'

'For a coffee.'

'Your rates have gone up.'

By the time I return with two flat whites, it's back in English.

I check my messages. They are mostly variations on what I predicted earlier – 'Where are you?' from Alex, Hannah. Several have landed since from guests invited tonight, including one from Charlie. I open hers first, and smile as I read it:

Coming tonight after all.

Charlie is really Lady Catherine Chadlington, family tree traceable back to centuries of kings and queens, but also one of the most direct, down-to-earth people I know. She is involved in a slew of charities including her main focus – an animal rescue for dogs and cats. She talked me into doing their marketing and media a while back, but I get more from it than the time I lose. Sometimes spending a few hours with a dog that doesn't judge or care who or what I was, or am now, is just what I need.

I'm scanning and quickly answering other messages when I spot one from the caterers for tonight, asking me to call. There are a few missed calls from them as well. There is a sinking feeling in my gut.

I call; it rings, rings.

'Hello?'

'This is Rowan Blackwood. You left a message about our catering for tonight.'

The news isn't good. There was a fire in their prep kitchen last night – no one was hurt but they are out of action for a while. She's all apologies, but there is nothing they can do – booking cancelled.

I drop my head into my hands. Everyone will be there tonight: Theo's family, co-workers and everyone who is anyone in Richmond and beyond. And part of that crowd? Gossips who'd love nothing better than a failure from someone like me. Even though I'm accepted as Theo's wife, no matter how hard I try there is always someone who is waiting for a slip-up, a chance to point out that I'm not really one of them. This can't be happening. Not tonight.

'Bad news?' Alex says.

'You could say that. Are Olly and Jack free tonight for a catering job?'

'Alas, no. Sally has them this week.'

I check my diary for the day, and it's full. What am I going to do?

I message Ellie.

So... the caterers have cancelled.

WTF?!?! Find another one.

I've got meetings all afternoon. Could you help?

There's a pause and I'm hoping she'll say yes; that she'll do it for her dad if not for me, but I should know better by now. Ten minutes later there is still no reply, which is answer enough.

There are emails to respond to and calls to return, meetings I can't get out of. After that I spend my lunch hour calling caterers in increasing panic. No one is free this last minute. Then I get a message from Theo's sister, Maxine:

Ellie tells me you need a caterer – try this one.

A name and number follow. So she did help, after all.

I sigh. I'd wanted something new and interesting for Theo's birthday. I'd picked everything myself – all Japanese, sushi, wines that match. But there is no real choice at this late stage. I call the number Maxine messaged. It's apparent that they'd been primed to expect me and can step in.

After lunch, Alex and I start to run through a campaign pitch for tomorrow – a less important client who is unlikely to change agencies so not the same stress as earlier. We're in the midst of sorting that out when we get the call that we've got the account from this morning. Alex is ecstatic. The bonus will be a good one. The money doesn't matter to me, not in the way it does to Alex – with an ex-wife and two kids the bonus is huge for him. But the buzz of nailing the presentation, getting the account, still makes me giddy, and I manage to throw off worrying about tonight. Moments like this are why I love my job.

But then Neil Fisher, senior partner, comes through from his corner office. 'Congratulations, Alex. Well done.' Back slapping follows. I stand, get in his line of sight. 'And Rowan.' A bare nod at me.

'Thank you,' Alex says. 'It was a good team effort.' Including me, but while that is true, it is also true that the main idea behind the campaign was mine.

'Let's leave early for drinks,' Fisher says, looking at Alex as he does so. Alex, whose dad went to the same exclusive school as Fisher. Years later, so did Alex.

'We'd love to,' Alex says, answering for both of us. This is when I should say that I can't, not tonight, but my phone rings – a call put through that I can't delay. I answer, half listening still to what they are saying. Fisher has moved on by the time I'm off the phone and I'm seeing others around us gathering coats, phones – everyone must be going.

I groan.

'You're coming, aren't you?' Alex says.

'I really can't. It's Theo's birthday and we're having a surprise party.'

'It won't be the same without you. But fair enough.'

It's an hour before my usual leaving time – so I could go,

briefly, then try to extricate myself – but Alex isn't pointing that out or insisting I come along like he usually would.

If I'm not there, all the toasts will be to Alex. Alex is a friend. But while he is careful to include me when I'm standing there, listening, will he do the same if I'm not?

I have to go.

We're at the usual pub nearby, being congratulated as a round is bought, but I insist on orange juice. I can't get home half tipsy and pull off gracious hostess tonight.

Someone has baby photos from a co-worker on maternity leave and they're gushing over her phone.

Alex runs interference, changes the subject, and gathers drink orders.

He brings me a glass of wine.

'I was only coming for one, remember?'

'The orange juice didn't count. Are you OK?' he says, concerned.

'Yes, fine.'

I never told him; we didn't discuss it. But when his second son was born three years ago, he somehow worked it out – or he thought he did, at any rate. He doesn't know all that is behind it – nobody does. But he didn't make a big deal about it, just never pressed baby photos on me and all the rest. And I was there for him last year when his wife asked him to leave. One of the few times I've bumped heads with Theo was over asking Alex to stay while he got a place sorted. We have three guest rooms, so why not? But then Theo relaxed about it, even suggested Alex have his corporate let in the interim – a flat he uses occasionally when he has to work late.

Half a glass of wine later, I finally manage to leave and rush for the Tube. It's almost half six – much later than I meant to be tonight. A train reaches the platform just as I do and I manage to slip into the crowded carriage. There is a close press of bodies all around as we go from stop to stop. At one station a woman pushes in just as the doors close, a baby strapped to her chest in some sort of sling. Facing out, legs dangling below. So small, probably just a few months old. Tiny little fists. Blue eyes. People shuffle along to make more room for her and her cargo, whether out of kindness or caution against possible crying or projectile baby vomit, but he – somehow, it looks like a he – is gurgling and happy.

He locks eyes on mine. I can't move, can't look away. Being this close to him reaches deep inside, to a well of pain and fear.

I need to get away but I can't, I'm trapped, people all around me. I'm dizzy and try to focus on breathing – consciously draw air in, out, in, out, slowly – but I can't, and I'm wheezing, barely breathing at all. I'm nauseous and breaking out in a cold sweat. We're slowing as we near the next stop. I'm already late but I need to get off, get away from her. But then I don't have to – she steps out onto the platform. She's gone.

Gradually, my breathing slows, my heart rate also, but my good mood from earlier is shattered. Wife, stepmother, respected and successful career woman. On the invite list for all the best parties and events in London; I have it all. Why isn't it enough?

Because no matter what I do, what I achieve, I'll always know: I'm not just a fraud. I'm a failure.

THREE

I remember to face the camera at the front door and it slides open.

'Welcome, wicked stepmother,' Vera says. Ellie must have added an enhancement to the system. I know our virtual assistant doesn't get humour or emotions, so why did she sound so amused?

'Ellie, honestly! Take that off the system at once.'

'I was on time. Needed to occupy myself somehow. But you're late.'

'I got caught up at the office.'

She raises an eyebrow as if she knows I'm lying. 'You smell like a pub.'

'How would you know?'

Then I realise that she was fishing. Now that people don't smoke inside them or even outside very often, there isn't really a tell-tale pub smell, other than the smell of drink, of course – but surely half a glass of wine hasn't lingered on my breath. I see in her smirk that she's clocked my lack of denial and look of guilt.

The caterer's van is out front and there are sounds coming down the hall from the kitchen. Ellie is ready for the party, in a little black dress – too short, really, but she has the legs for it. Long blonde hair, shiny and loose about her shoulders. Perfect make-up – she's better at it than I am. She doesn't look seventeen; she could easily pass for twenty.

'That dress is a little short, Ellie.'

'If you've got it.' She shrugs, then runs a dismissive eye over me. 'You look a mess. What's wrong?'

'Thanks. Nothing.' I shrug. 'There was a big presentation at work today. A client we've been trying to nab for a while finally signed up.'

'Congratulations,' she says, but couldn't look less impressed if she tried.

'It's taken it out of me, that's all,' I say, and as soon as I say the words, I wish I hadn't. It's best not to show any soft underbelly to someone with such sharp claws. I head for the stairs.

'Why bother?' she says. 'Be the kept woman you always aspired to be.'

Her words sting, even though they're not really true. There was a time early on with Theo – when our relationship was shiny and new – when I thought I could actually *become* someone else. Not just for pretend, but for real. When Theo said after our wedding that we should have our own child to bring us even closer together, I somehow convinced myself that fairy tales could come true. That we could have a child and our love would be enough to overcome anything. I even managed to imagine a different life with our baby and me staying at home, not rushing back to work. How perfect it could be.

That feeling didn't last. And even if it had – I'd never give up work. It is too much a part of who I am.

There is just enough time for a quick shower. Soon I slip into a new red silk dress that I thought Theo would like, but now I'm looking in the mirror, unsure: it clings more than I remember when I bought it a month or so ago, and not in a good way. But there is no time to dither or change.

I stand up straighter, smooth it. Remind myself who I am. I'll get through the evening without a slip. Everyone will be talking about what a lovely party it was, with such an elegant hostess. I push down the knot of dread in my gut that is always there before a big performance, and head for the stairs.

FOUR

Theo's sister Maxine and her husband Percy are early arrivals. I soon see why, as Maxine is bossing the caterers around as if this were her home, her party. I'm trying not to get annoyed; she did bail me out, after all. Soon there is a flurry of arrivals to distract me, champagne and wine on trays being handed around by the waiting staff.

Charlie arrives and finally my smile is genuine. 'I'm so glad you could come,' I say, and mean it. I have few friends – really, just her and Alex – and it's good to have someone on my side in the mix tonight.

She pulls me in for a hug. Charlie doesn't do the London sort of almost hugs and air kisses. She told me once that either she doesn't want to hug somebody or she does, and then she does it properly.

Ellie is watching for Theo on the CCTV by the gate on her phone.

'He's coming! Dad's coming,' she says. Everyone hushes, faces the door.

When it slides open a moment later, strains of Marilyn

Monroe singing 'Happy Birthday' ring out on the sound system – must be another Ellie touch.

'Surprise!' everyone says, and he does look surprised. I'd have thought he would have been alerted to all the arrivals via the app on his phone.

'Happy birthday, darling,' I say. A brief kiss and our guests come in ones and twos to greet him.

The doorbell rings – a late arrival who isn't programmed into the list for tonight. I open the door to our new neighbour. I'd invited her when we met briefly as boxes were being shifted in next door a few weeks ago.

'Thanks so much for coming.' I catch Theo's eye and he comes over. 'Theo, this is Margaret Lawrence, our new neighbour.'

'Lovely to meet you,' he says. I can see in her slightly widened eyes that Theo has made an impression. When he kisses her cheek she tilts her head, smiles flirtatiously, even though she looks to be in at least her seventies.

'This is for the birthday boy,' she says, holds out a bottle of red, a lovely French claret.

'Hardly a boy, but thank you.'

'You are to me,' she says.

'Welcome to the neighbourhood. Please excuse me,' he says, and goes to greet another arrival.

When Vera intones the name of the next one soon after, Margaret looks around to find who spoke.

'What was that?' she says.

'It's called Vera – our virtual assistant.'

'Gracious. What is that?'

'It's a bit like Amazon's Alexa but integrated into the house.'

'So, it plays music, tells you the weather if you ask it?'

'That and much more. Climate control, alarm system, lighting. It's a prototype Theo's company has been developing.'

'How did it know who was coming through the door?'

'There's a camera. If you look into it, if you're expected and we've inputted your image, the door unlocks and opens automatically.'

'I was going to ask if you could keep my spare key, in case I lock myself out. But then I can't return the favour.'

'Happy to, if you like. And you're right – we don't have keys.'

She's looking around the room. 'I don't see any light switches, either.'

'No. You just say lights on or lights off.'

'But you said that and the lights didn't go off.'

'You have to address the virtual assistant by name, like this: "Vera, what time is it?"'

'It is eight thirty-five p.m.,' Vera intones, in her almost but not quite human-sounding voice.

'What if it malfunctions, stops working? Could you get locked out, or trapped inside?'

A shiver runs down my spine. A locked door, no key – not even a keyhole. No way out. But that can't happen to me again. Not here. Not anywhere. I try to keep my smile in place, explain to Margaret and tell myself to listen, too.

'There's an app, on our phones. If there is any problem with the system, I can use that to unlock the doors, turn the lights on and off and whatever else.' I'm remembering now how Ellie had messed with my phone earlier. What if that happened and I was trapped? I have to ask Alex what he did to make it go back to English.

Margaret nods, clearly fascinated and not technophobic like you might expect for someone of her age. She reminds me of a bird – a tiny, inquisitive one that hops around the garden, looking everywhere at once. I've stopped feeling the sense of awe when I come through the front door that I saw on her face when she arrived, but sometimes it still surprises me that I actually live in a house as grand as this. No one in my family would believe it. But that doesn't matter, as they'll never come here. I've seen to that.

'Would you like the tour?' I say. 'And then I'll introduce you to some more neighbours.'

'Oh yes, please.'

This house was built to Theo's specifications. He and Ellie lived here from when she was a baby. Her mother never did so there isn't a sense of her about the place, and I'm glad for that. The sweeping entrance hall, gleaming wooden floors – spacious and double-fronted with reception rooms on either side of the entrance. The formal dining room and shiny kitchen and break-fast bar we only visit briefly as the catering staff are in a flurry of preparations. Grand wooden staircase. Everything is immaculate, shiny. Our cleaners are the best. The furniture and lighting are also the best, in terms of style rather than comfort – all in simple lines, black and white with touches of colour here and there. Seeing it through Margaret's eyes now it all looks... so sterile. As if every trace of life about the place has been scrubbed away. There's no real sign that I've lived here for over five years, other than in my dressing room, upstairs. Ellie's room – a wing of the house on the ground floor, really, with a bedroom, study and her own bathroom – is teenage chaos, but apart from that there is no clutter, no personal things anywhere downstairs. If I ever left a book on a table or my bag on a chair, Theo looked so pained that I stopped doing it.

The party drags on. Charlie is busily gathering support for a fundraiser, no doubt the reason she came. She corners Theo at one point and asks when we are going to foster a rescue dog – she does this every time she sees him. Theo would never tolerate that degree of mess and fuss. Instead, he promises to buy a table at the fundraiser – probably what she was angling for in the first place.

So many people want to say hello, make inane comments about the new Damien Hirst on the wall or the designer of my dress. I've never felt any kind of ease with most of Theo's friends, his family, but it's somehow bothering me more than it usually would tonight. Is there something going on beyond the usual barbs hidden behind smiles? I can sense it, see it in eyes that slide away instead of meeting mine. Titters and whispers. An urge to just leave them all behind – to go upstairs or even out the front door – is strong. That'd give them something to really gossip about. But hiding what I think and feel are survival skills I perfected at a young age.

Not even the wine is helping. It's the good stuff – of course it is – but it tastes like vinegar when I try it. There's an ache behind my eyes, a strange almost metallic taste at the back of my throat. An involuntary shudder passes through my body and I hurry excuses, rush to the downstairs bathroom, which is thankfully empty. Shut and lock the door. Lean on it, breathing, in, out, in, out, trying to control waves of nausea. Maybe I'm not just tired or menopausal. Maybe I'm coming down with something, have caught some sickness bug. In the mirror my face is pale behind the make-up.

When I finally emerge, Ellie is cross. They've been waiting to toast Theo and cut the cake. She hands me a glass of champagne and there are glances exchanged here and there. A few raised eyebrows and whispers and I'm checking I haven't splashed my dress when I washed my hands, that there isn't something stuck to my shoe, but can't see any reason for it. I'm not just being paranoid. Something is going on.

Ellie gives me a nudge.

I smile, face the room. 'I'd like to thank everyone for coming today to celebrate my wonderful husband Theo's half century.'

'Ouch. I'd like to second that,' Theo says.

'Happy birthday, Theo!' And we all raise a glass. 'To Theo!'

A sip of champagne isn't the treat that it usually is. It tastes odd, with an almost bitter aftertaste.

Two candles are lit on the cake – a five and a zero. Ellie says fifty individual candles would have been a fire hazard.

'Make a wish, Dad,' she says.

'What could I wish for? I have everything,' he says, smiling at Ellie, then me, then blows out the candles.

I can't stop myself from wondering if that is really true. If it is, do I – have everything I want? I have so much more than I could have ever imagined when I was Ellie's age.

My head is spinning – not so much nausea now, more that I'm dizzy.

No more champagne for me, not today. I spot a waiter with a tray and walk over to him to get rid of my glass, passing the wife of one of Theo's partners who is talking to a few other women.

'Looks like she's off to get herself another,' one of them says, in a low voice. I put my glass on the tray to have it taken away. Walk behind a few others in a huddle.

'... that's what I heard. Poor Ellie. And that's not all. Maxine had to step in at the last minute to get caterers, she didn't even manage—'

I've been spotted and whatever I didn't manage is left unsaid.

Smiles replace the vindictiveness. 'Such a lovely party, Rowan. You must have spent simply ages planning it.'

I'm on the edge – so close to demanding to know what they are saying about me. Instead, I dig fingernails into my hand and walk away.

The cake has been cut; pieces passed around. The thought of the sweet, rich icing – just, no. I manage a little of the cake and leave the icing.

I'm hit by another wave of dizziness, put a hand on the back of a sofa to steady myself. As I do, I scan the room. No one is looking at me directly, but when everyone is very purposively looking in another direction, you know that the one place they are really paying attention to is in the ignored void.

Theo comes over, takes my hand. 'Is everything all right?' he says, voice low, concerned.

Your friends and family are being even more charming than usual, is what I think. 'Just tired,' I say.

Theo stays at my side, and I'm glad. Arm linked in his. Facing everyone together, to remind them who I am and that any slight to me is a slight to both of us.

Maxine brings out photos of her grandson, insists everyone admire the nearly eighteen-month-old. Theo makes the usual comments, then calls Ellie over to show her.

'Ugh,' Ellie says. 'Don't get any ideas about having grand-children – I'm never having one of *those*.' She says it like the smiling chubby face hides the anti-Christ. Of course, if she ever had a child, maybe that would be a possibility.

It's after midnight by the time the last stragglers are going.

'Come and talk to me a moment,' Charlie says. I follow her out to the front step. 'Out with it. What's wrong?'

'Wrong? Nothing's wrong,' I lie. 'I'm just a bit tired.' I'm good at lying but she is good at seeing through me. I like Charlie, but it's always felt a bit risky being around her. There is something she's not saying and I'm putting that together with the whispers and glances earlier. Even though I know that Charlie doesn't play those kinds of games, she must know what was going around. 'Are you going to tell me my latest sins according to those vultures, or what?'

'Should I?' She rolls her eyes. 'Rumour has it that Ellie had to step in and organise the party. That you've been going to the pub after work and coming home drunk.'

'*What?* Seriously?' I'm shocked, angry, my face burning with embarrassment. Understanding now the looks I was getting, the fragments of comments I overheard. 'It's not true.'

'I know that. But I'm here if you need to talk.' A hug, a goodbye.

I've no doubt at all who started that rumour.

As I step back over the threshold, Vera reminds me of Ellie's other transgression. 'Welcome, wicked stepmother,' she says. I should have known she wouldn't have taken that off the system when I told her to.

'Ellie, really,' Theo says, shaking his head but looking more amused than annoyed. As usual. I'm about to demand a word with him, tell him the lies she's been spreading. But then I put it all together. It is true – I did go to the pub today. I barely had anything to drink there or since then, but what did everyone see? Me looking unwell and disappearing into a bathroom. Me, unsteady on my feet. And as far as organising the party goes – it is true. Ellie did go to Maxine, and she's the one who found a replacement caterer. It's not my fault the other one fell through, but it's still true.

She's outsmarted me. Anything I say she can counter. My guard was down when I got home. I was upset after what happened on the Tube. I gave her ammunition. I'll be more careful in future.

Theo calls me and Ellie over.

'Thank you both for a lovely birthday,' he says and holds out his hands, one to Ellie, one to me. I find a smile and we both go readily enough but Ellie resists when he tries to draw us closer to each other for a family hug.

He releases me first, gestures to the stairs. 'Give us a moment,' he says.

Maybe he noticed what was going on. Maybe, for once, he is actually going to tell her off.

FIVE

ELLIE

Dad waits until Rowan has disappeared up the stairs and I'm uneasy. Did she work out what I did? Did she tell him? No. She couldn't have. He's smiling.

'You really should try harder to get along with Rowan. Not wind her up so much.' Even as he says the words I can see the glint of amusement, even pride, in his eyes. Is it because I managed to reprogramme Vera in such a way that he didn't get notified of all the party comings and goings before he got home – that I'm a nerdy chip off his techy block? Or maybe it's because I'm as dysfunctional as he is, given his parents. Especially his mother. She died when he was a kid, but from what he's said she was hardly there before, so her death didn't change things much. I think I was five the first time he told me very seriously that he'd never be anything like his parents, that I'd always be the most important person in the world to him.

Of course, that was before he met doe-eyed Rowan – all shy smiles and long hair, looking like she needed rescuing. He never could resist being a hero, though why he couldn't see through her act I'll never understand. Before they got married, I overheard him talking to Auntie M. She was worried how fast things were happening and asked Dad what he really knew about Rowan. He said he loved her and that was all that mattered. Once they got married, Rowan did everything she could to drive a wedge between Dad and me. If she'd had her way, I'd have been carted off to boarding school straight after they said 'I do.'

'So, you'll remove that latest embellishment from Vera?' Dad says.

'Fine.'

'Goodnight, Ellie,' he says and I watch him go up the stairs, to *her*. Once he's out of sight I go to the kitchen, take an open bottle of white wine out of the fridge, and go to my room.

What a night. All the whispers and rumours about Rowan's drinking – she won't live that down in a hurry. I can only hope that the rumours will make their way back to Dad – that maybe it'll make him look at her more closely. See her for what she is. Know she can't be trusted.

Was she oblivious? I'm not sure. There were a few times when her eyes found mine and she looked even more unhappy that I was there than usual. Even if she worked it out, I don't care. If she says anything to Dad I'll both deny that I said anything and insist that Rowan does have a drinking problem. But I doubt that she will. She'd be too afraid he'd believe me over her to risk it.

For so long, it was just us – Dad and me. Since just weeks after I was born. So, what do I know about getting along with mothers or stepmothers or any woman, really? My mother took one look at me and scarpered, just like the nannies and house-keepers that followed.

If only Rowan would do the same thing.

SIX

ROWAN

Theo opens the door. I only got as far as kicking my shoes off, lying on the bed on top of the covers in my dress. I still feel dizzy but it's eased off to more of a pleasant buzz. I feel half drunk and I've barely had anything.

'Ellie apologises and says it won't happen again,' he says, but I don't know which of her sins he's referring to.

'For what?'

'The wicked stepmother comment by Vera. Why, is there anything else I should know about?'

'Nothing important,' I say. Managing to keep my face neutral.

He sits next to me on the bed, leans down. Kisses me so thoroughly I forget why I was annoyed, that I'm tired, that it's late. In this moment, I can almost be myself. It is all about feeling, being, in the now. The past and all the marks it left behind recede almost to vanishing.

Afterwards, Theo spoons me, kisses my neck. He's asleep almost instantly, a skill I don't share. Sleep has never been easy for me.

My second foster mum loved old movies and let me stay up

to watch with her when I couldn't sleep. We watched Audrey Hepburn in *My Fair Lady* before I knew it was based on a play – *Pygmalion*. Once I did, I got it from the library, devoured it, read it again and again. And then years later I discovered *Pretty Woman*, with Julia Roberts, loosely based on the same story. In the first film, Audrey is a girl who sells flowers in a market; in the second, Julia is a prostitute. Both women at the lowest rung of society. But all it took was changing how they spoke, how they dressed, and they became somebody new, completely different. They're both beautiful, of course, but it isn't just beauty: it's how they look at the world, move within it. I realised if Audrey and Julia could do it, so could I. All I needed to do was be somebody else. Look different, talk different. Think different, too, though that was harder.

I'd watch and rewatch anything I could find with the posh, refined accent I wanted and practice it over and again. At school and then university, I studied girls who had the confidence and poise that comes from being from the right background. Knowing the world would treat you right because you demanded it do so meant that it usually did. And if it didn't, the way to react to unexpected transgressions – outraged disbelief – put whoever it was who dared to cross you in their place. The way these people moved through the world, carried themselves, was probably more important than the right clothes or accent. I absorbed it, copied it all. And the more I became what I studied, the more the way I felt and thought followed along with it. If it didn't, I faked it until it did.

I still know what I was, where I came from. There are moments when things I did come back and it is almost overwhelming. But they have become fewer and less intense as time has gone on.

But lately something is changing and I don't know why. My thoughts drift to dangerous places more and more often. My control is slipping. Have I got too comfortable – has that made me lose focus on who I am meant to be?

Or maybe it is something much more essential and basic than that.

I watch Theo sleep. He knows about my problem with insomnia. There was a time when after making love he'd stay awake, talk about everything and nothing until I was sleepy. He'd hold me as I fell asleep and only then would he close his own eyes. There is a sense of longing for how things were then, and sadness, too. Maybe life and Ellie and his work and my work have all pulled us apart, bit by bit, until the only time we are really together is in the moment – the act. Orgasm, then sleep – for him, at least. That's all. And the less we are consumed by each other, the more the darkness is coming back for me. It isn't banished like it once was, just by being with Theo.

The movies never show what happens *after*. Could the flower girl and the hooker live happily ever after, or would what came before always be there? Richard Gere knew Julia's past, and it was overcome – this was implied, at least. But if they stayed together, year after year, when passion declined and life intruded, would he still feel the same?

I reassure myself that our situation is different. Theo can't change his mind about things he doesn't know.

It's much later when I finally drift off to sleep.

SEVEN

There's a sound reaching for me, pulling me towards wakefulness, but I resist. I'm afraid. Is he here? Play dead. Barely breathing, slower and slower, losing connection with my body. Floating away to a secret, hidden place, where no one can find me. It's a superpower, having an off switch. Nothing can hurt me now.

When I open my eyes later, I'm disorientated. It takes a while to calm my breathing, school my face. To note details, like how bright the light is under the curtains. That Theo is gone. I reach for my phone. It's after *ten*? There are missed calls – from Hannah, Alex.

I've overslept.

That wasn't a dream I had earlier – it must have been the sound of my alarm intruding into my dream. Someone must have turned it off before I woke up completely. Vera has all our personal alarm times programmed for each day of the week; mine gets gradually louder until it wakes me. Only my voice is supposed to be able to turn off my alarm, but Ellie must have found a way around that – a new game to play.

I call Alex.

'Hi Rowan. Is everything OK?'

'I'm so sorry. It was a late night and I slept through my alarm.'

'Don't worry. Hannah stepped in and covered for you.' Hannah, the whip-smart assistant with her eye on my job. 'I told the powers that be that you're unwell.'

'Thanks for covering for me.'

'It's fine. Take the day off and come up with a story for tomorrow.'

After more apologies and then goodbyes, I lie back in bed.

Despite oversleeping more than three hours, I'm still tired. I'm remembering now how sick I'd felt at the party last night, too. Later on – after the champagne – I'd felt so dizzy, and... hang on. Ellie had been telling tales about me drinking. She is the one who handed me the glass of champagne. I only had a few sips and I was dizzy, having trouble staying upright – backing up her story of drunkenness. And I'd thought the champagne tasted wrong, bitter.

Did she put something in my drink – a crushed sleeping pill, maybe? Imagine if I'd had the whole glass.

I shake my head. *Seriously, Rowan?* She may be a bitch but I can't see her going as far as spiking my drink. *Stop being so paranoid.* And anyhow, I'd felt sick before then, too.

I sigh. Despite my usual ban on all things medical except in case of emergency, perhaps I should drag myself in to the doctor's, face up to whatever is wrong. Maybe it'll help me feel less guilty about the unscheduled day off.

But I doubt it.

I call my doctor's surgery before I can change my mind. And I'm in luck – there's been a cancellation later this morning. This way I won't have much time to talk myself out of it.

Ellie is in the kitchen when I come downstairs, waiting for the kettle. She looks pale, tired, too.

'No classes this morning?'

'None I care to go to. No work this morning?'

'Well, yes, there was meant to be. But somebody turned off my alarm.'

'Oh?'

'Anything you want to tell me about that?'

'You probably did it yourself and fell back asleep. Don't blame me.'

'Can't you just be honest for once?'

Forgetting the kettle, she stomps down the hall to her room and slams the door. Well, a result. Not the one I was looking for – like, say, an admission and apology – but at least I don't have to wait for the kettle to boil to make tea.

Later, I'm walking to the Tube for the doctor's appointment when my phone rings – it's Theo.

'Hi,' I say.

'Ellie just called me, really upset. Says you accused her of lying.'

'Hang on, I'm not the one in the wrong here. She turned off my alarm – I overslept, missed work.'

There's a pause. 'After Ellie called, I checked Vera's log. The alarm was turned off by your voice in our bedroom.'

It's my turn to be silent. I know how good Ellie is with anything related to tech and computers. She must have changed the log to trick her dad.

'It wasn't me,' I insist. 'I didn't turn it off.'

'Maybe you were half asleep and don't remember, but either way – what is going on with you? You're not yourself.'

Now I'm angry. Either way – does that mean he thinks that either I forgot, or I'm *lying*?

I've reached the entrance to the Tube now.

'I've got to go.' I end the call without waiting for a reply as I go down the stairs.

Could I really have turned off the alarm myself and then forgotten?

I'm uneasy. I'd been dreaming about something trying to wake me – afterwards I thought it was my alarm. Maybe I really did turn it off, but it's not like me to forget things like that. Is this another sign of approaching menopause – forgetfulness?

If I did, there is a pang of guilt that I'd accused Ellie, though she gets away with stuff all the time, doesn't she? Unless... my champagne really was drugged. And that's why I didn't wake up completely. Even apart from that possibility, there are the rumours she spread about me at the party: she doesn't deserve an apology from me over this or anything else.

Just in case, I'll stop relying on Vera and go back to setting alarms on my phone. And I'll pour my own drinks.

By the time I get off the Tube, the anger is gone and the unease increasing. *You're not yourself,* Theo said. If he only knew.

EIGHT

I'm in the waiting room. It's a private surgery so not crowded, and they're not running late – I asked when I arrived, hoping for an excuse to reschedule. It's been years since I've been here. I'm mostly healthy, but that's not the only reason – more, it is avoidance and general dislike for anything and everything medical. And there is always at least one: a young mother, baby in her arms, a toddler in a stroller. She looks exhausted.

When my name is finally called it's not a GP I've seen before. She looks about twelve. I'd asked to see a female doctor and I'm sure she's fully qualified or she wouldn't be here, but I find myself wanting someone older than me, as if that would make them more able to understand.

But I'm here now.

'Hello, Mrs Blackwood. I'm Dr Khan. What can I help you with today?'

'I don't know, or maybe I do.'

She nods, waiting for me to say more, and now a rush of emotions I'd rather not feel are welling up inside.

'I think I'm probably menopausal. I've been so tired and

having trouble concentrating. I've been forgetful. And everything feels like too much, all of a sudden. But I'm only forty-two.'

'Perimenopause – initial signs of the menopause – can begin in the early forties, so it's not unusual. Do you have any other symptoms?'

'Sometimes at night I feel really hot and flushed. My appetite has been on and off, though I seem to have gained a little weight. I've been feeling sick sometimes, too – nauseous. I've nearly thrown up a few times.' As I say it I'm remembering other times over the last few months – when I've been sick or nearly so. I'd blamed it on what I'd eaten, but maybe this has been going on for a while.

'Have you been having periods?'

'Not lately, though I'm often irregular.'

'When was the most recent?'

Ignoring that was another part of avoiding all of this. 'I'm not sure. Maybe three or four months ago.'

She wants to check a bunch of stuff – do a health MOT, she says, as it's been so long since I've been seen. She arranges blood tests.

'Could you pee in this for me please?' She holds out a sample cup. 'Then give it to the nurse and I'll call you back in soon.'

I'm surprised. Don't they usually get you to bring that in the next morning? But I go to the ladies and comply, sit in the waiting room again. The doctor calls me in minutes later, and I stand by the door, hoping for a quick departure.

'Please, sit down,' she says.

Suddenly worried, I do. But she's smiling.

'Rowan, you're not menopausal. You're pregnant.'

I'm staring. She couldn't have said what I think she said.

'Rowan?' she says.

I stand up. I'm shaking my head. I'm not – I can't be – she must be lying. Why is she lying? I'm angry, then I'm afraid. She's getting up from her seat now, moving towards me. I back away, dizzy, heart racing.

Everything goes dark.

NINE

'Mrs Blackwood... Rowan...' A distant voice, calling a name. But who is Rowan? I'm trying to ignore it; I don't want to come back. No one can find me if I stay in the shadows.

'Rowan?' Louder, more insistent, and there is movement – someone's hand on my shoulder.

I panic and open my eyes. Rowan – that's me. I'm Rowan. I'm looking up, the ceiling far away. I'm on the floor. Dr Khan is kneeling next to me. A nurse has appeared as well.

'What happened?'

'You fainted,' the doctor says. 'Luckily I caught you.'

I start to sit up.

'Take it slowly,' she says. She and the nurse, one on each side, help ease me back to my feet and then into the chair by her desk.

Dr Khan checks my blood pressure.

'It's a bit low.'

The nurse brings me a glass of water, I drink it and Dr Khan nods at the nurse, tells her she can go. She closes the door.

'Have you ever fainted before?'

'No,' I say. 'I don't think so.' I'm confused. What happened?

Why did I faint? Then it rushes back all at once, and I gasp. 'Is it true? Am I really... pregnant?'

'You are.'

She's asking questions, gently. Concerned. Wanting to know if this is good news, and I'm having to remind myself who I am, something I haven't had to do for a long time: Rowan. Wife of Theo. The perfect, happy couple with the beautiful home and this is all that is missing. I reassure her. All is well. It was just the shock, that's all. After so long I didn't think it could happen. I hear my voice and I can't work out if the reasonable-sounding things I'm saying are true. Maybe if I say them enough, I'll believe myself.

She makes me have more water and checks my blood pressure again.

'Are you sure you're feeling all right now?'

No. But I want to get away from her, from here.

'Absolutely. I'll be fine,' I lie.

She's writing appointments down on cards and telling me things I can't take in when all I want to do is leave. The room feels smaller the longer I stay in it, as if the walls and ceiling are coming closer, and I'm struggling to breathe. I'm smiling, nodding. Lie again and promise I'm being collected before she'll let me go.

Once out on the street, I breathe deeply, in and out, and again. I could get a taxi but want to be alone, anonymous. I get the endless bus instead of the Tube, not wanting to go underground, to feel trapped, but it's not much better.

She's mistaken. She must be. Either she did the test wrong or it was a false positive or something else went wrong.

I get off early to stop at a chemist. Look all around as if someone will see what I'm buying and care or judge, but no one is paying the slightest attention. After I pay for it, I hide the pregnancy test deep down in my handbag and walk the rest of the way home. All the while I'm thinking, it can't be – *I* can't be. No. She must have made a mistake.

I'm glad when I get home that Ellie is out. Theo shouldn't be back for hours still, though sometimes he surprises me. Not wanting to be interrupted or have to explain, I go to an en suite in one of the guest rooms and lock the door. Read the instructions.

Pee in the cup. Dip the stick. Take it out, lie it flat and wait.

It doesn't take long. Two thin red lines, one above the other. Dr Khan was right.

'I'm pregnant.' I say it softly, almost whispering, as if hearing the words will make it feel more real. I say it again, a little louder this time: two words that change everything.

Nausea, tiredness, not feeling like myself – the dizziness, too – all signs? I haven't had a period for three or four months but thought I was menopausal, and I often skip them for no reason. How did I not think of this? I suppose because after over five years of no birth control – something we agreed when we got married – I didn't think it was possible. After so long, I was so sure it wouldn't happen that it didn't even enter my mind as a possibility. Or maybe I didn't want to know.

Dr Khan said I need to have a dating scan – an ultrasound where we can see how far along I am and check everything is OK. She insisted on scheduling it for the start of next week, another appointment with her a few days after that. She tried to run through a bunch of antenatal stuff with me, but I was in so much disbelief and shock I couldn't take much in.

Going by my last period, I could be maybe four months along – enough to be showing? I stand sideways, pull up my top. Look in the mirror. When I'd put on that red dress last night, I'd thought it clung too tight. Could this really be a baby bump? Already?

I'm here and I'm somewhere else, both at once. A long time ago, terrified and trapped. But I'm not that girl, not any more.

Everything is different now. I tell myself this but I'm going past scared to terrified, breathing too fast, feeling dizzy, and I sit down on the side of the bath. Head in hands, breathing, in, out, in, out, until the faintness passes.

Can I do this? Can I *be* this? I don't know.

Inside me, right now, is a life. It's part of me but also separate. It could be a daughter – I hope so. A boy would be harder.

But either way, a tiny defenceless life is hidden inside me. Fragile both now and after it is born, needing care and love to grow, to thrive.

This time, I get to choose. Nobody can make me do this. And maybe that is all that I need to know.

And could this be what we need – Theo and me? To make things more like they used to be between us. To make loving him enough to make me someone new; someone he believes in. Enough that I can believe in myself.

That's a lot to ask of an unborn baby. Our child will be their own person, too, with wants and needs all of their own.

I place my hands over my tummy, cradle my arms around myself, caught in a surge of emotions – fear, confusion, others hard to identify – but over all of it, fierce protectiveness. I'm startled by how strong this feeling has become, how all-encompassing. Just hours since I found out they exist, I'd do *anything* to protect this baby.

This time, I'll do everything right. I promise. This time, it'll be different.

TEN

I spend the rest of the day in a daze, going between being unable to accept or grasp what I can't refute, and slipping into daydreams of how everything will be. Our child, mine and Theo's. Will they look more like Theo or me? His blue eyes, my high cheekbones. Dark hair, of course – we both have dark hair. Cherubic smiles and giggles and OK, sleepless nights and the rest of it, but it will all be worth it.

Which room would make the best nursery?

This one, I decide, and settle on a chair in the corner of one of our guest rooms that overlooks the front garden. I imagine making the room the way it should be – with nursery furniture, toys and pictures on the walls, picture books on shelves. Everything they could ever want, for the idyllic childhood I never had. And a rocking chair, for nursing our child, just here where I'm sitting.

I want Theo. To hold him close, tell him. It's only five, he's not usually home until seven or eight. I want to call him, tell him to hurry home, but I don't. Instead, I wait, anticipating his reaction. He'll be so happy. Won't he? What he wanted when we got married is finally coming true.

There is a faint sound below and I get up, look out the window, hoping Theo is early, but it's Ellie walking up to the door. While I can imagine Theo's reaction, I'd rather not think of Ellie's just yet. Then I remember this morning, my alarm. I'd assumed it was her, but Theo put enough doubt in my mind about whether I did it myself and forgot; perhaps that wasn't fair. I'd also suspected she tampered with my drink. But the doctor said I had low blood pressure – that's why I fainted. That must be why I was dizzy the night before, too. It didn't have anything to do with Ellie.

I head down the stairs, find her in the kitchen.

'Hi Ellie. Have you had a good day?' She shrugs, gives me a dark look, and opens the fridge. 'Sorry about this morning.'

She closes the fridge and turns around, a can of fizzy drink in her hand. 'Just to be clear, what are you apologising for? For assuming it was me who turned off your stupid alarm, or calling me a liar?'

'That's not quite what I said—'

'It's what you implied.'

I'm in a good enough mood to be conciliatory, and even to feel a twinge of guilt. Despite her messing around with my phone and the rumours she spread about me at the party, she might not be the culprit this time. 'You're right, and I'm sorry.'

'Whatevs.' She takes the drink and goes to her room down the hall, slams the door.

At least by the time our child is a teenager, we'll be ready for it.

When it's edging past 8 p.m. I can't wait any longer and message Theo, to ask what time he wants dinner.

It's half eight, and the dinner I prepared of Theo's favourites is almost beyond being rescued, when a reply finally comes.

Meetings tonight. Don't wait up.

And nothing else, not an apology for not telling me sooner or even the usual xx at the end.

Tears are smarting in the back of my eyes. I'm hurt, want to call and tell him so, but then remember that the last time we spoke, I hung up on him. It feels like a lifetime ago to me but it was only this morning. I think for a moment, then reply.

OK. Sorry about this morning. I apologised to Ellie also. Love you xx.

When I go to bed a few hours later there is still no reply.

I'm uneasy. It's not like Theo to be so uncommunicative. Is he still angry about this morning, or is something else going on?

I'm past tired, caught in a deep fatigue that makes my thoughts sluggish, my very bones feel weary. Sleep while you can, I tell myself. When this baby joins us, you won't get as much chance.

ELEVEN

I'm running as fast as I can but it is never fast enough. Not when what I'm afraid of comes with me, wherever I go. Everything is in slow motion, each second dragged out. My feet – *thud, thud* – on the ground. *Thud, thud.* The sound repeating until it starts to become something else – a ringing that echoes with my feet. The fear, the dread, are more, not less.

Which is worse, dream or reality? I don't know, but before I can decide, it's too late. I'm awake.

I turn off my phone alarm. I'm alone, then realise with dismay that not only is Theo not here, but his side of the bed is also as neat as it was before I went to sleep. He never came home at all.

My other alarm starts now.

'Vera, alarm off.' It cuts out as I check my phone; there is a message from Theo. It came after midnight.

It was so late when we wrapped up that I stayed at the flat. Love you too xx

It's the same flat he let Alex stay in for a while last year, in the London offices. Theo stays there now and then when there is some big deal going on and he's working all the hours, but he's never done that before without telling me ahead of time.

Love you too, he said, and I focus on those three words, try to put the rest of it out of my mind. Everything is fine with us. Isn't it? And even if there has been some distance between us now and then lately, once he knows about our baby, it'll change everything. I know it will.

It has to. I can't start over again – I *can't*. Especially not with a baby. I could never do that alone.

Getting up and ready for work seems harder than usual. Now that I know, it seems obvious that none of my clothes fit quite right. After a while I find a dress that is loose enough and head downstairs.

Ellie is at the breakfast bar. 'No Dad?' she says.

'He worked late so stayed at the flat.'

She's eyeing me as I put bread in the toaster. 'You need to go on a diet,' she says.

'Gee, thanks.' I stand straighter, not wanting her to have any inkling, not yet.

'Maybe you should cut down on the carbs or something.'

But soon I'm buttering toast, smearing on Marmite. I don't normally eat much bread – especially not with Marmite – but it just felt like what I wanted. Is this a craving? Halfway into eating two pieces I put another slice in the toaster.

'Of course, there are plenty of thin women out there if you pork out,' Ellie says.

'Yeah, thanks for that thought.'

'I mean you said he was at the flat, but was he really?'

'Ellie, that's enough.'

'Or maybe he was there last night, but not alone.'

I give her a hard stare, but Ellie is impervious. She grins as if she knows that she's hit a nerve. Gets her bag and heads for the door.

She's seventeen, I remind myself. She'll be gone soon.

I'm so away with the fairies on the Tube that I nearly miss my stop, only just getting off as the doors start to close. I've only missed one day, but it seems so much longer – the divide between before, when I didn't know, and after, when I did – is a chasm so wide I can hardly see to the other side.

Then I'm rattled at the words I used, even silently, to myself. *Don't* call it that. Not before and after. That was another time. This is nothing like my life was then.

'All right?' Alex says when I get to my desk across from his.

I nod. 'Thanks again for covering for me. I didn't mean to sleep in, but as it turned out the day off was just what I needed.' There is curiosity in his raised eyebrow, as if he knows there is something I'm not saying, but then Hannah is coming over and I don't have to deflect any questions.

'Hope you're feeling better,' she says. No, she doesn't. She hopes I disappear and she can step into my desk, my job. Then I realise that I am going to have to leave, probably for at least a year. Or maybe even longer. I hadn't really thought of that yet. Will I come back? Will I want to? I'm sure I will. But either way, she'll get her wish soon enough.

Other co-workers ask after my health at various points during the morning, and I find myself saying I'd felt sick – true – and went to the doctors – also true – and that I'm feeling better today. And I am. Once I got over having to wake up this morning, not even Ellie's insinuations could knock me from this feeling that I can hardly explain. A mixture of joy, well-being; I feel like I'm actually glowing. Isn't that how pregnant women are described? And I'm relishing this secret, keeping it close. Knowing something this huge, that apart from me and Dr Khan, nobody knows. At the moment the joy is enough to push away the fear.

I'm working through my inbox when a box of pains au chocolat for someone's birthday is brought around. I take one on a napkin to my desk and I'm about to take a bite when the buttery richness reaches my nose and all at once I'm holding back nausea, running for the loo and only just making it in time to throw up in a cubicle.

A bit later I'm staring at myself in the mirror as I splash some water on my face. The glow I thought I felt earlier is well and truly gone.

Hannah comes through the door, hesitant. 'Are you all right?' And she looks genuinely concerned.

'I will be. Could you bring my bag? So I can fix this,' I say, and gesture at my face.

'Of course.'

She hurries back with it and I do my best to repair the damage, breathe in deeply. I still don't feel great but don't think I'll be sick again. I head back to my desk.

Alex comes over. 'Rumour has it that you've been sick in the loo,' he says.

'Oh?'

'Let's consider the evidence.'

'You can't. I flushed it.'

'Ugh. You've been tired, moody, sick, and the mere sight of your favourite pastry made you violently ill. I ate yours, by the way.'

'Good.' I was afraid it'd still be sitting there when I came back. 'But I'm not sure it was violent, exactly.'

'That's not what I heard from someone who was in the cubicle next to you at the time.'

'Huh. And it wasn't the sight of the pain au chocolat; it was the smell.'

'That just confirms the results of my investigation.' I'm starting to get nervous about where this is going.

'Add to that the fact that you had orange juice at a drinks celebration and only a few sips of wine,' he says, then checks around us, making sure no one is listening. 'Rowan, could you possibly be pregnant?'

'Seriously?' I say, and cross my arms. 'Just based on that flimsy evidence?'

'I've been there, done that, twice. Well, in an observing capacity. I recognise the signs.'

'Of course not,' I say, but maybe I want a friend – someone who cares about me – to know.

He must see it in the smile I can't stop from taking over my face.

'I'm right, aren't I?' Even though he brought up the subject, his eyes are wide. It's like he said it for me to refute it, and now that I haven't, he's not sure how to react. 'Wow, Rowan,' he says, finally. 'Congratulations.'

I should probably try to convince him he's wrong but I'm grinning even wider and then he's giving me a hug.

'*Don't* say anything.'

'You know I won't.'

'Just one question. What did you mean by... *moody*?' I fake glare and he springs away, returns to his desk with a look of mock terror.

'Let's go out for lunch today,' he says, a moment later.

'Why not?'

'You choose. I don't want to accidentally pick the wrong type of pastry.'

We get back to work but I'm having trouble concentrating. If Alex worked it out, will anybody else? Maybe, but most people wouldn't front up to me like Alex did.

It feels wrong that Alex knows and Theo doesn't. I have to tell him. It has to be tonight. But what if he works late again?

I think for a moment, then message him.

Really need to spend some time with you tonight... alone xx.

He answers a moment later – says he'll be home early.

There is a fizz of excitement inside. Theo will be so thrilled; I know he will. Having a baby was something he wanted so badly when we got married, and, OK, it took a little longer than we thought it would, but why would anything have changed? But we haven't even spoken about it in years and it's like until he knows, I'm holding my breath. Waiting.

Anticipation can be both pleasure and pain. Like a child at Christmas: before you rip the wrapping off a gift, it can be anything you imagine it to be. Once it is revealed and you hold it in your hands, that's it.

Maybe that is why I'm holding my breath, waiting. My gifts never lived up to my imagination.

TWELVE

ELLIE

I'm staring out the window in maths, twirling my pen when I should be taking notes. Thinking about Rowan this morning. She's not usually that easy to wind up. It's got me wondering if there was something behind it that I don't know about.

She does look like she's put on some weight, but she was pretty thin to start with. Maybe she's feeling insecure. Could it be that Dad actually *is* seeing someone else, and she either suspects or has found out, somehow?

And I feel... weird about that. I wouldn't cry if she left tomorrow – in fact, it'd be a good reason for a party. But it is just possible that if there is another woman and they do split, Dad might end up with someone worse.

Or – devil's advocate – better?

No. I shake my head internally. I can't imagine Dad ever getting together with someone I like.

Maybe it's another sort of devil: better the devil I know.

I'm thinking back, also, to her apologising for accusing me of turning off her alarm. *That* surprised me, and not just because I did it. Normally if I prank her, she reacts in one of two ways:

pretends it never happened, or tells me off. So far so Rowan when she told me off in the morning, but why did she apologise later?

She's not herself; something is going on.

I need to find out what it is.

THIRTEEN

ROWAN

Alex gets a glass of red and I go for ginger ale. We find a table in a quiet corner – no one close enough to overhear.

'OK, tell me everything,' Alex says.

'Like?'

'When did you find out?'

'Yesterday. I went to the doctors. I haven't been feeling well and thought I was coming down with something.' I substituted that in quickly for *thought I was menopausal*. Somehow, I don't want to admit that out loud, certainly not to six-years-younger-than-me Alex. 'Turns out what I'm coming down with is having a baby.'

'When are you due?'

'No idea. I'm having a dating scan on Monday.'

'No idea? There are clues, or so I've been told.'

'This is getting a tad personal, but I'm not very regular, so they need to check.'

Even though I desperately wanted to talk to someone about this – and I trust Alex – I'm feeling increasingly weird that he knows and Theo doesn't. If Theo found out, he wouldn't take it well. Both that anyone knew before him and specifically that it was Alex.

He must see it on my face. 'Is something wrong?'

'No. It's just – well, Theo doesn't know yet. He was... away for work last night.'

'Are you worried how he'll react?'

I shake my head. 'When we got married, we planned to have at least one.' Or at least, Theo did and I was so in love, I went along with it, with not using birth control. But that is best kept to myself. 'After five years, I didn't think it could happen. So, it'll come as a surprise, but it's what we always wanted.' I'm saying the words out loud, much the same ones I'd told myself earlier, but realise now that maybe Alex is right: I am more worried than I want to admit, even to myself.

'You know if you need a friend, someone to talk to about this or anything else, I'm here for you. Right?'

Slight stress on the word *friend*. There was a time he thought he wanted more from me. A message there, received. 'Right. There's nothing to worry about, I promise.'

He nods but I can tell he doesn't believe me and I'm feeling even more uneasy to be having this conversation with Alex.

This is the biggest news; it'll change everything in our lives. For the better. Of course. But I've known Theo long enough to know that, with the possible exception of birthday parties, he doesn't like surprises.

FOURTEEN

Ellie is out with friends when Theo gets in – at half six. Very early! And it soon becomes apparent he assumed when I said I wanted to see him alone that it wasn't for talking. He takes my hand, leads me up the stairs to our room. I'm glad for the delay. Once he knows, even before this baby arrives, will we ever be completely alone again? They will always be with us.

After, Theo is kissing my neck, his hand stroking my hair. I can tell by his breathing he's almost asleep. I can't put this off any longer.

'Theo?'

'Hmmm?'

'There's something I have to tell you.'

His hand stills. I shift to lie on my back.

He goes up on one elbow. Sleepy blue eyes, he smiles. Sated. Content. 'Intriguing,' he says. 'You've softened me up thoroughly for whatever it might be. Let's see... you'd like a new car? What colour?'

'No. Guess again.'

'Uh... a holiday? It'll take some juggling, but in a few weeks, I could probably manage a week. Where would you like to go?'

'Nuh-uh.' The sound of a *no* buzzer. I pull his face down to mine, kiss him. 'I have the most amazing, wonderful news. The thing we hoped for, waited for, thought we couldn't have...'

He's looking lost. 'OK. I give up. What is it?'

I take his hand, hold it against the slight new curve of my stomach. 'I'm pregnant.'

His eyes, on mine. Not comprehending, not reacting or even hiding a reaction. He pulls away, lies back on the bed.

I go up on my elbow now, search his face but his eyes don't meet mine and I still can't see what he is feeling.

'Theo? Say something.'

'Are you sure?'

'Yes. You know how I wasn't feeling well at your birthday party? And I've been really tired, not myself. I went to the doctor yesterday and she did a test. I did another one at home later. And I am most definitely pregnant.'

A mix of emotions too swift to follow cross his face, and I can't read him, don't know what is going on inside him.

'Theo?' I say, uncertain, scared now that I've got things wrong, that I should have found another way to tell him. Or maybe there isn't a right way; maybe he doesn't want this any more.

'I just – you're sure? This is for real?'

'Yes. We're going to be parents.'

His eyes turn back to mine. He studies my face. 'Are you sure this is what you want? Hasn't Ellie put you off?'

'Ha. Not completely. Yes, Theo. It's what I want, more than anything.' As I say the words, I'm gripped again by this fierce protectiveness wrapped around with joy.

'When?'

'I don't know. They've booked an ultrasound for Monday afternoon.'

'An ultrasound?'

'The doctor called it a dating scan. To check things and see how far along I am.'

'Now that I know, I can't believe I didn't notice,' Theo says.

'Thanks a lot.'

He's laughing, pulls me closer for a hug. 'Just winding you up. You're as gorgeous as always.' He kisses me and the worries I'd felt before about telling him melt away.

I'm glad Ellie is out for the evening. We get up after a while and Theo makes me dinner – not something that happens very often, with all the hours he works. He looks alternately dazed and buzzing with happiness, and maybe I'm the same. Everything feels new, like we're starting over again – as if we're still in that early phase of both of us longing to be with each other but not yet sure what it means. A mix of butterflies and anticipation swirl inside me. We're about to become something new and different, and it's both exciting and terrifying. Like a leap of faith should always be.

Late that night Theo is spooning me, his hand caressing the curve of my stomach. Usually that'd make me want to stretch out, to make any imagined bit of round belly disappear. I've never had any serious problems with my weight but that doesn't stop me from worrying about it like anyone else. But things have changed. This bit of soft roundness is something to treasure.

It's an odd weekend. It's like everything is different, but because we haven't told anyone, nothing has changed. Theo stays close but sometimes I catch him studying me at odd moments, as if he's trying to work out who I am, where I came from – how this all came to be. Then he catches my eye, smiles. Holds out his arms.

FIFTEEN

Monday afternoon finally comes. Theo by my side, I'm settled on the table, shirt pulled up. Gel – it's cold. I've never had an ultrasound before but being in a hospital is taking me back to another time, another place, and I flinch, have to stop myself from jumping down and running away.

The sonographer must notice. 'Are you OK? This won't hurt, I promise.'

'I'm fine,' I lie.

The probe goes back and forth slowly in the gel and I'm reminding myself: that was then, this is now. That was then, this is now. All thought of it leaves my mind when I look at the screen.

Our baby, inside of me. Moving in and out of focus, both as the sonographer moves the probe and as our baby moves. And she's pointing things out on the screen, explaining what we can see, so much detail on a 3D screen, even the four chambers of a tiny heart. Arms and legs already recognisable as our baby, the child they will become. It makes it all more real, and I'm drinking it in, being in this moment and only this moment.

'Does everything look OK?' I say, needing reassurance.

'Perfect.'

'Can you tell if it is a boy or a girl?' I say.

'Yes, with a fair degree of certainty, though errors can be made. Do you want to know?'

'I don't know.' I look to Theo but he bounces it back to me. I want a girl. If it is a boy, is it better to know now or when he makes an appearance? I'm not sure.

'No. Let's wait,' I say.

'And how far along is she?' Theo asks.

'We can estimate with good accuracy at this point, using measurements and what we can see on the screen. The due date is estimated to be the twelfth of October.'

Seriously? Only just over four months to go?

I glance at Theo. His eyes turn to mine and he smiles and there is a sense of rightness, despite the initial shock for both of us; a sense that this was always meant to be. I'm suffused with joy so complete I can't speak, can only pull him closer and kiss him. Forgetting where we are and that we're not alone. He kisses me back and there is a throat-clearing noise nearby. He pulls away but his eyes are still on mine.

This baby will be so loved. *Nothing* that happened before matters.

We're soon in the car, on our way home. There is a wide grin on my face that I can't suppress. My hand is on Theo's knee; I want – *need* – physical contact. I feel giddy, my thoughts scattered and fast like my heartbeat. Our baby, made with love. Inside of me. The images on the screen. More real to me now that I've seen her. Or him, I add hastily. Either way. I'm warm, tingling with joy. The happiest I can remember ever being.

'There's something – someone – we need to talk about,' Theo says, and his words are like a sharp pin popping a balloon.

I sigh and sit back in my seat. 'Let me guess. Ellie?'

He nods. 'Let's tell her tonight.'

He's right. We have to tell her. It'll be obvious soon enough. But somehow I wanted this to be just us for a while longer, as if we are the only people in the world. 'OK,' I say. Even thinking about it is making me anxious. She's made it obvious so many times she'd rather I wasn't around. How will she react to a baby on the way?

We stop at a light and Theo glances across.

'Don't look so worried,' he says. 'It'll be fine.'

'You must know some other definition of fine than the one I'm used to.'

The light has changed, his eyes are back on the road. 'You know, she may surprise you. There'll be a moment of shock, yes. But I think Ellie will like not being the only child, having a brother or sister.'

I hope, so much, that he's right. But the more I think about it, the more my misgivings increase. If Ellie is so annoyed that she ups her game with the pranks and the lies, is that something I should have to cope with on top of being pregnant? Maybe Theo might side with me for a change, and this'll be a way of having things out with her, clearing the air, and starting again. Even if he doesn't – I'll do whatever I have to do to stand up for myself. It's not just me to consider now.

Ellie, you don't know what I'm capable of. Don't start a war that you can't win.

SIXTEEN

Theo asks Ellie to join us that evening. She comes out of her room with a sigh, no doubt wondering what unreasonable thing we're going to demand of her now.

'We've got some news,' I say.

'It's exciting and surprising and lots of things all at once,' Theo says.

Ellie must catch that this is something more serious than usual. She even puts her phone down. 'What is it, already?'

'We're having a baby,' Theo says, smiling.

'You're kidding me. Right?' Ellie looks between her dad and me, our beaming faces. Her eyes widen, she takes a step back. 'Oh. My. God. You're not kidding.'

'No. It's for real,' I say. 'You're going to be a big sister.'

'*Half*-sister,' she hisses. 'This is sick. You're both, like, way too old. And don't think for even a second that I'll be babysitting or having anything to do with it.'

'Give us a minute, Rowan?' Theo says, and I want to say no, that this is something we need to deal with together. But I can tell that he really wants me to go and I bite back my reaction. Be gracious. No matter what Ellie thinks or wants, there is nothing she can do to change reality. There will be a baby in this family, just months from now. She'll have to accept it.

'Of course,' I say.

I leave the kitchen, reminding myself as I do so that she is seventeen. Another year and a bit and she'll be gone, won't she? University or a gap year, travelling, or – slim to no chance for Daddy's little princess, but can't rule it out completely – she might even get a job. I walk through the dining room and the lounge to one of the sofas opposite to sit down. But then something happens, something amazing and magical, and I hold my hand against my bump. A flutter, inside. And another. Our baby – she or he is moving – kicking? And I have to share this with Theo, right now, and rush back the way I came.

'—promised me!' Ellie's voice. 'You promised this wouldn't happen. So can you explain yourself?'

'Calm down. Wait and see, Ellie. Everything will be fine.'

'How? How will it ever possibly be fine?' And before I can back away, she's up, across the room and to the doorway where I'm standing.

'Didn't anyone ever tell you it's rude to listen at doors?' She pushes past me and goes down the hall to her room, slams the door.

Theo's face... a raised eyebrow and a quizzical look; he thinks I was eavesdropping, too.

I shake my head. 'I wasn't trying to listen to you and Ellie. I had to come to tell you – just now – she's kicking, I can feel it!'

'She?'

'I don't know, she just *feels* like a she.' I gasp. 'She did it again.' I take his hand, hold it across my bump. 'Can you feel it?' He waits a moment, shakes his head.

'I think she's stopped now,' I say, disappointed for him. 'But back to Ellie. Don't you think we need to deal with her together? We're a family. She has to accept that.'

'Of course we are. But sometimes I think Ellie needs to hear things from me. And slam doors for a while. She'll come around.'

I rest my head against his chest and his arms wrap around me. He kisses my forehead. I know he wants me to drop it, but some of what Ellie said doesn't make sense.

'What did she mean that you promised her this wouldn't happen? Did you tell her we wouldn't have children?'

'Of course not. Before we got married, I did my best to reassure her that things wouldn't change between us. She was much younger then, she must have misunderstood.'

Ellie is a champion at interpreting things to suit herself, so it isn't hard to believe. I look up at Theo. He leans down, kisses me.

He leads me upstairs and all thoughts of Ellie are banished from my mind.

SEVENTEEN

ELLIE

He *promised*. How could he let this happen? Just thinking about it makes me want to vomit. Rowan looked so impossibly smug, like she's done something amazing. Any idiot can get pregnant; it's not exactly an achievement.

She's done this on purpose, hasn't she? To push me out. To get rid of me like she always wanted to. The only surprise is that it's taken so long.

She's been scheming against me from the beginning. It started with her trying to get me sent away to boarding school when I was twelve. She tried to convince Dad it'd be better for my *education*. As if she cared about that. Every now and then I almost relax – think she's nearly human – that maybe we can just ignore each other and peacefully co-exist for a while. But then something she says or does gets back to me. She is always trying to turn Dad against me.

She probably thinks having a baby will make me want to get as far away as I can. But she's in for a surprise: I'm not going anywhere.

Is she trying to disinherit me, too?

I know about their prenup. Dad explained it before they got

married. He said I would still inherit his company and almost everything, not Rowan. That if they got divorced, she wouldn't be entitled to any of it. But does Rowan being pregnant change things?

Phone out, I do a search: *is a prenup still valid if you have a baby?*

I wade through the first page of hits, but the answer isn't clear. It may depend on the wording of the prenup, but even if it clearly says I inherit and Rowan's child doesn't, judges could overrule the agreement if they think it isn't fair.

Dad promised me they would never have children. How could he do this to me?

There's no way I'm going to let Rowan get away with this.

First things first: I need to find the prenup.

EIGHTEEN

ROWAN

There is a meeting between the partners and creative teams the next morning. I decide to go for a visual update, at the end of all the account and client news.

'There's one final project I'm involved in that I'd like to share with everyone,' I say, and drop the ultrasound image into my presentation. It takes a moment for everyone to catch on, for the looks of surprise, congratulations.

'You always did have a flare for the dramatic,' Alex says.

Hannah looks particularly happy with my news but I don't even care. I'll be too busy to be bothered who covers my maternity leave. There are a few sidelong glances between some of them, and I know what they are thinking: isn't she too old? A few days ago, I might have agreed with them. But as it turns out – no. I'm not.

'When are you due?' A question from the head of HR.

'That's where I was yesterday afternoon – having a dating scan. It should be in mid-October, so about four months.'

Now they're really surprised.

'A bit more notice would have been good.'

I glance at Alex, his eyebrows raised a little – he's surprised, too.

'Yes, I totally get that. But I only found out last week.'

More surprise. Disbelief, too. Do they think I'm lying?

Word spreads fast. By mid-afternoon I've almost given up trying to work because of the steady stream of surprised congratulations from the curious. A few pointed comments about biological clocks. A certain male gaze from some, that they always knew I wasn't really serious about this job and now they have proof. But they have children, don't they? Why should it be any different?

A message buzzes on my phone – from Alex. I glance across our desks. His eyes look to my phone and up again. I open the message.

Drinks after work?

Drinking isn't a thing I can do just at the moment.

You look like you could use one. But I'll do the drinking this time.

I hesitate. He's worried. I'm going to have to talk to him eventually; it might as well be now.

OK. A quick one.

End of day we bypass the usual pub – it's busy, and co-workers and clients are likely to be there. Instead, we take a backstreet to a more out of the way place, one we've been to before when we want to talk without ears around us.

A quiet table at the back and he gets a large glass of white while I have to make do with sparkling water.

'So...' Alex says.

'So.'

'Four months?'

'Indeed. I got the feeling there wasn't much belief in my honesty on that front. Should I get my GP to write them a letter? Because I actually fainted when she told me last week.'

'You did?'

'It's OK. She caught me.'

'Are you going to be all right with this motherhood caper? Because fainting at the news sounds like a sign. I know you avoid babies like some avoid people coughing on the Tube.'

He knows me well – at least, he thinks he does. But only as much as I want him to; he certainly doesn't know *why*. I need to give him something so he'll stop watching, worrying, examining me for cracks. But I don't want to lie to him, either.

I sigh, searching for something I can say that is at least partly true. 'It's kind of like this. After trying for so long, I thought it wasn't possible for me to be a mother, so I didn't think about it, tried to keep away from reminders. If there is something you desperately want that you can never have, you maybe convince yourself that you don't want it.'

His eyes on mine, concerned, thoughtful. A nod. 'Because wanting and not getting it will only make you miserable?'

'Exactly.'

He studies me a moment longer and I look away. 'There isn't anything else behind it?' he says.

I shake my head, but when I meet his eyes, he knows I'm lying. Doesn't he? And he's disappointed I won't confide in him.

I'm unsettled that I have been so transparent, that he can read me like this. I've let my guard down too far. This has to stop. Realising I won't go any further, he changes the subject.

'I'm guessing since it came up in a work meeting that you've told Theo. Everything OK there?'

I nod. 'Of course. He didn't faint when I told him, but it took a little while to sink in. We're both delighted now.'

Are we? *Yes.* Of course we are. When I'm with Theo, the certainty is there. The further away he is, out of sight, the more unease ripples around me, and being with Alex isn't helping.

He finishes his wine and we leave soon after. When we say goodbye and head for different platforms at the Tube, there is something in his eyes that shouldn't be there. We both pretend it doesn't exist.

I think through what I said. There was more truth than I realised to the words I chose. It's not so much that I convinced myself I didn't want a baby because I thought I couldn't have one. More, I never thought I could actually *be* a mother. Not the getting pregnant part, but all the rest. And here it is. It's going to happen. Somehow, I've got to find a way to take on this new role, new identity.

But I don't know if motherhood is something I can learn, or copy. What if it is either in you, or it isn't? What then?

NINETEEN

The next day I escape all the eyes and curiosity at work by taking a road trip to a client's offices. I'm halfway through a presentation when I start feeling something I shouldn't be feeling. I wrap things up as fast as I can, then head to the loo. I wasn't imagining it. Spots of blood. Bright red, accusing – *you thought you could do this, did you?*

No, no. It can't be – I can't have a miscarriage. Not this baby; please, no. Despite all the mixed-up feelings and fear to start with, the thought that it could all be over? I call the doctor, so hysterical by then that I'm put straight through. She's reassuring, saying spotting happens sometimes in completely normal full-term pregnancies and miscarriages are less common after the first trimester. But I should still come in for a check, today – to the private hospital.

I get a taxi, call Theo on the way. He doesn't answer. How do I leave a message about this? I hang up. Try again when we're nearly there.

This time he answers. 'Hello, darling.'

'I'm on my way to the hospital. I've had some spotting.

Blood, I mean. I'm scared something is wrong.' He's calm, soothing, says he'll meet me there as soon as he can.

At the hospital while I wait, I cross my hands over my barely-there bump, as if holding, cradling, this tiny life inside of me will keep it where it should be. I promised to look after you. I promised that things would be different. I can't fail – I *can't*. I'll do anything, devote all that I am, or may yet become, to my child. If only she – or even he – is all right.

A calm doctor. A monitor – the baby's heartbeat, reassuring and real. A blood test. A scan. The gel and the probe and I'm afraid to look.

'Mrs Blackwood? Everything is looking absolutely fine.'

'Are you sure?'

'I am. Look, I'll show you.'

I manage to raise my eyes to the screen. The heart, beating. Small movements and arms and legs all present and correct. 'No sign of miscarriage,' she says.

I don't know if it helped or not, all the promises I made to myself. But there are tears of relief in my eyes.

Theo is shown in.

He sees my tears and misinterprets. He takes my hand. 'What's happened?'

I shake my head. 'It's fine, things are fine. Just some spotting, they said.'

The doctor comes back now to speak to both of us. He says that things are progressing as they should, that having some spotting during pregnancy isn't unusual, but that we need to be vigilant. At my age – thanks – I need to be particularly careful. Don't ignore symptoms. Rest. Take it easy as much as I can.

Theo brings the car around, gets out to open the passenger door and settle me in. When he gets back in, he doesn't drive off straight away. He takes my hand.

'They said to rest and take it easy as much as you can,' he says.

'I know.'

'Rowan, you need to think carefully about work. Do you really want to be rushing around on the Tube, going to meetings, working late? You can quit your job. We don't need the money.'

'I know that, but...' My voice trails away. But what? I won't know who I am if I don't work. Even more: I can't stay still, be alone in my thoughts. Shut in, only myself to talk to. Day after day. While the end may be in sight it is still too far away. I couldn't bear it.

I can't.

TWENTY

The door opens, closes. Vera welcomes Ellie home. I'm not up to dealing with her just now and hope she walks straight through, but her footsteps pause.

'What's with you?' she says. I must have caught her eye. Being wrapped in a blanket on the sofa in the afternoon isn't usual for me.

'I've had to go to the hospital.'

She turns towards me, concern in eyes that meet mine. 'Is everything all right?' She's doing a decent impression of someone who cares. Despite saying *half*-sister the way she did when we told her, is she more invested in having a sibling than I thought?

'I think so. They said to take it easy for a few days.'

Theo comes out from the kitchen, a mug of mint tea for me in hand. 'A few days?' he says. 'I thought it was more, take it easy, generally.'

'So, I'll lay off running marathons. End my burgeoning stunt double career. Maybe stop the regular bungee jumps and sky dives.'

'Excellent. And?'

'I've got an appointment with my GP tomorrow. I'll see what she says.'

Theo gives me a hug, extracts a promise that I'll rest, and heads back to work.

I hope, so much, that the GP says everything is fine and there is no risk whatsoever to continuing work and all the other things I do. But I made a promise, to myself, to this baby. I need to give this new life every chance to thrive. If I don't and something happens, I'll never forgive myself.

Ellie disappears into her room. It's too quiet. I want to get up, do something, anything, but I promised. I put the TV on for a while, but the voices and background of people that aren't really here is jarring. I turn it off. I'm enfolded in silence. Ellie's door must be shut as no music or TV escapes. All I can hear are faint traffic sounds, muffled through triple glazing; the grandfather clock I hate that we have to keep because it belonged to Theo's grandmother. Usually, I manage to ignore it.

Tick... tick...

Tick... tick...

It's dragging me back to another clock that ticked, another time I was silent and alone. My heart rate is increasing, my skin clammy.

If I do what Theo suggests I'll be home, alone, most of the time. Like this. Listening.

Tick... tick...

The darkness inside me is too hard to ignore in the silence.

Alex should be home from work by now. As soon as the thought is there, my phone is in my hand.

He answers on the fifth ring, just as, disappointed, my finger is edging to end the call.

'Hi Rowan,' he says. I can hear the sounds of mayhem in the background – two little boys at close to top volume.

'Hi. Sounds like you're busy.'

'Give me a sec.' He puts the phone down, calls for attention and promises a video. Louder whoops and then... near silence. Apart from a video that goes fainter as he moves further away.

'I'm back. Is everything OK? I thought you were coming back to the office after that meeting.'

'Well, I was going to, but instead made a trip to hospital.'

'Oh no. What's wrong?'

I give him the summary. I reckon he can take the details, having two of his own.

'So, it's rest for a few days?' he says, and starts running through meetings he can handle on his own, others to postpone, and as he does so I'm thinking how I'd speak to one client, what I'd suggest for another, but that isn't what this is about. He pauses for a breath.

'Alex, the thing is, I'm not sure I'm going to come back. I'm going to see my GP tomorrow, see what she thinks. I'll call HR after that, but I wanted to talk to you first.'

'Of course, do what the doctor says. If you need more rest, take it.'

'I need to make this baby my first priority. Work is an added stress and strain. Maybe it's time to take a step back.' I hear my voice saying words I'm not sure I want to be saying, almost like I'm trying them out, seeing how they sound.

There is a pause. 'Are you sure that's what you want?' Slight emphasis on *you*.

'I think so. I mean, yes. But I'll let you know what happens tomorrow. Sorry if I end up leaving you in the lurch.'

'Don't apologise. I'll cope – we'll cope. It'll be fine. Do what is right for you.' He pauses. 'I wonder, sometimes, if things would have turned out differently for Sally and me if we weren't both rushing here and there all the time. If she could have done just that – taken a step back. We couldn't have handled our mortgage then without both of us working, but if we could have, things might have been different.'

I'm surprised. From everything he's told me before, work commitments weren't the problem with Sally.

We say our goodbyes.

Maybe Alex said that because he doesn't want me to come back. Maybe he wants to be the lead for real and not just in Fisher's chauvinistic estimation, and me leaving would give him a clear run at moving up. Then I feel guilty for suspecting him of that kind of machination. After all, he did ask, too, if that was what I really wanted – implying it might be Theo behind it.

But this isn't about Theo, or anything he said or didn't say.

I can't fail. I just can't.

That night I can't sleep. Not getting enough rest has to be on the list of things that aren't good for my baby, but worrying about what is or isn't good for them is what is keeping me awake. And worrying, too, why I always want to talk to Alex when something is troubling me. Why do I feel uneasy about it? That is what friends do, isn't it? And that is what we agreed: to be friends.

Anyhow, as far as work goes, what about what's good for *me*? That must be good for my baby, too.

I finally drift away, trapped in nightmares, one after another, each darker than the last. Bookmarked by the *tick, tick* of the clock.

They've found me.

It's because I'm pregnant – my unborn child is a beacon, drawing them ever closer. They'll never stop, never let me go.

I run as fast as I can, but no matter how I try, footsteps are close behind me; the *thud, thud* keeping time with the clock. Getting closer. Then I trip, frantically try to right myself.

Reaching for supports that aren't there, I fall. So scared I've hurt my baby, but all I can do now is close my eyes and hide inside.

Part of me knows I'm dreaming, that it can't be real. If I wake up, I will leave it behind. But I can't. I'm trapped in darkness.

TWENTY-ONE

Theo and Ellie are gone by the time I drag myself out of bed the next morning. A pale face, dark circles under eyes that stare back from the mirror as I brush my teeth, still feeling shaken by last night's dreams. When I'd finally managed to wake myself to escape the horror, it was 4 a.m. I'd stayed awake, counting minutes, then hours – afraid if I fell asleep again that the dreams would return.

He can't find me here. I've made sure of it. Even if he could, he has no power over me or my future any more.

I know these things are true, but still can't shake off the residual fear. Can't forget the threats he made all those years ago. I'd been caught in-between for too long, suspended, neither awake or asleep. A liminal place, where nightmares leave traces that won't easily let go.

Somehow, I get through the morning; manage to eat. Shower and attempt to cover the evidence of a difficult night with make-up. Make it to the GP in time for my appointment. The waiting room today has an older man. A mother and teenage daughter. Another pregnant woman, much younger than me. Her stomach is straining against her maternity dress – she must be nearly due – a blush of happiness and good health on her cheeks. I'm studying her, wanting to emulate her in months to come. She gives me an odd look and I realise I was staring, look away.

A door opens – it's Dr Khan.

'Mrs Blackwood? Please, come in.'

Once in her room I settle myself in the chair opposite her desk.

'How are you feeling today?'

No point in lying; she has eyes and no doubt can tell that I'm exhausted. 'Not great. I couldn't sleep.'

'Sorry to hear that. Have you been worried about the spotting and hospital visit?' I nod, though that is just one on my list of worries. 'I've seen the scan and other results. Everything is looking just as it should.'

'You're sure?'

'Yes, absolutely. I'm sure they told you that if you have more spotting or other symptoms like pain, cramping and so on, you need to go back straight away and be checked again. But please be reassured.'

'I'll try. Thank you. I have a question.' She nods for me to go on. 'They said I should take it easy, rest for a few days. But I'm thinking of giving up work.'

She asks about my job, the demands, the hours. We discuss the pros and cons. She thinks it's not necessary to give up work, but at the same time, can't promise that nothing will go wrong. In the end I get her to sign me off for a week instead of a few days, to think things through.

When I walk back to the Tube after my appointment, I can't shake the feeling that something, someone, is watching me, following. I turn again and again to look but no one is there.

I'm off the Tube and walking home when I'm sure I can hear heavy footsteps behind me, getting closer – so like my nightmare that I feel like I'm sleepwalking, that this isn't real. I spin around. He's not there. But people look at me oddly, give me space.

Get a grip, Rowan. Lack of sleep is making me imagine things. That's all. No one is following me home.

TWENTY-TWO

ELLIE

Not taking any chances of being interrupted, I put Vera on instructions that no one is to get in or out of the house without her checking with me first. Not Rowan or even Dad. No doubt he could override it in the app – even Rowan might manage to figure out how – but it'll take long enough for me to get clear.

I open his study door, go across to the built-in wooden filing cabinets that line the back wall. Dad is organised, methodical. Files everything alphabetically and keeps every receipt and statement *forever*. All I have to do is work out where to look. What would their prenup be filed under?

I try P for prenup – no.

Under Rowan's name? She's not under R. But there is a file under Blackwood, Rowan. Full of things like credit card bills, bank statements. I take a quick photo of her account details for both – might come in handy. Then I can't stop myself from snooping into her credit card bills. That red dress she wore to Dad's birthday party cost a packet. It'd go a good way towards buying me my first car. Dad wants us to do a rebuild of a classic, together – like he did for Rowan, and for his first car, a long time ago. I think that is a delaying tactic to keep me off the roads, and

I'd rather shiny and new. Anyhow, going by Rowan's dress, I need to demand an increased allowance. But there is definitely no prenup in her file. I'm pushing it back in place when I notice the file before hers, and my stomach twists. Blackwood, Naomi. My mother.

Everything goes still, inside and out. I know so little about her. Once I knew she left me, I didn't want to know more – that's what I said if anyone asked. But as much as I want that to be true, there are days when I can't stop myself playing *what if*. What if she never left? What if she came back? I made up stories when I was younger, all different but with one main premise: she never meant to leave me at all. She'd been kidnapped, say, but managed to escape. Or she had a bump on the head and forgot who she was, but then her memory came back. She'd run to me and I'd run to her and it'd look like some TV ad of a mother and daughter, running into each other's arms in a field of daisies.

I've grown up enough now. I don't believe in fairy tales, in happily ever after. She left me – that's it. Nothing to add.

But I can't stop myself from looking in her file.

Her credit card bills. The month she left, over seventeen years ago, and then no more. Either she stopped using her credit card that Dad paid or he cancelled it. Her last few credit card bills are full of baby stuff. Picture books. Baby clothes. Toys. She was shopping, big time, for a baby she was about to abandon. She must have bought all this stuff because she felt guilty. Didn't she? I hope so. I hope she never got over it. I hope that it ate into her every day of her life and it still does until she dies, hopefully of a horrible incurable illness, alone.

Stop getting distracted. It's unlikely that Dad would come home in the mid-afternoon but with Rowan off this week, I've no idea where she is or when she'll be back. I put the file back as it was.

Where else could the prenup be filed?

Maybe under Rowan's name before she got married. What was it?

I'm struggling to remember. I was only twelve. She doesn't have any family that visit, so it's not like her parents come by to remind me what it was. Rowan had a few friends from university that came to the wedding, but no long-time friends from before then. I haven't seen her university friends around since. She never goes away for girls' weekends or anything. Now I think about it, it's like she never had a life until she showed up and started wrecking mine. But no one appears out of nowhere. She must have had parents, maybe siblings; friends, enemies. Schools and jobs and all the rest. I've tried finding Rowan on social media before and didn't come up with anything beyond a vanilla Facebook page – very little on it that was personal. Just work stuff mostly. But maybe if I try harder, I'll find something in her past I can use against her.

How about her present? There were a few people she worked with that came to the wedding. Alex was one of them. I remembered him from the wedding when he came to stay for a few nights last year when he split from his wife. I wasn't likely to forget him. Even when I was twelve, I thought he was totally fit – the complete tall, dark and handsome cliché. But it wasn't just how he looked, he had something – a kindness, I suppose – that extended even to an unhappy and unfriendly me. He made an effort to get me talking about non-wedding stuff. His wife didn't come to the wedding – home with their son, he'd said – so I don't know what she was like. He was going to stay with us for longer when they broke up, but then Dad let him stay in his work flat until he got something sorted.

Dad didn't like Alex – it was obvious. So why did he help him with the flat?

Apart from being fit, Alex is also much younger than Dad – I'm pretty sure he is younger than Rowan, too. Was Dad jealous? Did he let him stay at the flat to get him out of the house?

Was there something going on between Alex and Rowan? That didn't occur to me at the time, but now I'm wondering. Even if there wasn't, maybe I can use that somehow.

Something to think about after I find the prenup.

I scan through the alphabetised files, looking for anything on Rowan, but there are so many files. I'm sure her surname was something unmemorable, ordinary. I skip ahead to Smith. Nothing. Then try Jones, and there it is: Jones, Rowan. I flip through the file. There isn't much. Some notes in her handwriting. A quick glance confirms – love letters. I grimace and put them back. OK, I guess it's cute that he's kept them, but in a filing cabinet? Then there is her old ID before the name change to Blackwood when they married. There most definitely isn't a prenup.

So, where the hell is it? I know Dad; he keeps everything, he'd have his own copy for sure. I'm staring at the filing cabinets, willing them to offer up their secrets. Opening drawers randomly as if it'll jump out at me. The last drawer, bottom right – it doesn't open. Is it jammed? No. I think it's locked. I bet all the interesting stuff is in there. I hunt around in the desk drawers for keys, but don't find any.

Though he'd have no need to hide the prenup. Rowan signed it and I know about it, so why bother?

A flash of inspiration hits me: maybe it's filed under the name of the law firm he uses.

'Ellie, Rowan is at the front door. Should I let her in?' Vera's almost but not quite human voice. I scrabble quickly through the files, find one marked Abel & Johnson. Bingo. Rifle through it and there it is – a cover letter, agreement attached. Grab it, turn off the light and run to my room.

'Vera, let Rowan in.'

TWENTY-THREE

ROWAN

I stand this way and that, hold my face at different angles to the camera, but the door stubbornly refuses to open. I could really do without this just now.

I fish my phone out of my bag, tempted to call Theo and ask him to take care of it. But I need to be able to do this myself. What if I'm left standing here in the rain with a crying baby?

I open the app, go through the menu, find the front door. Just as I'm about to slide the switch to open, the lock clicks and the door opens.

I roll my eyes, step through. Give the door a bit of a slam. 'Vera, thank you *so* much for letting me in,' I say, sarcasm at full tilt. It's like she was watching, giggling, waiting until I found the right part of the app and then opened the door.

'You're welcome, Rowan.' Vera is very literal. While she has the basic please and thank you of human manners down well, she doesn't get humour or sarcasm.

Now I'm wondering if someone else was doing the watching and giggling.

'Vera, is Ellie home?'

'Ellie is in her room.'

I'm not up for any kind of confrontation with Ellie just now. Instead, I make some peppermint tea and retreat to the guest room upstairs to think. The one I'd picked as our future nursery. I sit in the chair in the corner, where my rocking chair will be.

When I sat here just days ago, I was caught in daydreams of our smiling baby and perfect lives. I know babies are hard work, but Theo and I love each other. This baby will make our family complete. And I felt optimistic that I could keep my previous life and the things that happened to me where they belong – in the past. That I could protect and nurture this child. Theo is such a good parent; any shortcomings I might have he could balance out. And I would strive to be a good mother, the best I could possibly be.

That all-encompassing sense of feeling protective of this tiny life is still there. But now things feel more... unsettled. Why?

It's a combination of things. How the ticking clock got to me yesterday. The nightmares that followed. Lack of sleep. The feeling I had earlier that someone was following me. But most of all, I'm afraid what these things may represent. Is being pregnant going to bring everything back? Can I really cope with this?

Not alone. But I can, with Theo. With us as a united front, together.

At least there was the good news today that Dr Khan doesn't think there is any need at all for me to quit work, so long as I'm sensible and don't wear myself out. I'm so relieved. I know myself. I need to have enough to do, to occupy my mind, to keep the things I don't want to – *can't* – think about at bay.

A message pings to my phone: Theo. Asking how things went with my doctor's appointment. I feel guilty. I should have told him straight away.

I answer.

All is fine. Have you got a few minutes to talk?

He rings a moment later.
'Hi Theo.'
'Hi. So, what did she say?'
'She's happy with my general health, and while a few days off might do me some good, there's no need to cut back on what I normally do. She's signed me off for a week, but no problem going back to work after that. I just need to be sensible and get enough sleep.'
He doesn't answer straight away.
'Theo?'
'You don't need to work.'
'I know that.'
'So why not take the time for yourself? To take care of the two of you.' His voice is gentle, concerned. He wants what is best for me, but how can he know what that is when there is so much that he doesn't know? There are voices in the background at Theo's end. 'I have to go in a moment. I won't be home tonight – there's a late meeting. We'll talk tomorrow. Love you.' The phone clicks and he's gone.

There were times when we were first together – when loving Theo was so overwhelming, amazing – that I almost told him, at least part of what I went through when I was young. But when I tried, he said whatever may have happened in my life before didn't matter. I could tell him if I wanted to, but it was my choice. I didn't *have* to.

And that made me love him even more.

Now, after so long, hiding who and what I was is so much a part of me, and who I've become. The more time passes, the more impossible it feels to go there. Especially now. The stakes are so much higher. I can't risk telling him anything, not when it's not just me I have to protect. I can't mess things up.

All Theo knows is that I was raised in care and have no family. That is all true – sort of.

I was in care from age sixteen. And I have no family by choice.

TWENTY-FOUR

ELLIE

Rowan never comes to my room; Dad doesn't, either. This is my domain and only the cleaner gets in once a week. So, the chances of being interrupted are very low. But they're not nil and I'm risk-adverse.

I go into my bathroom with the documents and lock the door.

The prenup is in legalese and I concentrate as I go through the clauses, not sure I get every detail, but as far as I can tell it all seems much as what Dad told me. But then, a clause towards the end. Black words on white paper, stark and definite: *this agreement is null and void if there is a child of the marriage.*

I read the words over and over again, but there is no grey area. It's definite enough.

I'd destroy it if I thought there'd be any point. There'll be another copy of it, somewhere – with the lawyers. Or maybe Rowan has a copy. She should do. She probably had her own lawyer when this was being drafted; they might be the ones who insisted on that clause.

Maybe Dad was so sure they'd never have a child that he thought it didn't matter. Or maybe, this is how he always meant things to be: me deposed. Replaced. Not the most important person in his world, not any more. Not with Rowan and a new baby.

Dad promised me this agreement protected my inheritance. He also promised me they wouldn't have children.

Two broken promises, wrapped together in a pink or blue bow.

I can't stay here, between these walls, not tonight. Dad's not going to be here and I can't face dinner with Rowan, alone.

I try Maisie, then Amy – both are busy. Other friends, too, but no one can make a night out tonight.

I don't care; I'll go on my own.

I book an Uber, find a dress – the one Rowan said was too short. Brush out my hair, do my make-up. When I come through, my timing isn't great. Rowan is just coming down the stairs.

'Going out?'

'Clearly.'

'Do you want some dinner? A snack?'

'No. I'm going to a party, there'll be food there,' I lie. 'Don't wait up.'

TWENTY-FIVE

ROWAN

Now that she's older, sometimes Ellie and I seem to have reached a kind of understanding. She's always been such a schemer – she always has a plan. Things she says often seem innocent enough but have double meanings, ones that Theo can't, or won't, see. And somewhere along the way I mostly stopped reporting things she has said and done to Theo. It did little good. He either didn't believe me or she'd find a way to explain things away. Now most of the time we keep out of each other's way. I don't meddle in her life any more than I have to. But with Theo away on an overnight business trip, when she says she's going to a party and tells me not to wait up, that is exactly what I decide I should do. Well, wait, anyhow, half awake and half asleep on the sofa. Music on low to mask the ticking clock.

The sound of the door makes my eyes open. Ellie lurches through from the hall, almost falls, catches herself.

'Ellie? Are you all right?'

She turns slowly, faces me, confused, like she can't quite focus enough to see who is there. Her make-up is a mess. Has she been crying?

'Ellie?'

She leans against the wall, slides down until she's sitting on the floor. I get up, go to her, and hold out a hand.

'Come on. Up you get. Time for bed.'

She shakes her head, arms crossed against her stomach. 'Feel shick,' she says, and she looks it.

I run to grab a bin and get it to her just in time as she starts to retch. Not much comes up, as if she's already been sick, but the smell of it is making me feel like I might be about to join her. I manage to hold it off.

Finally, she stops.

'Soz,' she says, sounding like she means it.

'No big deal. Come on.' I help her up, to her room. Bed. Take off her shoes, start to pull a blanket over her and she's already snoring. I put her bin next to the bed, just in case. And leave her to it.

Going back through, I see – and smell – the one she was sick in. I'm not washing that out. I take it to the bins outside and chuck it in.

It's after 2 a.m. What, if anything, do I do or say about the condition Ellie was in when she got home? She said she was at a party, but if they'd gone to a pub or a club, she'd easily pass for old enough to get in. Not all her friends would, though. I hope she wasn't on her own.

I sigh. I'll try to talk to her tomorrow, though no doubt she'll misinterpret everything, no matter what I do or say. Maybe it is impending parenthood making me feel this way, but I'm actually worried about her.

TWENTY-SIX

'What on earth are you doing?' It's Ellie, having finally emerged from her room at almost noon. She is staring at the mess on every worktop and me pulling things out of cupboards. Her face is pale, looking a bit green from last night still.

'Reorganising the kitchen cupboards.'

'Because why?'

To have something – anything – to do, is what I'm thinking. 'To make them more organised,' is what I say.

'By making a mess.'

'That's how it starts.'

She takes a can of fizzy drink out of the fridge; finds a glass in a cupboard I haven't got to yet. She pushes the button in the fridge door for ice to clang into her glass and flinches at the sound. Then she stalks back the way she came.

Is something wrong, beyond a well-earned hangover? In the set of her shoulders, more than the usual storm clouds in her eyes?

'Ellie, wait a moment.'

Cue a tragic sigh as she turns and faces me. 'What?'

'About last night.'

'What about it?'

'Don't you remember not being able to walk straight and vomiting in the bin?'

'Oh, that,' she says, and she looks like she might need another bin, just thinking about it.

'You're underage. Where were you? Were your friends with you? You said you were going to a party.'

'So?'

'I'm only worried about your safety. When you're that drunk, you're more vulnerable – anything could happen to you.'

'Like that would be my fault!' She's angry now, and I get it. I really do. And I'm thinking, what if this was my daughter? What would I say?

'Look at it this way. You wouldn't leave the front door wide open with your keys and purse on the side in case someone stole them. It'd be wrong if they did – it's not like you're asking to be robbed – but some people are dishonest.'

'So?'

'You should be able to be safe no matter how much you've had to drink. But the reality is there are nasty people out there. And that's not all. You could fall over, hurt yourself. Cross the road without looking and get hit by a car. Just please be careful, that's all.'

'Fine.' She hesitates. 'You're not going to tell Dad, are you?' The bolshy teenager retreats and the little girl is back, the one who doesn't want to ever disappoint her dad.

I'm torn. 'Do you think I should?'

'No!'

I sigh. 'OK. I won't. But if you come home like that again, then I will. Got it?'

'Whatever.'

'Is something else wrong?'

Her lips form a thin line, a look of contempt. 'You should know. Why don't you answer your own question?'

'I honestly don't. Why don't you tell me?'

'As if you care.' And she's gone.

What was that about? Suddenly tired, I sit at the breakfast bar. Admire the mess, as Ellie called it. More than one mess, maybe.

As if you care, Ellie said. I don't know if it is the impending baby that's making me feel this way, but somewhere under all the petty annoyances... I actually do care for Ellie. Maybe more than I realised. It's been over five years now: why does she still resent me so much? If I can't get along with my stepdaughter, who's to say it will be any better with my own child?

I don't know how I'll be with a baby. It's not the practical aspects; I had younger sisters and brothers I had to help with, so none of that will be a surprise. It's having the mother–child bond between us that makes me nervous. What if they're born and I hold them, and there is just nothing there? I want with all of my being to protect and nurture this child – to love them and keep them safe. To give them what I never had. But what if they look at me with Ellie's eyes, want nothing to do with me?

Maybe my relationship with Ellie is so difficult because of me, not her. Maybe the family I escaped from has left marks so deep that no child could ever truly love – or even trust – someone as damaged as I am.

Maybe they'd be right not to.

Between the lack of sleep, Ellie's animosity and my dark thoughts, my interest in a better-organised kitchen has disappeared. I manage to stir myself enough to put everything back in the cupboards, more or less where it was to start with.

I go upstairs to our room, draw the curtains. Close the door so I can't hear the clock. Curl up on my side of the bed, wishing Theo were here but it'll be hours before he's back from work.

I close my eyes. Images – faces – words said and worries whispered only to myself – all tumble randomly in my thoughts. I slow my breathing and slide into sleep even as I'm not sure if I should. When I'm asleep, I'm not safe. That is where the monsters hide. The things I don't want to think about come closer.

They said he couldn't find me. They were wrong.

I saw him get out of his car. I should have run. But as soon as I saw his face, it was like every vein opened and blood and resolve flowed out of me. Fear left me empty, powerless. He dragged me by my hair, out of the house and into the street. His hands around my neck. His words before the police came and pulled him away:

No matter where you hide, I'll find you, I'll kill you – to save you from the devil.

I know he meant it. He's searching for me, still. He'll never stop until I'm dead.

Vague shadows coalesce, threaten me and my unborn child.

They've found me. He's coming for me now—

Wake up, I tell myself – shout in my mind – but the more I try to move, to speak, I'm held down, frozen like I was all those years ago. Powerless. Unable to move, to free myself.

Then I'm struggling, fighting, caught in blankets. Pushing at the weight holding me—

'Rowan! Wake up.'

I open my eyes. Confused, lost. Slowly, here and now come back.

Theo is rubbing his shoulder. 'You've got a good right hook.'

'Did I hit you? I'm sorry. I was having a nightmare.'

'I'll say. You were screaming the house down.'

'I was?'

'What were you dreaming about?'

I shake my head. 'I don't remember,' I lie.

I get up, shower. Ellie has gone out. We make dinner together and I manage to eat it. I'm exhausted and don't argue when Theo suggests I go up to bed early.

But I can't close my eyes. I'm too afraid.

TWENTY-SEVEN

The next morning, I feel more tired than when I went to bed. Taking it easy isn't working for me – it's not a good strategy. The more time I have to sleep, the less I can do it. The more I try, all I can think of are nightmares. I'm exhausted after just days at home. I need to go somewhere, anywhere. Away from these four walls. I would normally email the roughs for the charity dinner marketing for Richmond Rescue. Instead, I print them out, force down some toast and get in the car for the short journey.

Halfway there, I stop at a red light. Then jump when a loud horn sounds behind me. The light is green. I drive forward. Did I actually fall asleep? Maybe I shouldn't be driving when I'm this tired, but I'm almost there now. The fear of falling asleep again keeps me gripping the wheel so tight my hands ache. When I pull in, Charlie's car is in the car park. Maybe this was a bad idea. I try to get past her office but the door is open and she sees me, waves me in.

'Hi Rowan, lovely to see you.' She draws me in for a hug.

'I've brought the roughs for the dinner.' I hand over the file.

'You didn't need to run them over. What's wrong?'

'Nothing. Just thought I'd see if there is anyone who needs some company.' She knows I mean one of their furry friends.

She raises a sceptical eyebrow, but lets it go and tells me about a new arrival. They've called her Sasha. A blue roan show cocker, she was freed from a puppy farm. Not much more than a few years old but likely had multiple litters, one after another, in miserable conditions. Charlie takes me to her kennel.

Sasha is beautiful, from what can be seen – she is turned away from the kennel door in a corner, shaking. Bed, toys, food all ignored.

I go in, quietly. Sit on the floor very near the door so as not to crowd her. Stay very still.

I speak in a low, soft voice. Tell her that she is a good dog. That things will get better. Not all people are cruel. Someone will love her and she'll love them back and her life will be better than she ever dreamed it could be. And I hear my words and wonder who I am speaking to – her or me? Do either of us believe in fairy tales?

I don't know how much later it is when I stir. Half curled on the floor and half on the dog bed. Sasha is asleep, too, on the floor, not touching me but close. Her eyes open soon after mine do – liquid and beautiful brown. I want to stroke her, but I'm afraid any movement will spook her. She's sniffing, then so quick and soft a touch it could almost be missed, her head darts forward and she gives a tiny lick of my arm. And like that was all she could manage for the day, she goes back to her corner. At least she's not shaking any more. I get up quietly, go back through the door. Promise I'll come and see her again.

I mean to slip away to my car but Charlie spots me as I go past her office and calls me in for a chat.

'You were so long that I'd gone to check how you were getting on, and saw you both asleep.'

'Sorry, I was so tired – I didn't mean to take a nap.'

'Don't apologise. It was amazing how close to you Sasha came.'

'Less threatening unconscious, I'm guessing. I should get going—'

'Not so fast. I'm worried about you, Rowan. You weren't yourself at Theo's party; now you're so exhausted you fell asleep on a dog bed. Are you going to tell me what is wrong?' She's not prying in the way some people do – to learn things for gossip or advantage. She genuinely cares, I know she does. But I bet she wouldn't if she knew everything about me.

Though there is something I can tell her that won't be a secret much longer. Everyone will know soon enough.

'Well, I do have some momentous news. We're having a baby.'

'Oh, Rowan! Congratulations. That's amazing.' Another hug, then she pulls back and studies me. 'But you don't seem that happy about it. Is everything OK with Theo?'

'It's not him, it's me. It's just – I'm not sure I...' I'm too tired to string a sentence together even after my nap. I'm afraid I'm going to cry, that she'll see me for what I really am. Pathetic and weak. 'It's just I'm not sure I'm cut out to be a good parent.'

'And you're scared.'

I nod, not trusting my voice.

'I was, too. Though it's long ago now, I remember the fear. There is no rule book for being a good parent. All you have to do is be yourself. Dogs love you – they vouch for you. They tell me how kind you are inside, Rowan. I know by how you were with Sasha and others before her that you will be an amazing mother.'

I'm struggling to keep myself together, afraid if I let go what else may spill out. And I'm not sure dogs are the best judge of character. The one that lived next to us when I was a child loved his owners no matter how they treated it. People are different. I never forget. And with that thought I'm all right again. Held in. Contained.

'If you ever want to talk, I'm here,' Charlie says.

'Thank you, I appreciate that. Now I must get on.'

She's giving me yet another hug, but I'm switching off, keeping myself away from Charlie inside if not outside.

'I hope you can come and see Sasha again.'

'I will. I wish I could foster her,' I say, and mean it. She's scared, locked up in a strange place, alone. She doesn't know yet that it is better than where she was before.

'I know you do. It should be in all marriage vows – a promise to love, honour and rescue dogs.'

I can't complain, not really. Theo might not want to rescue a dog, but he rescued me. And I'm far more trouble.

TWENTY-EIGHT

I stay awake on the drive home – that nap with Sasha must have done me some good. I even manage to get a casserole in the oven for the three of us to eat later. I try to read a book, but can't concentrate. Flick through channels on TV. Nod off, come to, nod off again.

Finally, I call Alex.

'Hi, Rowan. How're things?'

'OK. But please tell me you miss me and that the company will collapse without my immediate return.'

'Of course, we all miss you! But we're coping.'

'Any time you want to call to discuss clients or anything, I'm here.'

'You're bored, aren't you?'

'I am. Any suggestions?'

'Well, when Sally was pregnant the first time, she went through a massive nesting phase. Cleaned every inch of the house. Made extra meals for the freezer. Darned socks. It was amazing.'

'Huh. Anything that doesn't involve domestic chores?'

He starts listing the latest popular series, but I've never been one for sitting and watching TV for hours. My mind always wanders. Maybe that is because – in part, at least – it was forbidden when I was a child. When I was first in foster care, I went through a phase of wanting to watch it all the time, my eyes and ears hungry for what had been denied. When that wore off, it all seemed so boring, so samey, and anything that didn't take my complete attention let my mind wander to places I'd rather it didn't go. Instead, I began to read my way through libraries, which led to my grades going up, getting into university. In words and stories – trying on other lives through the characters – I found an escape.

Alex runs through the initial campaign strategy for our new major-catch client, but we wouldn't have that client if it wasn't for me, my ideas. And now the development is happening without me.

Alex has to go to a meeting.

After our goodbyes, I'm sitting here, holding my phone. More bored and unhappy than before.

Ellie gets in from school. Says nothing, gets a drink and goes to her room. Distant slamming of the door. I guess being the cool parent – stepparent, Ellie corrects me in my mind, as if she can hear my thoughts – has completely failed to make her more favourably disposed towards me. I sigh, not sure if I'm doing the right thing in not telling Theo the state she was in last night. I mean, I could tell her again that her behaviour could be dangerous, but she won't listen to me. If Theo said it, she'd probably be more inclined.

But I more or less promised not to, didn't I? So long as it doesn't happen again. Though maybe I'm just telling myself that because it's the path of least resistance.

It's heading for eight and I set the table, then go to check the casserole. But when I open the oven door – it's cold. I'm sure I turned it on. I remember setting the temperature. I mean, I think I do. Could Ellie have turned it off? Why would she, other than to be annoying? I can't accuse her of that without proof or I'll end up apologising to both of them again.

I'm slamming the oven door shut when Theo comes in.

'Did the oven do something you object to?'

'No.' I sigh. 'Dinner should be ready now but I must have forgotten to turn it on. If I do it now, dinner won't be ready for hours.'

Ellie comes in now, gives Theo a kiss on the cheek.

'What's for dinner?' she says, an innocent look in her wide eyes making me wonder again if she's behind it.

'Raw beef casserole,' I say.

'Yum.' She pulls a face.

'How about we go out for dinner?' Theo says.

'Not me,' Ellie says. 'I've got homework. But I need pizza money.' She holds out her hand and he complies.

'Get ready,' Theo says to me, 'and I'll see if I can get a reservation at our place. If not, I'll try some others.'

Our place – what we call the French restaurant he took me to on our first date. Get ready? I glance down, realise that what I'm wearing is not for public consumption. Theo rarely sees me in trackies and T-shirt.

Upstairs I find a dress that still almost fits. I need to go shopping for maternity clothes. That is something I could do on one of these endless days off.

I can't stay home like this for months, just waiting. I can't. I need to pull myself together, show Theo – and more importantly, myself – that I'm with it enough to go back to work next week.

The fit of the dress in the mirror is acceptable. It does show my baby bump a little but that's OK, now I know that is what it is. But my hair is a mess. I brush it out, then put some extra effort into my make-up. Dot and blend concealer under my eyes to hide the dark circles.

Finally, I head down the stairs. Theo is finishing a cup of tea; he says we have a table booked.

'Thanks. Sorry about dinner.'

'Shall we take your car, and you can drive back?' Theo says. Double downside of being pregnant: I can't drink, and I'm stuck being designated driver. I almost protest – I'm so tired, my driving is probably as suspect as if I'd had a few glasses of wine. But I don't want Theo to worry. I'll take extra care.

Then I'm hunting in my bag and jacket pocket for my keys.

'Looking for these?' Theo says, holding them up.

'Where were they?'

He's shaking his head – amusement in his eyes. 'I found them in the fridge.'

TWENTY-NINE

ELLIE

I slam the door behind me. Maisie's Mini pulls in just as I get through our gate.

'What a fucking day,' I say, and collapse into the passenger seat.

'Oh no, babes.'

'At least operation ruin dinner worked, and thus I am free.'

'Excellent. Where shall we go?'

'Where do you think? I need a strategy session. I messaged Amy; she's meeting us there.' *There* being a particular King's Arms we've found – a pub we quite like where the guy at the bar quite likes me, so no ID required. Bit off the beaten track and down-market enough that we're unlikely to be rumbled by parents or their friends. But now we're nearly there, I'm uneasy and wishing I'd suggested somewhere else. I ended up here on my own the other night, didn't I? It's all a bit hazy. All I have are flashes of memory – being sick in the loo. Gross. And how did I even get home? I can't remember, but I won't forget the hang-over in a hurry.

But it's too late. A message from Amy that she's there comes just before Maisie pulls in. Before long the three of us are at a table in the corner of the beer garden.

'Can you go?' I say to Amy, give her the pizza money to go to the bar.

She's back a moment later, shakes her head. 'He wants to see you.'

I go to the bar. 'Hi, Stuart,' I say, and manage a smile.

'Hi Ellie.' He's tall, long streaked blond hair. Not at all bad looking, maybe twenty-five. But there's no chance I'm getting together with a guy who works at a bar, no matter how handy that is until I'm eighteen.

'You look hot tonight,' he says. His eyes do that thing where they roam from my face, down my short dress and back up again, slowly, and he whistles. 'Can you get rid of your friends later? I'll drive you home again.'

Again.

I'm feeling sick. More flashes of memory from the other night are coming to me now – of Stuart, his car. He just drove me home. Didn't he? That's all. I start backing away then remember why I'm here.

'Can we get a bottle of white and three glasses?' He turns to get wine out of the fridge, a cooler. The glasses. I pay, then feel his eyes on me as I take the wine and glasses out and to our table.

'What's wrong?' Maisie says, instantly.

I shake my head, pour a large glass of wine. I have a long sip. It's almost chilled enough to mask how crap it is compared to the stuff I pilfer at home and I try to remind myself why we're here, what I need to talk about – Rowan. The baby. Push away all thoughts of Stuart.

'What is it, Ells? Are you OK?' Amy says.

'You know me, I'm always OK. But I have some news. You seriously won't believe it. I mean, I barely do.'

'I knew something was up,' Maisie says. 'You haven't been yourself all week. So, spill.'

I haven't told anyone yet. Maybe because saying it out loud will make it seem more real.

I sigh. 'It's Dad and Rowan. They're having a baby.'

'No way. How old are they?' Maisie says.

'Dad is fifty. She's forty-two.'

'Well, that's not too old,' Amy says. 'One of my aunts had my cousin when she was forty-seven.'

'This isn't about being ageist, it's about being Rowan-ist.'

'Is that a word?' Amy says.

'It is now. You see, she signed a prenup. If they split, she doesn't get half of what he has, and if he dies, she doesn't inherit.'

'You do.'

'Right. Or, rather, I *did*. Because I found the prenup and it's void if they have a baby. That bitch is doing this to disinherit me.'

They exchange a glance. 'There might be other reasons she wants to have a baby, you know,' Amy says.

'Are you saying the world doesn't revolve around me?' I say, hands on hips – mock outrage.

'I wouldn't dare.'

I almost laugh but I can't, not at this. It's too serious.

'You're on my side, remember? Anyhow, if you'd been there when they told me, and had seen Rowan's face – she was so *smug*. Like, nauseatingly so. But the thing is, I'm almost sure that there is something else going on. I can feel it. And I'm wondering if the baby is even Dad's.'

'No way. Has she been playing away?'

'I don't know for certain. But there is this guy she works with – Alex. It feels like there's some sort of connection between them. And he split with his wife last year. But that's not all. Dad has a flat at his London offices. Lately he's been staying there more often.'

'So maybe he's got someone else, too?'

'Maybe. Or maybe he just doesn't want to come home to her, I don't know. But I need to find out.'

'It's like a soap opera,' Amy says. 'Or a thriller, where everyone is watching everyone else and you can't work out who did what to who.'

'Speaking of which, what are you going to do?' Maisie says.

'I think just stir things up a little between them, see what happens. If I'm wrong and they're blissfully happy together, or even if one or the other or both of them have been cheating but they decide to stay together because of the baby, there's not much I can do about it.'

'It's not like this baby will completely disinherit you,' Maisie says. 'You might just have to share.'

'That's not what Dad promised me when he married Rowan. And anyway, I just feel, in my gut, that there is something going on, that it could change things if I could find out what it is. And another thing: when I was looking for the prenup, I found there was a locked drawer in Dad's filing cabinets. I want to know what's in there.'

'Do you know where the keys are?'

'No, or I'd be telling you what was in it. I looked through his desk but no luck. Don't suppose either of you knows anyone who can pick locks?'

They shake their heads.

'In the meantime, it's operation stir things up between Rowan and Dad,' I say.

Amy gets a notebook out of her bag. She always has a notebook in her bag.

'Suggestions?' she says, pen poised.

By the time we finish the bottle of wine I have a long list of ideas. Some of them may even be legal.

THIRTY

ROWAN

It's a lovely restaurant but everything on the menu is so rich. The nausea I hoped would be behind me is threatening to stir again. I'm not sure I'll cope.

We order drinks first. Sparkling water for me; red wine for Theo. When they return and pour him a taste to try, I'm jealous.

'Very nice,' Theo says, and the glass is filled.

After the waiter is gone, I take Theo's glass, swirl it around. Sniff appreciatively. Sigh and hand it back.

I order the blandest thing I can find on the menu.

'Are you still feeling unwell?' Theo says, concerned.

I shrug. 'Nothing major, just don't fancy anything too heavy tonight.'

'I'm worried about you, Rowan,' Theo says. 'You're looking brighter than you did this morning' – the extra swipe of make-up must have done the trick – 'but let's have a look at the last few days. You had a nightmare yesterday that had you screaming and taking a swing at me. You were tossing and turning last night.'

'Sorry if I disturbed you.'

'You did but not for long. I went and slept in a guest room eventually, but that's not what I'm worried about. I just thought you might sleep better if I wasn't there.'

And despite being sure I'd been awake for ages, I didn't notice he was gone. Maybe I slept more than I thought.

He's not finished. 'Then there is dinner made but the oven not turned on, and the pièce de résistance – keys in the fridge. You're not yourself, Rowan. What can I do to help?'

'I'm not myself, because I'm not good at having too much time on my hands. I need to get back to work next week.'

'Are you sure?'

'Yes. But it's not just me. The doctor said it was fine to continue working. And she's the medical expert, Theo.'

'But I'm the Rowan-expert.'

How can he be when there is so much about me that he doesn't know? And there is something else going on with Theo, I can sense it. I stay silent, giving him time to find the words.

'You have to understand – with what happened before, with Ellie's mother, Naomi. I don't want that to happen again. I couldn't deal with it.' He almost never mentions Naomi. I'm not sure if I've ever heard him say her name before. I know the basics. That she left him and Ellie when Ellie was just a few weeks old and never came back. How hard that must have been. A new baby to care for on his own, and his business wasn't the success it is now. He raised her and worked and built up his business and he did it all on his own. Ellie might have some issues with me, but still, she is generally happy, healthy, does well in school and has good friends. She's confident and independent and, as annoying as both of those things can make her, I can see Theo's influence in both traits. He's been the best parent he could be for her – two parents in one.

'That will never happen,' I say. 'I promise you: I'll never leave you. You're stuck with me – with both of us – forever.' He looks in my eyes. Nods. He leans across and kisses me; not passionately, more a kiss that is also a promise. A pact that can never be broken. And I meant every word.

'You've never really talked about Naomi before.' I hesitate, wanting to know more but unsure how he'll react to questions. 'Do you know why she left?'

'I'd rather not discuss her. The past is a foreign country, one I don't want to visit,' he says. How can I argue when I'm just the same? 'She has no bearing on our present. I love you, Rowan. Let's focus on here, now. On us.'

We eat, not talking much now but it is a silence that feels all right. I'm glad he opened up a little about Naomi, but it has made me realise: I was worrying about the things in my past Theo doesn't know about, but it goes both ways. I know almost nothing about Naomi and his life with her.

Is that unusual? Do spouses usually dissect previous relationships with each other? My reticence about my own past has made me good at deflecting talking about myself. But maybe as a result we don't talk about his past, either – we don't exchange stories.

It never occurred to me before that Theo might have secrets, too.

THIRTY-ONE

The next morning I'm up and in the kitchen before Theo even stirs. I had another uneasy night, dreams that left an unpleasant feeling behind even though the details were gone when I opened my eyes. Talking about Naomi, however briefly, has made me feel unsettled, and I'm not sure why. Is it just because thinking of Theo being with another woman – loving her – and being hurt by her leaving, made me realise the blindingly obvious: that I'm not the only woman he has ever loved?

Once he mentioned her, I wanted to know more. He didn't want to discuss her any further and I didn't press him, and now I'm asking myself why. When I went to university, I very consciously reinvented who I was, how I spoke, even changed my name. Over time, the act became my reality. The past couldn't hurt me any more; it didn't define who I was. If I was uncertain what to do or say in a given situation, I'd focus on this new person I was becoming, and think, what would she do? Part of this was being able to hold my ground and stand up for myself. Be assertive in a way that was not tolerated in my childhood. But if I'm brutally honest, have I ever done that with Theo? Maybe I've always been happy for him to take the lead, to sort things, for both of us. And why that may be is something I don't want to think about too closely. But there is a whole other human being arriving in just months. It's not just myself I have to look out for any more.

Despite all of this, I'm starving. I start preparing a cooked breakfast: bacon, eggs, tomatoes, mushrooms. The works. It's nearly ready, the kettle is on and bread is in the toaster when Theo comes in.

'I woke up ravenous this morning,' I say. 'There's enough for two or three?' Meaning if Ellie appears also, though I doubt she will. In my mostly sleepless night, I heard her coming in some-time after one. So much for her alleged homework. But with Theo home, any reaction to that or the time she got in I'll leave to him.

He comes over, kisses me. 'Smells good but I'm not that hungry after last night,' he says. The kettle clicks off and he's pouring water in the teapot, getting milk from the fridge.

'Are you sure I can't tempt you?'

'Just some toast. Thanks.'

The bacon is done, on a plate. I reach across the stove for the pan with the eggs, pause as maybe they're not quite done.

'Rowan!'

'What?'

Theo yanks me away from the cooker and that's when I see my dressing gown sleeve – it must have touched the gas ring – flames are licking up the sleeve and I'm screaming and he's pulling the dressing gown off me, stamping on it on the floor. My eyes, horrified, on his now.

'What the hell is going on?' It's Ellie, eyes half open and hair mussed every which way, in her pjs.

'I just accidentally set myself on fire.'

'Oh.' She wanders across, grabs a few pieces of bacon, and wanders back down the hall towards her room.

'Rowan, you need to pull yourself together. If that had

happened when I wasn't here, you might have been seriously burned.'

'It was just an accident, that's all.'

'I know, but there have been too many accidents, things you've forgotten or lost. It's starting to make me worry.'

'What is that supposed to mean?'

'How are you going to look after a baby if you can't even look after yourself?'

Stunned, I stare back at him. Unable to believe he just said that. He forgets about having tea or anything else. Walks out of the kitchen.

'Vera, open the door.' And he's gone.

Tears are sliding down my face. I look around at the mess. Turn the cooker off. Stumble upstairs to our room. Close the door, curl up on the bed. Wrap my arms around myself as if to give the hug I needed from Theo. To hold and protect our baby, too.

Is something wrong with our relationship? For a while now I've thought that things between us felt a little off-kilter. There have been moments of discord over the last year, usually to do with my work. He works long hours, always has, but if he happens to be home early and I'm not here, he doesn't like it. It's like he wants me home, waiting for him, all the time, just in case. Which is ridiculous, of course it is; it's a twisted double standard. But despite that, I didn't think there were any serious problems between us – it was just occasional blips in an otherwise happy marriage. If anything was wrong I'd put it down to me, because I was looking back too much.

I'd put it all out of my mind with the baby news; I'd thought it would bring us closer together. But maybe I was wrong.

It could have something to do with Naomi leaving him after she had Ellie. Is the problem that he still hasn't dealt with that, and he's insecure and worried that if I'm not coping, as he put it, I might leave him, too? He doesn't come across like that. But he's never been really open about his feelings. He's always – almost always – calm, rational. Which might make it harder for him to understand what is going on inside him. But how can I help him if he refuses to talk about it?

Who might tell me what happened between Theo and Naomi all those years ago? There's really only one answer: Maxine, Theo's sister. I go back downstairs, find my phone where I left it.

I'll message her, I decide. What should I say? Even though she can be annoyingly bossy, we generally get along. But we aren't particularly close; we've never got together without Theo and other family being there. I can't think of a ready excuse for wanting to see her, so go with the truth:

There is something I really need to talk to you about. Are you free at all today or tomorrow? Thanks.

I start tackling the congealed mess in the kitchen when my phone pings with a message. It's Maxine.

I am intrigued. I've got a busy few days, but you could come over today at about three for afternoon tea. Does that suit?

I'm relieved; I was afraid she'd put me off for days. Even though she doesn't work, has a full-time housekeeper and her children left home for families of their own years ago, she's one of these women who constantly tells anyone who will listen how unbearably busy she is.

Perfect. Thank you.

I finish sorting the kitchen, manage to eat some toast. Tell myself that Maxine will help me understand Theo and everything will be OK, but I feel uneasy, uncertain, as if the very ground under my feet is less convincing in its support than it used to be.

There is a buzz at the gate. I check the camera: a white van has pulled in.

'Yes?'

'A delivery for Rowan Blackwood.'

'Just a moment.'

I go to the gate, enter the code, and he hands over a box containing a huge bunch of flowers – red roses. I take them in. There's no card when I search through, but of course they are from Theo.

No card: does that mean that he can't quite manage to say sorry in words, so instead, says it in flowers? The knot of worry around my gut eases, just a little.

THIRTY-TWO

Maxine answers her front door herself.

'Rowan, you look amazing! Positively glowing.' She air kisses both cheeks.

'I take it Theo told you our news?' It hadn't occurred to me to wonder if he had or hadn't until I was driving over.

'He did, indeed. Congratulations. I'm so happy for both of you.'

But I know I don't look amazing or glowing, despite the lift I had earlier with the flower delivery. 'You're lying, though. I look dreadful. I slept terribly last night and was sick this morning.' The toast I had earlier didn't stay put in my stomach for long.

'You poor thing. I remember the joys. That's usually mostly during the first trimester, though?'

'Guess I'm just lucky.'

'I've got Alison to set up for tea in the conservatory. Shall we?'

Their conservatory is lovely, spacious. Warm with even today's weak sunshine. Alison appears with a full teapot to add to the spread of little cakes and sandwiches arranged on a stand. By tea, Maxine didn't just mean a cuppa.

'I'll be mother,' Maxine says, pouring the tea. She's about sixty, ten years older than Theo. From what he's told me, in some ways she was more his mother than their mother was; he was only a child when she died. Maxine always looks so elegant and I don't think of her as that age, but now and then she says something like that to remind me.

'This is all so lovely. Thank you.'

'Go on. You're eating for two.'

I select a few of the dainty quarter sandwiches. They go down well and my appetite seems to be coming back.

'Now, what did you want to talk about?'

Will she go back to Theo with this? I don't know, but I can't see any other way to learn anything about Naomi. I'm hesitating, trying to work out what to say.

'You said you didn't sleep well. Is something worrying you?'

Several somethings, but only one I'll share with Maxine.

'It's Theo. Something about his reaction to having our baby feels, I don't know, mixed. And I think it might be tied up with Naomi somehow. It's like he's scared of something – not that he'd put it that way.' Scared? Not sure that is the right word, but he definitely didn't want to talk about her beyond the few words that he said.

'Ah, I see. It's maybe understandable.'

'Can you tell me about her? Theo won't. But if I understand better what went on with her, it might help. There's nothing of her anywhere in the house. Not even a photo.'

'There were a few framed photos – one from their wedding, I think, and one of Naomi with Ellie when she was only days old. Ellie had a temper tantrum of epic proportions, must have been, oh, seven or eight years ago. She destroyed them.'

Seven or eight years ago she would have been nine or ten, a few years before I met her. A child acting out against a mother who abandoned her and, despite everything that is wrong between us, my heart aches for Ellie. Our situations were very different but feeling abandoned by a mother who should have protected me is something I can relate to.

'Wait a moment,' Maxine says. She leaves the room, returns a few minutes later. A photo album in her hands. 'I brought these photos of Naomi together, and kept them for Ellie – one day, she might want them. Do you want to see them?'

I'm unsure if I want to see Naomi as a real person, one Theo loved. But I say yes.

She moves the cake stand across and opens it on the table between us. Photographs of Naomi, of Naomi and Theo together. Their engagement party. Wedding invitation – her full name, Naomi Lee Baxter. I knew so little of her that I hadn't even known her name before she married Theo, or if she changed it when they married. And then there are wedding photos. The best man is Maxine's husband. The maid of honour looks so like Naomi.

'Is this Naomi's sister?'

'Her younger sister – Pamela.'

'And are these her parents?'

'Yes, Ellie's grandparents. And our dad, just next. He died the year after they got married.'

'I've not seen or heard anything of Naomi's family. They're not in Ellie's life now?'

'No. They blamed Theo when Naomi left and didn't want anything to do with Ellie.'

I'm shocked. Ellie wasn't just rejected by her mother, she was rejected by her mother's family, too. And she was a tiny baby, their granddaughter. How could they turn their backs on her, walk away?

There is a close-up of the bride and groom together. Naomi was beautiful – blonde hair, so like Ellie's – and her dress was stunning. There's a hint of blue at her throat – a sapphire pendant on a delicate gold chain – that brings out the blue of her eyes. It hurts to see how happy they are, how perfect they look together.

And then there are photos of a pregnant Naomi. Is there a shadow even then of what was coming? Her lips are smiling but it doesn't seem to reach the rest of her face.

Then photos of baby Ellie in Naomi's arms. Ellie is tiny – just days old. Naomi is holding her, not looking at the camera – gazing at her daughter in her arms with a look of pure joy.

'She looks so happy. What went wrong?'

'I'm not really sure. Theo said she was crying uncontrollably. Refused to see a doctor or any visitors. Postnatal depression, most likely. He had to get a nanny in soon after Ellie was born because Naomi couldn't cope at all. Then one day, Theo was at work, and he got a message from Naomi that she was leaving. And she did. Left Ellie with the nanny, went out and never came back. Theo raced home after he got her message but she was already gone when he got there. And he never saw or heard from her again.'

I'm shocked. I knew she'd left them and wasn't in contact; I didn't know she disappeared like that.

'If she was depressed, everyone must have been worried for her safety. Did anyone try to find her?'

'Absolutely. Theo tried everywhere he thought she might go, her friends, family. The police tried to find her, too, but no trace. Theo even hired private investigators but they came up with nothing.'

'So, she could be out there somewhere, living in another place, maybe with a different name.'

She nods. 'Or maybe not.' She hesitates. 'Naomi loved the sea. Theo said he could imagine her walking out into the waves.' And with these words I can see her, this young woman who should have had so much to live for. Alone in the sea.

'Did she leave a note?'

'As in, a suicide note? No. But not everyone does.'

How could she leave Ellie and not even write a note to say goodbye?

'I'm not sure if showing you this has helped. But if Theo doesn't seem quite himself with the baby news, he went through so much before. He's not very good at saying how he feels, is he?'

I shake my head.

'If you want any advice from me, you need to be there, reassure him as much as you can. He'll be fine once your baby is here and he sees you're OK.'

If I am OK. I'm far from certain about that.

'There is something else I want to talk to you about, Rowan. I was actually going to call when I got your message earlier.'

'And what's that?'

She looks uneasy, awkward. 'I don't like to meddle.' Yes, you do, I think. It's high up on your list of enjoyable activities.

'Go on.'

'It's your drinking, Rowan.'

I'm staring back at her. So much has happened since Theo's birthday party that I hadn't thought of Ellie and the rumours she was spreading.

'You can't be serious. I barely drink. And I certainly haven't touched a drop since I found out I was pregnant.'

A raised eyebrow. 'Are you sure? Because at Theo's party—'

'At his party I was exhausted after a long day and had morning sickness, not that I knew what it was then. I only had a few sips and that's it. Anything you heard from Ellie was exaggerated.'

She doesn't believe me over Ellie, that's clear. I make excuses, leave soon after. So angry to be questioned by her like that. Are other people going to think the same thing?

I try to put it aside, think about Theo and Naomi. Theo thought she was suicidal. That the reason she couldn't be found was because she killed herself, maybe got swept away in the sea.

I feel I'm getting more of a sense of who Theo is, the things that shaped him. He loved Naomi – I can see that in the photos. And he thinks she killed herself; that having their child led to depression so severe she saw no other way. But in doing so, she didn't just leave Ellie – she left him, too. Grief and abandonment, together, and having to raise Ellie on his own. The abandonment issue might be even worse because of his mum dying when he was young – the two women he loved most in his life to that point left him.

After Naomi, no wonder he's worried about having another child. And likewise, no wonder any signs of weakness he perceives in me are making him scared the same thing will happen.

Maxine said Theo needs reassurance, but I think it's more than that. I need to be strong; capable. Show him I'm not going to fall apart like Naomi did.

THIRTY-THREE

ELLIE

'There you are,' Maisie says, and sits on the sofa next to me in the sixth form common room. I'm slumped there with a coffee and my maths coursework, trying to decide if I'd rather stay on this sofa or just go home already. But with Rowan off work this week I likely won't have the house to myself, and more Rowan is just what I don't need.

'How're things?' she says.

'Don't ask. But I've solved the lock-picking problem.'

'Excellent. Did you put an ad in the paper for local burglars?'

I raise an eyebrow. 'Now, why didn't I think of that? Instead, I found videos on YouTube on how to use an electric lock pick. It looks pretty easy. Ordered one and am just waiting for it to be delivered.'

'Won't your dad wonder when he sees the credit card statement?'

'Maybe. But I put it on Rowan's card.' I'd managed a quick look in her purse when she was in the loo to get the security code. Added to the card details from her file, my shopping horizons are unlimited.

'Sneaky. Pub night tonight?'

'If we can find a new one. I think we should stop going to the King's Arms.'

'How come?'

'It's Stuart. He's getting too creepy.'

A concerned look. 'Did something happen?'

And I want to tell her, but tell her what, exactly? That he drove me home and I have no idea what happened on the way? I'm so embarrassed, angry. It's not my fault, it's Rowan's. If I hadn't been so upset about her and the baby I wouldn't have gone out on my own. I wouldn't have had so much to drink, either.

Before I can decide what to say, my phone vibrates – a notification from Vera. I glance at the screen. Rowan is heading out the front door, a bag of rubbish in her hand.

I show it to Maisie. 'I've tweaked the notifications from the door camera and the ones inside, so it notifies me if there is any movement either side of the door. If anyone who shouldn't visits Rowan, I'll know about it.'

'You're such a geek.'

Guilty as charged. By all accounts, I look like my mother – the blonde hair, blue eyes – a wide-eyed look from me fools people who don't know me well into thinking I'm sweet, angelic, and not particularly bright. I use that when I want to. But my brain is wired like Dad's – mechanics, maths, computers, programming, any of that. I just get it. It's weird that it seems genetically predetermined; according to Dad, no one else in his family is like us.

I watch my screen as Rowan goes around the side of the house to the bins. This could be fun.

THIRTY-FOUR

ROWAN

I take out the kitchen rubbish. The cleaners would do so tomorrow but I'm convinced smells of uneaten cooked breakfast linger with it and it's making me queasy. Vera opens the front door on request. I walk around the side of the house to the bin store and in it goes. Turn around and go up to the door, face the camera, and... nothing.

Not again. I line myself up with the camera repeatedly, turning my face this way and that in case it helps, but the door remains resolutely closed. And where is my phone? I thought it was in my pocket but it's not. It's probably on the worktop in the kitchen. Or – who knows? – it could be in the fridge, looking for my car keys. Maybe I even tossed it in the bin along with the rubbish, but the thought of looking for it there is making my stomach protest so much that I have to breathe in and out slowly to have a chance of not being sick on the doorstep.

Theo won't be home for hours and I have no idea when Ellie will get back; she might be even later. I have a sudden urge to pee, and I'm not going to be able to wait for long. Is it from this baby pressing on my bladder? Tears are coming up in my eyes. I'll have to try neighbours, get someone to call Theo so he can open it using the app, but most of them will be at work this time of day. I walk to the front gate, glad there is a simple keypad option to open it and not another camera.

I'll try Margaret, I decide. She's retired and I'm hoping more likely to be home. I'm walking funny, trying not to have an accident. I feel so pathetic and my eyes are smarting again. She has a long drive – or so it feels today – no gate. I press the button on the video doorbell.

'Hello?'

'Hi, it's Rowan. From next door. I've locked myself out.'

'Oh dear. On my way.'

I can only assume she was in the furthest reaches of her garden as I'm waiting, waiting, legs awkwardly half crossed in a standing position.

The door finally opens. 'Come in. Would you like some tea?'

'Sorry, I just really need the loo.' I'm blushing, embarrassed.

'Of course, dear, it's just there,' she says, but I'm already on the way before she finishes speaking; I know where it is from being here before with the previous owners. I fumble with the button on the top of my jeans and it's almost tragic but I make it. Just. Wash my hands, head back to the hall.

'Thank you. The door camera wouldn't work and I didn't have my phone on me so couldn't use the app.'

'It's no bother.' Her face is kindly, concerned. 'Is everything all right, dear?'

Everything isn't even close to all right just now, and the thin edge of control I have is undone by her kindness. I burst into tears. She's leading me to the sofa, handing me tissues, making soothing noises and I just cry harder. Struggle and finally get some control.

'I'm so sorry,' I manage to say.

'You're absolutely fine. I'll put the kettle on.'

'I don't want to impose.'

'You're not imposing at all. I was just about to make some tea before you arrived.'

She makes tea and chatters on about her grandson – he's in the Met – and the fact that he and his wife and her three great-grandchildren are coming next weekend. Great-grandchildren? She must be older than I thought. She keeps filling the airwaves so I don't have to as I get myself back together.

She brings in a teapot, cups. Pours and hands me one.

'If there is anything you want to talk about, I'm a good listener. And I'm very discreet.'

Somehow, I believe her. But I can't, *won't*, talk about Theo with someone I barely know. He'd be horrified. But I can't blank her after she's been so kind.

'You probably don't know our news. I'm pregnant. The hormones are making me crazy.' I try to smile.

'Oh, how lovely! I'd wondered but didn't like to speculate in case I was wrong. Congratulations! Is it your first?'

'Yes.' The usual lie comes easily. We drink the tea; she tells me more about her family. Five children, twelve grandchildren. Just the three great-grandchildren so far.

'Is that your Ellie walking past?' She's looking through the window over my shoulder and I turn, and yes, it is Ellie, with one of her friends, going past to our gate. 'Thank you so much. I'll go now and get in before they disappear.'

'No problem at all. Rowan, anytime you need someone to talk to – I'm usually here.' She comes to the door with me. 'Take care.'

'I will. Thank you.' I'm touched again by her kindness; the kindness of someone who knows almost nothing about me. If she knew the truth, would she still be the same?

I hurry over to our drive, through the gate, and get to the door just as they're going in.

'Hi Mrs B,' Maisie says. Ellie ignores me.

'Hello. Have you had any trouble with the door camera today, Ellie?'

She sighs, turns to face me. 'No, why?' The picture of inno-cence. Of course *she* hasn't had any trouble with the camera. That was the wrong question.

'Never mind,' I say. They're exchanging a glance and I'm realising I have to always make sure I have my phone on me, even if I'm just going to the bins.

'Oh, these are beautiful,' Maisie says, as they go past the roses on the dining table. They disappear down the hall to Ellie's room. Whispering and giggling about something. Ellie must be rubbing off on me as now I'm rolling my eyes.

As I sit down there is a flutter inside that is quite unlike any other sensation. Our baby, changing position or waving their arms around, and I can feel a real smile spreading over my face.

I hug my arms around myself. Nothing else matters. This child will be so loved. Safe. Cared for in a way that I never was. *Nothing* is more important.

But to achieve this, I have to make sure everything is right with Theo. Whatever it takes.

Maxine said, reassure him. And now that I have more under-standing of why, I get it. He was out of order with what he said this morning. But he's just worried that the same thing will happen to me that happened to Naomi. Any signs that I'm not with it have scared him. Fear made him less supportive than he should have been, but there isn't any need to belabour what he said. Accept the roses and the apology they represent, and move on.

Maybe the way to reach Theo is to be more who I was when we met. Reassure him that I'm not changing, not going anywhere. But that isn't enough. I have to show him that looking after myself and our unborn child is the most important thing.

Phone out, I think for a moment, then tap in a message:

You'll be pleased to know that neither my clothes or the house are on fire, my keys are at normal room temperature, and I've got something important to tell you, too: you were right.

His reply comes a moment later:

Excellent news on all fronts. What am I right about?

This is what I need to do to make Theo happy, but I still have trouble tapping in the words. I stare at them a moment before pressing send.

I'm going to leave work. Concentrate on family. I love you xx

There's a pause, a long one, and just as I'm worrying that I've read him wrong, a message lands.

That's wonderful news. I know you've made the right decision. I love you too xx

Do it now, I tell myself. Before I have the chance to second guess or talk myself out of it.

I email HR at work. Explain I have to leave work for health reasons and wish to resign with immediate effect.

An email response lands in my inbox a moment later:

If you don't plan to work out a notice period, I presume you have medical documentation to support this?

Much as expected, so I'm ready. I know my company and how they operate. The only thing that will get through is going straight to what is always most important to them: the bottom line. I answer.

Look at it this way. If I get a medical certificate, I'll be entitled to sick pay, followed by maternity pay for a year. If I don't get a certificate and return for a few months, ditto for maternity pay. How about instead of either option, you accept my resignation, effective immediately?

There isn't an answer straight away, which is good: he must be talking about it to the partners. They're going to be so annoyed.

Finally, it drops in later.

Resignation accepted. There's nothing about regret or best wishes, no come back in the future suggested. Just two words that hurt and twist inside.

I message Alex:

Did you hear? I've resigned. I'm not coming back.

That might explain why I've been summoned to the board-room – on way there now. Sorry you're going, hope you're OK.

Am I OK?

I don't know. There is a flutter of panic inside to go with the baby's movements. It's almost four months before he or she makes an appearance. Sixteen weeks. Over a hundred days. I manage to stop myself from working out hours, minutes, seconds. With no work to keep me busy, to distract me, there'll be nothing to stop me thinking obsessively about both the past and the future, all the while counting down to something I'd rather not think about too closely. Once it's over and I can hold our baby, I'll probably forgive what he or she put me through, but the less time I spend thinking about what is involved, the better.

I've heard other women say that after your first it gets easier, that you know what is coming and your body remembers how, too. But maybe that depends on how things went the first time.

Everything will be fine this time, or so I try to convince myself. I was a child myself then, unprepared. Uncooperative. Now I'm a grown woman, and I don't have to do this alone: Theo will be there, loving and supporting me all the way.

But it isn't just the birth I'm worried about. The carefully constructed me – the one Theo fell in love with – is an articulate career woman. Everything, from how I talk to how I dress, is part of this. In Theo, I found the perfect husband – successful, attractive, generous – to be part of the life I had by design; we agreed back then to try for the ultimate accessory, the perfect baby. So far, all part of the plan. But I didn't really think it through, did I? If the confident, working woman part of me is taken away, what if the rest disintegrates along with it? If it does, what will be left behind?

I get up, go to the window. Look over the drive, the garden. The high fence and locked gate that seem to be moving closer. Shutting me inside.

THIRTY-FIVE

As afternoon becomes evening, the feeling of being trapped intensifies. My chest feels constricted, my breathing an effort. But it's crazy to feel this way. I know it is. I can leave whenever I want, do anything, go anywhere. Just not to work.

Our baby is having a busy day, as if they are reflecting my feelings and trying to break their way out. A future kick boxer, maybe. I guess it's not a big space to hang out in for nine months, but I wish for some peace. The sense of wonder the first times I felt a flutter has worn off and I'm feeling uneasy, uncomfortable. As if the more they move about the less they are part of me and the more a separate entity, with their own will and needs. What if they are different to mine?

I set the dining table. Adjust the arrangement of the roses in the vase. The fragrance I thought beautiful when they were delivered is filling the room, sweet and cloying. I sneeze, then relegate them to a side table.

When I hear Theo's car, I go to the door to greet him as it opens – to catch some fresh air – then it closes. Shut in again.

He leans down, kisses my cheek.

'How is my lady of leisure?'

'Excuse me, I've been busy making dinner.'

'Something smells good so you must have even turned the oven on.' Gentle teasing or a touch of condescension? Either way, I choose to ignore it. He comes through. Red wine is breathing on the table. He turns to the side table, the roses.

'What are these?'

'Aren't they beautiful? Thank you.'

Theo shakes his head. 'Nothing to do with me.'

'Seriously? There wasn't a card. I assumed they were from you.'

'Well, they weren't.'

I frown, both confused – because who else would send me red roses? – and upset. The flowers I thought were Theo's apology for this morning weren't anything of the sort. Which means he never apologised. And I did just what he wanted, as if he had. I push away the annoyance. That's not the only reason; it was Maxine, the things she explained about Theo. About him needing reassurance, not a hormonal, unpredictable wife.

'Who are they from?' he says. 'You must have an idea.'

I shake my head. 'I really don't.'

A raised eyebrow, like he doesn't believe me. 'When will dinner be ready?'

'About twenty minutes.'

He pours a glass of wine, takes it to his study and closes the door.

I go into the kitchen. Caught between feeling hurt and wanting to throw dinner in the bin, or better yet, at Theo's face. And curiosity, because if he didn't send the roses, then who on earth did?

My phone vibrates with a call. It's Alex. Could he have sent the flowers? No. Why would he? And if he did think to cheer me up with some flowers, he wouldn't have picked red roses. Hardly the sort of flowers a friend would choose.

'Hi Alex.'

'Hi Rowan. How're things?'

'Fine, I guess.'

'That doesn't sound good. Anything wrong?'

Nothing I'll tell Alex about. 'Just tired. What's up?'

'Hannah is moving to your desk.' Surprise, surprise. Even though I expected it, that was quick work. 'Did you want to clear out any personal things yourself? Or I could do it for you, if you'd rather not come in.'

I'm trying to remember what is there. So many years of bits and pieces. A photo of Theo and me. Lipstick and mints. Spare stockings. A soft toy from a campaign we did, a few other mementos of success. Tampons.

'There might be some girly stuff in my drawers.'

He wolf whistles.

'Grow up. If you can handle that, if you could chuck my life in a box for me, that'd be grand. Don't really feel like running the gauntlet to do it myself. Make sure you take my stapler.' Petty, maybe? I haven't got much cause for stapling at home. But I did buy it myself.

'No problem. We could meet at lunch for the handover?'

'Sounds good.'

'When are you free?'

'Is tomorrow any good?'

'Perfect.' He suggests a time, place.

'Now tell me what I've missed.'

And he does – all the infighting, sabotage and one-upmanship that is our workplace – I mean, Alex's workplace. Not mine any longer. I put him on speaker while preparing the vegetables. And as I do, his stories get more and more outrageous.

'Now you're just making things up.'

'OK, maybe some exaggerating.'

'I've got to go; dinner is nearly ready.'

'Call anytime. I'm here if you need someone to talk to.'

'Thank you, Alex. Bye.'

Hit end call on the screen and as if I can feel his eyes, I turn. Theo is standing in the door. A cold look on his face.

'I thought you resigned.'

'I did.'

'So why do you need to hear all that?'

'Have you been standing there, listening, for long, then?'

'Long enough.' He turns. Goes back to the dining table. Sits down and pours another glass of wine.

The urge from before – to throw dinner in the bin or in his face – is strong. But then the front door opens; Ellie is home. I won't give her the satisfaction of seeing us row.

'Am I in time for dinner?' she says.

'Just.' I push annoyance aside, and bring in roast chicken, vegetables. Fresh homemade bread, still warm – OK, made in the bread maker, but it still counts. Then apple crumble. I even made custard from scratch to go with it, vanilla pods and all. I don't usually go to this much effort but it's not like I had anything else to do.

My appetite is poor, whether from being upset with Theo or morning sickness making an appearance at the wrong end of the day, and I push things around my plate. Theo, on the other hand, is – as usual – enjoying his dinner without any thanks. If Ellie notices any atmosphere between us, she doesn't mention it. But then she doesn't seem quite herself, either. Gives short answers to Theo's attempts at conversation.

After dinner, Ellie leans over the roses, breathes in. 'They're lovely,' she says. I watch her go down the hall, hear her door open and shut. Then I turn to Theo. Hold his eyes – he's looking back at me, but I can't see what he is thinking, feeling, as if he's not sure of his hand and doesn't want me to know. He breaks gaze, says he has paperwork to do, goes to his study.

I load the dishwasher. Is this my life from now on? Kitchen drudge. One who doesn't object to any treatment. Years ago, when we met, I wouldn't have let any of that go. If it didn't fit who I was trying to be, modelling myself on, I'd have pushed back straight away.

I need to hold on to who I became. I'm not letting it go now, either.

I make tea; peppermint for me, Assam for Theo. Tap on his study door and open it, step in, without waiting for an answer. He looks up from his desk, and admittedly there is paperwork everywhere and his laptop is open, so that was for real.

'Cup of tea?'

'Thank you,' he says, and I place both cups on the desk. Seeing mine next to his, he must realise I'm not planning to go anywhere just yet, and he leans back in his chair.

'Theo, what's going on? Is something wrong?'

'*Is* something wrong? You tell me.'

'Are you jealous – is that it? Because of the flowers?'

'Should I be?'

'Stop answering questions with questions. I have no idea who sent them. You can't blame me for something somebody else did.'

'You're right.' He closes his laptop, gestures for me to come around to him. I lean on his desk and he takes my hand. 'I actually went to the kitchen earlier to apologise, but when I did, I caught you talking to Alex.'

'What do you mean – caught me? If I was trying to be secretive, he wouldn't have been on speaker. Alex is a *friend*. He was just trying to cheer me up.' I'm staring at Theo searchingly, trying to understand. Is Maxine right? Is this the rejected husband – the image she painted of Theo? Is it reassurance that he needs? 'Theo, you're the only one for me. You have no reason to worry, not now, not ever.'

He holds out his arms, pulls me onto his knee. Kisses me and I nestle into his arms.

'You're right. I'm sorry,' he says. 'It's just the thought of you being with someone else – I don't know what I'd do.'

'It's not going to happen. I promise.'

Another kiss, more passionate this time. He takes me by the hand, up the stairs, to bed.

Afterwards, he's asleep almost instantly. I cuddle up against him, a weird mix of feelings, sensations, floating through my mind. I should be happy, that we talked about things – he didn't avoid it, deflect; that he apologised, then reached for me, wanted me. But I'm feeling unsettled, and I don't know why.

My unease must transfer to my dreams. They make no sense, like some kind of art house movie where the focus is skewed and you can't work out who anyone is or what they want. One dream bleeds into another and another, until I wake up at nearly 3 a.m. and decide that I've had enough.

I stay awake, watch each minute tick down. Each slower than the one before.

THIRTY-SIX

I'm still awake when Theo's alarm gets him up the next morning. I follow soon after, have a quick shower. Dress in day-off clothes – jeans, a shirt. My jeans are uncomfortably tight. I glance in the mirror. So pale, anxious – a light pinch of my cheeks. I smile at myself and I look something like I should, but instead of the usual confident mask it feels more like a thin veneer.

I need to get this right. Things have changed – my life has changed – and I have to become a new version of myself. I'm a happy new-mum-to-be and I should be thinking of happy mum-to-be stuff, like these too tight jeans. Shopping – that's it.

Theo and Ellie are at the breakfast bar. She's staring at her phone, thumbs flying across the screen. He glances up from his tablet – reading the news.

'Good morning, Rowan.' I kiss his cheek, reach for the kettle. Fill it. 'Any plans for the day?'

'I need to get some maternity clothes. Nothing fits quite right.'

He nods without comment, back to reading his tablet. But

Ellie looks up, glancing first at her dad, then me. A raised eyebrow. She can sense the atmosphere isn't quite as it should be. She's right, but I don't know what to do about it.

I make toast with Marmite, but it tastes like dust.

THIRTY-SEVEN

ELLIE

I get home early afternoon. Vera confirms Dad and Rowan aren't home, but I can't stop myself from having a quick check through the house, to make absolutely sure.

I fetch the electric lock pick I bought from its hiding place, then watch the YouTube video on how to use it one more time. I can do this. Inside the case with the pick, there is a slender piece of metal with a short bend at the end; I slot it into the keyhole. The electric pick has another piece of thin metal, shaped like a fork. I fit it into the keyhole above the other piece already there. Flick the switch – a vibrating whine, enough like a dentist's drill to put my teeth on edge. Jiggle it and the other bit of metal goes in and out a little and – yes! The lock turns and the drawer pops open. I'm surprised it was so easy.

I pull the drawer out. There's a lot in here to go through and I don't know how much time I've got. Dad should be hours still, but Rowan went shopping and I've no idea when she'll get back.

Some files I shuffle through quickly – bond and share certificates, our passports. The next few contain contracts and other business stuff. There is a thick file with plans of our house – architectural drawings, specifications, all kinds of stuff. Why does he keep them locked away? The plans are folded up, too large to be easily photographed, but there are a few copies. It's unlikely to be missed out of a thick file; I take one to look at later. There's a file of specs and master codes for Vera – that could definitely be useful. I quickly take images with my phone.

Next, there is a file labelled Blackwood, Vera – Dad's mum. She died when he was younger than I am now. Vera, the name of our virtual system, is an acronym for Virtually Enabled Reliable Assistant, but it was really named for her. Curious, I open the file. There are some press cuttings from when she died. There was an inquest into her death? I didn't know that. All Dad ever told me was that she died in a car accident.

The inquest gave an open verdict.

Does that mean... she might have done it on purpose – that she deliberately killed herself? I'm shocked and a little shaken.

There are photos in the file, too. She was so beautiful: you can see an echo of her in Auntie M, but she had something few women have. A presence. There is one of her with a baby on her knee and a girl standing next to her – must be Dad and Auntie M. Why does he have these in a file that is locked away instead of in an album, or framed and on the wall?

Focus: I don't know how much time I have.

Next, there is a file labelled King, Grace. I don't recognise the name. Who is she?

The file is full of information on this woman. Date of birth, names of her parents, a big family with a long list of siblings. There are photos of a house with an address scrawled underneath. What looks like legal stuff – pages and pages of court documents – from over twenty-five years ago. And an invoice dated almost six years ago. When I look closer, the invoice is from an investigative agency. What – like private detectives?

Did Dad hire someone to find out about this woman? That's weird enough for me to take photos of everything in the file, trying to stop myself from reading it all as I go. I need to hurry.

The rest of the files in the drawer don't seem interesting. I almost don't notice the small box at the back of the drawer. Inside is a necklace – so pretty! – gold. A pendant of what looks to be sapphires. Why is it hidden away? I put it back where I found it.

I better get out of here; time to lock the drawer. I put the curved metal pick back into the keyhole, the electric thing in place. Just do the same thing, but this time it isn't happening. I try again, moving the pick around, pushing harder on it and it slips out of the keyhole.

Damn. The lock pick has gouged into the wood under the keyhole.

Maybe Dad won't notice, but slim chance of that. Every inch of this house – apart from my rooms – is pristine. If any little thing is out of place – say, the salt and pepper shakers not quite lined up – he notices, straightens them. Should I try to lock it again? I might make it worse. I decide to leave it as it is.

Dad is going to notice the gouge in the wood, that the drawer isn't locked. He'll go through the contents, make sure nothing is missing. Then he'll want to know who did it. I bite my lip, thinking, then open the drawer and take out the box with the necklace inside.

I head up the stairs, to Rowan's dressing room. I can't leave it anywhere too obvious so she finds it straight away, but not so hidden Dad won't find it if he goes looking for it. This way he'll think it was Rowan who broke into his locked files, not me. I tuck it in the very back of a drawer full of scarves. Done.

I go to my room. All right, Grace King. Who are you?

I start skimming through the documents I took images of on my phone. She lived in Wigan. Big house, though it looks run down, front garden a mess of long grass, children's toys. Then I notice her birthday – the sixth of February. That's Rowan's birthday. That can't be a coincidence, can it?

Then I find a copy of a deed poll record.

She changed her name from Grace King to Rowan Jones when she was eighteen years old. They are one and the same person.

Dad seemed not to care about Rowan's past, said he loved her and that was all that mattered. But here is proof that he paid someone to track down every detail they could find out about her.

Did Dad already know about the name change? Rowan might have told him and he was checking into it – so he didn't trust her. Or maybe she never told him anything at all about this other name and life. Either way, the fact that he's had her investigated like this is a huge breach of trust. Maybe it would make Rowan angry – so angry that she'd walk out on him.

Should I show her the proof of what he's done? Or maybe it would be better to leave it somewhere, so she comes across it.

Perhaps... there is more I can do with this. She must have changed her name for a reason.

I go through the court documents and read them all carefully. My eyes open wider and wider.

THIRTY-EIGHT
GRACE

Two thin red lines. One above the other. I had to steal the money from Mam's purse to buy the test and I know she'll notice and work out it was me. Even if she doesn't tell Father, I'll be in so much trouble. When I bought the test, still thinking, it can't be, I can't be, that was what I was worried about the most. Not any longer. I'm sweating, feeling sick. Lean my forehead against the cold metal wall of the toilet cubicle. I'm at school, didn't dare do this at home. I read through the instructions again, looking for a loophole or something I did wrong or misread, but find nothing.

Two thin red lines: positive.

They're so very wrong. *Positive* for me would be one line. This is about the most negative thing I can imagine.

I'm pregnant.

THIRTY-NINE

ROWAN

The train from Richmond is late. I should have left earlier, but struggled to get myself together this morning after another night of weird dreams and troubled sleep.

Alex is already there when I rush through the door of the restaurant, at a table in the window. He stands up, gives me a kiss on the cheek.

'Sorry I'm late,' I say, a little out of breath.

'Well, you know us gainfully employed types,' he winks, 'always on a schedule. But don't worry, not much going on this afternoon.'

'Did you bring it?'

'Oh yes.' He looks both ways, reaches under the table. Not even a box, it's a carrier bag. 'Though I confiscated the mints. Carriage charges.'

'So long as you brought the stapler.'

'Feel free to take inventory.'

I make a show of peering in the bag, then put it back under the table.

'How was Fisher after I resigned? Are they really annoyed with me?'

'On a scale of five minutes late to large scale embezzlement, you're ranked closer to the latter.'

I shrug, say it doesn't matter, but it does. If I need a reference, how is that going to go? Advertising is a small enough industry. News will travel. I remind myself I don't need to work, that I can rely on Theo, but it doesn't make me feel any better.

'How are they changing the teams?'

'Well, I've got your job as the lead now. Hannah is going to work with me.'

I knew it. But what does it matter?

'She's a quick learner,' I say. 'No one will even notice I'm gone.'

'I think you're wrong, but either way – *I'll* notice.'

'Any time you want to run something past me, I've got time on my hands. I even baked bread and made crumble yesterday.'

'Custard, too?'

I nod, and he whistles.

'Wow. You must be bored. Are you OK?'

'Physically, mentally?'

'Either. Both.'

I shrug. 'I'm fine. Honest. I'm just really tired and occasionally run out of the room to vomit.'

'So, if you make a sudden dash, I won't follow.'

'Though if you did, you could hold my hair?'

'Ah, sure. Though come to think of it, I might get in trouble if I go into the ladies.'

We order lunch, talk about various customers and accounts, and despite the lack of sleep I'm starting to feel more like myself, or, at least, the version of myself that Alex knows – intelligent, capable, a good conversationalist – and less like I did last night. Staring at the ceiling and waiting for morning. Remembering that, I can feel the smile leaving my face.

'Rowan, are you sure you're OK?'

I hesitate, not sure what to say.

'You know you can talk to me,' Alex says. 'It's about time I returned the favour.'

He told me the whole Sally saga last year when they split and he needed tea and sympathy. I trust him, but there is something about all of this that I feel I should hold close and I'm not even sure why.

I try to come up with something sensible and truthful without telling him my worries about Theo and our relationship.

I sigh. 'I'm not sure what I've told you about Theo's first wife, Naomi.'

'I seem to remember you said that she left Theo when Ellie was a baby.'

'That's right. And that was about all I knew until recently. I thought if I knew more about what happened with Naomi, it might help me understand Theo better. I asked him about her, and he won't talk about her at all. So, I went to see Theo's sister, Maxine.' Saying it out loud doesn't sound that good – that I went behind his back like that. 'Anyhow, it turns out that Naomi didn't just leave Theo and Ellie – she left her entire life behind. She was a missing person. The police were looking for her.'

'Seriously? That's a very different story to what you thought you knew.'

I nod. 'I know. Maxine said Naomi had postnatal depression and that Theo thinks she killed herself. I keep wondering what happened to her.'

'Why didn't Theo tell you?'

'I don't know. Maybe it's just too painful for him. Anyway, it is a long time ago now.'

'Perhaps you need to try to talk to him about her again.'

'Maybe. I'm not sure how he'll react if he finds out I was talking to Maxine about it, though.'

'Take it from one who knows. Keeping secrets from your spouse is never a good idea.'

'You're probably right,' I say, but he doesn't know Theo like I do, or all the other secrets I've kept for so long.

Alex glances at his watch.

'Do you need to go?' I ask.

'Soon-ish. Sorry.'

'Don't apologise, it's fine.'

'It's been great to see you, Rowan. Any time you want to get out for lunch, or need someone to talk to, you know where to find me.'

Alex is concerned for me; it's in his words and the way he holds my eyes. I've had so few friends in my life beyond the superficial sort, I don't want to lose contact with Alex just because I've left work. Thinking about this has my eyes smarting. I blink hard.

'Thank you, Alex.'

We split the bill and go out together. He gives me a hug when he says goodbye. I hold on to him a little too tight, then turn and walk away. I've only gone a few steps when I realise that I've left the bag of stuff from my desk under our table. I quickly turn, almost walking into someone coming out the door of the restaurant.

'Sorry,' I say, but he doesn't answer. He turns his head and disappears up the road. I go in, find the bag, and resume the walk to the Tube.

That's odd. The man I almost crashed into – he looked familiar. I've got a good memory for faces but can't place him. It feels as if I've seen him somewhere recently. Maybe he was on my train this morning.

And he ended up at the same place for lunch? What a coincidence.

FORTY

I'm sorely tempted to head straight home after lunch with Alex, but the pinching waistband of my jeans reminds me of the official reason I came out today: shopping for maternity clothes. I'd made a list of places to try, starting with a shop Charlie recommended in Kensington.

I used to love shopping, especially when university was over and I got my first job in London. Even though rent in my flatshare was a killer and I had to be careful with money, it really was the first time in my life that I could pick something I loved and buy it myself. I could spend hours comparing, choosing. Though even then it wasn't just a pleasure – it was important to dress like the person I wanted the world to see. After I married Theo and there was no need to budget, the frisson wore off quickly. It became more about making sure I was wearing the right clothes – the right designers – for every occasion. All part of the masquerade, and what I liked, personally, was less important than projecting the correct image for the life I was living. But I guess having a little of something that you've worked for yourself is more satisfying than being able to buy a roomful of posh frocks.

It's not busy when I arrive – just a few other women on their own, both visibly pregnant. Both decades younger than me. I feel out of place and I'm thinking of leaving, just buying some regular clothes in a bigger size. I must be giving off confused shopper vibes because an assistant cuts me off before I can reach the door.

'Can I help you with anything?'

I hesitate. 'I'm not sure.'

'Are you shopping for your daughter, a friend, perhaps?'

I wince. 'Ah, no. It's me. Four months to go.'

She blushes, apologises profusely. Tries to turn it round by saying I don't look expectant, I look amazing, nothing like five months. *Expectant* somehow sounds much nicer than pregnant, like waiting and looking forward to something.

I feel sorry for her embarrassment and decide to stay. 'I guess I need quite a few things. My clothes are all a little tight.'

Soon I'm deposited in a changing room while she brings me all the things I simply must have. Once I start trying on clothes, it's OK, and I can see how cleverly they make things to fit now but grow as I do. In the end it is easier to take most of it than to have to decide and her eyes are round when I pay without asking how much. I hope she gets commission. I keep a few dresses and trousers to take with me now; they'll deliver the rest.

I head down the street to the Tube. It's one change from Kensington. By the time I get off at Earl's Court to change, it's the start of the commuter rush. The platform is packed and so is the train when it pulls in. I manage to get into a carriage. The doors are shutting before I see her: another woman with a dangling baby strapped to her chest. I try to edge further down the carriage, avert my eyes, but it's no good. I can't move. I'm frozen, transfixed.

Her baby is fretful. She's bouncing up and down a little, trying to distract him. I'm breathing too fast, heart thudding in my chest. Sweating and feeling faint at once. I try to breathe in slowly, out slowly, repeat. It's not helping, not working. My eyes are on his red face and little fists just as he draws in a lungful of air and starts a proper howl, a high-pitched cry that has everyone in the crowded carriage pull away as much as they can. I'm moved along a little with the people around me.

Please. Please let her get off at the next stop. I can't breathe, I feel faint. If I wasn't held up by all the people around me, I'd sink to the floor.

We're slowing, doors opening. She's getting off – thank God – but the relief is short-lived. I still can't breathe. I try to focus, make myself draw air in, then out, holding on tight to the back of a seat. The last time I was close to a baby on the train, my panic attack eased when they got off. Things have changed since then; now I know. *I'm going to have a baby*. If just seeing one on a train makes me panic, what will happen when my baby is born? I can't do this, I *can't*. Someone gets up and I sink into a seat. There are people all around me but my eyes are clenched tight, they all fade away.

I remind myself who I am. Rowan doesn't panic, she isn't afraid. I start to claw my way back to myself, my surroundings. Open my eyes. A few people around me are looking worried; more are ignoring whatever just happened as all good commuters should.

'Are you all right, love?' A concerned face, elderly woman.

'Yes. I'm fine. Thank you.' Sweat is drying cold. Breathe in and out, counting, slowly. Gradually the faintness goes and leaves behind a headache, worse than a hangover.

Finally, we're approaching Richmond. My shopping and bag from work aren't heavy but they feel that way. I head to the doors. Glance back and halfway down, facing the other way – I can't be sure, but it looks like the man I almost ran into after lunch. He turns his head now and he's looking directly at me, and there is something in his eyes – recognition, as if he knows not just who I am now but who I *was*. I get off the train, watch as the doors close. He's still on the train, by the door. A glint of gold on his neck and then the train pulls away.

It was a cross. Wasn't it? A gold cross around his neck – just like the ones the men wore in Father's church.

They've found me.

I'm numb, shocked. People are going past me to exit the platform and I'm still standing there, watching as the train disappears in the distance.

If he was on my train this morning, at my restaurant at lunch, on my train home again – it can't be a coincidence. Was he following me? Though if he was, surely he'd have got off at this station. But maybe he didn't because he realised I recognised him.

Think about it logically. I wasn't sure he was on my morning train – I just wondered if that was why he looked familiar at the restaurant – but if he commutes on this line regularly I could have seen him any other time, really. Also, lots of people wear gold crosses. It doesn't mean anything.

But I can't convince myself that it was all just chance. It was his eyes – I feel like they are following me now, even though I know he stayed on the train.

Walking home the short distance from the station, I pull my cardigan closer around me. It's June but the temperature is dropping and I walk quickly, still ill at ease. Listening.

There is a faint echo behind me – footsteps? – that seem to increase in pace with mine. Maybe he didn't get off the train because he was with someone else who took over. Maybe this second person is following me now.

I spin around. No one is there. My heart is thudding. Every sense is on alert, in hyper focus. I feel a prickle on my skin like eyes are watching me still. Now, they are hiding. As soon as I turn around, they'll start following me again.

Run.

I pelt up the road as fast as I can go to our gate. Spin around, breathing heavily. I can't see anyone. I enter the code, go through and then quickly lock it behind me. Vera must like what she sees today; the door opens straight away and I close it behind me.

That's when it hits me. I'm a fool. I shouldn't have come home. If someone was following, watching, didn't lose me when I ran... now they'll know where I live.

I look on my phone, check the CCTV cameras out front. Watch, wait. No one is there. No one walks up to the gates. The odd car goes by; that's it.

Now I'm doubting myself. Was someone following me or did I imagine the whole thing?

It's early enough to collapse on the sofa with a tea before I need to think about dinner. But my thoughts wander back to the baby on the train, how I reacted. I'm scared – past that, terrified. How can I look after a baby if the mere sight of one does that to me? That was the worst panic attack I've had in years.

I make myself get up from the sofa and gather my shopping, the stuff from my office. Take it all upstairs. I put on one of my new dresses – casual and cute, sort of boho – and instantly feel at least a little better. Stare at myself in the mirror. You can do this, I tell myself. You can because you must; no other option is available. Pretend, like you always do; the rest will follow.

I go downstairs, decide to prepare a simple dinner tonight: fresh pasta, salad. Garlic bread from the rest of the loaf I made yesterday. I'm slicing it when Theo gets in.

He kisses me on the cheek. 'How was your day?'

I shrug. 'OK. Mostly shopping – do you like?' I do a twirl around the kitchen and my new dress spins out around me.

'Very nice. Did you get some lunch out as well?'

I turn and get salad dressing out of the fridge, thinking quickly. He doesn't need to know I met Alex, not after how he reacted when he heard us on the phone the other day. 'Just grabbed a quick bite,' I say.

Ellie isn't home yet but everything is soon ready. We take dinner through to the dining table, start to eat. Something feels odd with Theo, as if his mind is elsewhere. And now I'm questioning myself again – am I imagining that, too? When the front door opens for Ellie and she asks if she is in time for some dinner, I'm almost happy to see her. I get up to fill a pasta bowl for her in the kitchen.

'Thanks,' she says when I place it in front of her. 'How did your meeting go today, Dad?'

'Good. We're getting close to a US distribution deal on Vera mark 3. I'm going to New York for the final negotiations.'

That is the first I've heard of this trip. But then I didn't ask about his day, didn't even know about this meeting. Ellie did.

'When are you going?' I say.

'Tomorrow morning.' I give him a raised-eyebrow look, one that says, were you planning to tell me at some point? 'Only booked it this afternoon,' he adds.

Theo heads to his study after dinner. I sort the dishwasher, and then, suddenly exhausted, go upstairs.

Why didn't he tell me about this trip straight away? It felt like he only mentioned it because of Ellie asking about his meeting. How many other secrets is he keeping from me?

I remind myself Theo said he only just booked this flight. I'm sure he was about to tell me.

Even as I'm trying to reassure myself about him, I'm also trying not to think about what happened on the train today when I saw that baby. Or that man with the gold cross.

Suddenly it hits me: I'd assumed he looked familiar at the restaurant because he might have been on the same train on the way in. What if, instead, I recognised him from so long ago that his name is gone from my memory? He was maybe ten years older than me, so would have been in his twenties when I left the church. Could he be one of them? I'm trying to think back, to remember anyone he might have been, but even just trying to recall faces has me trembling, my chest tightening. My memory is in pieces.

Theo's footsteps are coming up the stairs. I rush to the bathroom, lock the door. Splash water on my face. Stare at my white face, panic not far from the surface.

I'd decided that I need to reassure Theo; to show him I'm calm, rational. In control. Instead, I'm about as close to the edge as I can get without going over.

FORTY-ONE

ELLIE

We haven't gone back to the pub where Stuart works. But something about finding out about Rowan's past has me thinking about my – admittedly much more recent – past. What really happened when Stuart drove me home? The way he looked at me the last time we were there – I shudder. I can't avoid this. I have to know.

I slip out after dinner and go on my own, not sure it's a good idea but I'm unwilling to tell any of my friends what is going on. Maisie has been my best friend forever, but she's crap at keeping secrets. And the more I thought about telling someone, anyone, the less I could do it. One thing is for sure: I won't be drinking tonight. I'm not sure I ever will again.

Stuart's face lights up when he sees me come in. It's not busy. I go to the bar.

'On your own again tonight?'

'Maybe.'

'Bottle of white? On me.' He's reaching behind him into the fridge.

'Not so fast. I've gone off drinking after the last time.'

'Here's a glass for when you change your mind.' He pours a

large one, pushes it in front of me on the bar, and despite what I thought just a moment ago, I'm tempted, I really am. To make everything go blurry around the edges.

'Come out with me tonight after work,' he says. 'I can't stop thinking about you.'

'What exactly is it you can't stop thinking about?' I tilt my head, trying to look flirtatious when I just want to run. I need to know.

'You. Me. The backseat of my car.' His smile is making me feel physically sick. I try to hide it.

'Oh? I have a question. Just what, exactly, happened on the backseat of your car?'

'How could you forget?'

'Did we? *You* know.' And I'm smiling at him, trying to get him to talk, even though maintaining it nearly makes me sick.

A raised eyebrow, a smirk. I can see it on his face even if he doesn't say it out loud.

I find I do want the glass of wine, after all. I pick it up and throw it in his face.

I head home, trying to convince myself on the way that he's just pretending there is something between us, to make me go out with him. He's playing a game, that's all. There's just no way I'd have let him do that. There's no way I wouldn't be able to remember it now if I did.

But I can't take the chance. I buy a pregnancy test on the way home. Lock myself in my loo, read the instructions over. Pee on a stick. Wait. Relief swells through me that it is negative, but then I read through the instructions again. It might be too soon for a reliable result.

I go online. Is it too late for a morning after pill? Yes. It is. They have to be taken within three days for one type, or five days for the other. Either way it's too late.

But while I'm reading about that I find something else – drugs that cause abortion. For sale online if you look in the right places. I don't know if I even need it; my period isn't due for another week. But 'be prepared' is my motto. I make the order – use Rowan's card details again.

All I can do now is hope that what Stuart implied didn't happen. Wait for my period. Do another test if it doesn't come.

I can't stop myself thinking of Rowan. What happened to her? Grace, I mean, as she was then. Pregnant at fifteen – two years younger than I am now. Did she get drunk, too? Is that why she warned me about getting in that state?

No. Don't feel sorry for her – *don't*. It's her fault that I went out on my own, drank so much. Remember what is at stake.

It was Maisie's idea to send Rowan red roses without a card – using Rowan's account again to buy them. That worked a treat, didn't it? Dad was definitely unhappy about them. If he notices the roses on her statement and thinks she did it to make him jealous, he'll be even more angry. Since then – maybe before, as well – I've felt there is something going on between Dad and Rowan, some problem I don't know about. She looked positively delighted to see me when I came in late for dinner, as if she didn't want to be on her own with Dad. And they were so weird at dinner. She didn't say anything but I could tell she was cross to hear about his trip away, too – that he hadn't told her.

It's time to escalate things with Rowan. Anything to distract me while I wait.

FORTY-TWO

GRACE

I am fear. Fear is me. There is nothing else.

I want to run, as fast and as far as I can, but where is there to go? The thing I am most terrified of would come with me. I can't do this, *be* this. But the only way out is a sin so big my mind can't encompass or contemplate it. Is it a worse sin to take another life, or your own? I don't know.

I book an appointment at the clinic. I'm told I don't have to tell my parents, but they advise I do so. They don't know my parents.

I get through the few days between. Manage to get up, pray, go to school, go to church, do my chores, pray. Without saying anything. Without screaming.

Finally, it is the day, the time. In the morning when I should be going to school, I get a bus, instead. When I arrive for my appointment, the nurse seems shocked when she realises who I am – what I am. It's hard to miss us, the way we dress. The long skirts, kerchief around our hair and the no make-up, no jewellery. Even this far from Wigan we're always recognised. Usually avoided.

She quickly hides it. Talks through options, but there is only one I want to know.

How soon can I get rid of it?

FORTY-THREE

ROWAN

Theo leaves very early in the morning for the airport and I only half wake up to say goodbye. But once I hear the front door close behind him, I can't get back to sleep.

Everything from yesterday crowds in for my attention. I feel ridiculous now that I'd convinced myself I was being followed, that the church had found me. How could they? The man I saw may or may not have been the same person at the restaurant, but either way, he was just some random man wearing a gold cross, that's all. But despite telling myself there was nothing in it, despite how claustrophobic I feel at home, I can't convince myself to go out.

I get up after I hear Ellie leave. Go to the kitchen and sit at the breakfast bar with my laptop and start looking at all the baby things we'll need. I make some lists, order some things, all the while thinking how ridiculous it is that I'm planning for a baby when just being near one makes me tremble, panic.

A courier comes with my maternity clothing delivery. I spend ages unpacking and de-tagging, washing some things, trying not to watch the clock, the minutes slowly ticking down.

Theo should have landed in New York by now. I check my phone; no messages.

Make some mint tea, take it to the sofa. There is a thriller I've been wanting to read that I left on the sofa when I came down earlier, since Theo wasn't home to get annoyed at clutter – as if a book qualifies as clutter. But when I try to pick it up, I soon put it down again. As much as I want distraction, I can't concentrate enough for the words to make sense.

Instead, the photos Maxine showed me of Naomi fill my head. The look of joy on her face with her baby daughter, Ellie, in her arms. That's the way I desperately want to be with our baby. But then Naomi left, so the feeling either didn't last, or other feelings were stronger. From what Maxine said, Naomi had postnatal depression, perhaps took a long walk into the sea with no return.

But no trace of her was found. If she walked into the sea, wouldn't her body have washed up on a beach somewhere? Or if she ended her life in some other way, same thing: wouldn't her body have been found?

Still no message from Theo. I'm uneasy. He always messages on arrival when he's away for work, just to say he's there and that everything is fine. But nothing.

Is he really on a business trip? Or maybe it is what Ellie mocked me with before – that he has another woman. If he is seeing someone else, they'll be in for a surprise if they think there is any chance of getting rid of me. They don't know who I am, what I can do. What I am capable of.

Stop it. You have no reason not to trust him.

Should I break the usual trend and message first? I consult the mental manual of who I am supposed to be, and that particular answer isn't in place. It hasn't had to be before. Being needy – no. I sigh. But one message must be allowed. I hesitate, finally send this.

Hi darling, hope your flight went well, miss you xx

I watch for a reply that doesn't come. Then try to read again, give up, pull my feet up and close my eyes.

It's much later when I'm startled awake, not sure if I heard something or a forgotten dream prodded me awake. Stiff, I stretch. Long shadows outside say evening. I reach to check for a message from Theo but I can't find my phone. Has it fallen on the floor, gone under a sofa cushion? No. There is music on low in the background – the radio? I don't remember turning it on. Is Ellie home? But she generally only puts music on in her room. I wander into the kitchen, yawning, grateful for the absence of nightmares – ones I can remember, at least – and a few hours of much-needed sleep. Have a glass of water. Look on the surfaces for my phone. Where could it be? I'm sure it was next to me when I drifted off. I go back and look around the sofa. Did I get up for the loo? I check the downstairs one; it's not there.

'Vera, is Ellie home?'

'No, Ellie isn't home.'

I don't know if she'll be home for dinner but I should eat something, anyhow. I start looking through the fridge, decide to make a stir fry.

It takes a while to register that the music I can hear isn't the radio; there is no speaking between songs. It's a little louder now and following me room to room as if I'd programmed it to do so, but I didn't. Most are songs I've heard before, all on a topic, one after another: Roy Orbison, 'Crying'; Dionne Warwick, 'Walk On By'; Adele and 'Someone Like You'; even Taylor Swift and 'The Tortured Poets Department'. It's a break-up playlist.

'Vera, music off.' It continues. 'Vera, why didn't you turn off the music?'

'Command override.'

OK. Great. 'Vera, are you sure that Ellie isn't home?'

'Yes.'

'Vera, has Ellie been home in the last few hours?'

'Yes.'

OK. I've identified the culprit. I'd message her if I could find my phone. I'd use the app to turn off the music, if I could find my phone. I might even have a message from Theo on said phone. Putting on broken-hearted music that I can't turn off to annoy me, yes, I can see Ellie doing that. Stealing my phone? That seems less likely. So, it's probably here somewhere. And now I'm taking all the cushions off the sofas and chairs and looking under furniture and checking my bag, coat pockets, and – why not, given my keys were found there once? – even the fridge. No phone. I'm shifting from annoyed to angry to stressed. I try upstairs next, though unless I was sleepwalking, I haven't gone up since I last used it. Everything seems as usual, nothing out of place.

And then, all at once, stress turns to fear. If I don't have my phone, I can't even open the door. I'm trapped. I run down the stairs so fast I lose my footing, grab onto the banister and only just manage to stop myself from tumbling down the stairs. There is a lurch of fear in my gut: what if I had fallen? I cradle my arms around myself, around my baby, trying not to cry.

'Vera, open the door.' The door slides open. I breathe easier.

'Should I close the door?'

'No.'

'Should I close the door?' Vera says again a moment later, and I swear her unanimated voice sounds puzzled, then realise I said 'no' without her name.

'Vera, leave the door open.'

A moment later Ellie walks in, surprised first at the open door. Then she looks at the sofas, cushions still scattered everywhere.

She raises an eyebrow. 'Were you having a pillow fight with yourself?'

'No, I was looking for my phone.'

'Did you find it?'

'Of course I didn't. Where did you put it?'

'Hang on a minute; I haven't touched your phone.'

'Really?'

'Are you going to call me a liar again?'

But now the anger is dissipating and there are tears in my eyes.

'Geez, get a grip. Vera, where is Rowan's phone?'

'It is one point two metres right and three point six metres back from the door.'

Ellie steps out approximate meters and arrives at the side table next to the sofa. She lifts up my book. Underneath it is my phone. I can feel my face turning pink.

'I'm sorry—'

'Save it. I don't care.'

'But—'

She holds up her hands in a stop signal. 'Don't. Care.'

She goes down the hall, slams the door to her room. I sit on the sofa, head in hands. I can't remember if I checked under my book. Could Ellie have slipped it under there when she lifted it up? I doubt she could have managed that without me noticing. Vera said where it was before then, anyway, so it must have been there while Ellie was still across the room. I pull a few cushions up from the floor, tuck them behind my back. Adele's 'Hello' is just starting, the broken-hearted playlist still in full swing.

'Vera, how did you know where my phone was?'

'All phones in the house and perimeter can be located in the grid.'

Sure. Whatever that means. At least I'll be able to ask next time I can't find it.

There's no message from Theo. I go to the app, slide the music to off just in time to cut full anguish mid-word – hell instead of hello.

FORTY-FOUR

ELLIE

Rowan looked like she was really about to lose it. Is that what being pregnant does to you? I hope I never find out.

I message Dad.

How's it going in the Big Apple? Are you coming home soon? Because you've left me with a crazy woman. I could call the authorities.

He answers a moment later.

All good – we've signed the deal. I might regret asking, but what's going on with Rowan this time?

She couldn't find her phone, turned the house upside down and it was on the table next to her the whole time.

There is a pause. 'Turned the house upside down' are not words Dad likes to hear.

He answers:

Try to get along. I'll be home tomorrow night.

I can't say we get along exactly, but we peacefully co-exist the rest of the evening. Rowan messages to see if I want some dinner. We eat at the same table. It is on the quiet side – she doesn't say anything – but that is fine with me.

She leaves the dishes, goes upstairs. I sigh, eye the table. Take the dishes into the kitchen and load the dishwasher. The sofa cushions are still all over the place, but I didn't contribute to that mess, and so I leave them where they are.

I go to my room and try to work on coursework, but I can't stop seeing the look on Stuart's face, hearing the things that he said. I almost wish Rowan had stayed downstairs, that we could have watched TV or something so I'm not alone with my thoughts.

Almost, but not quite.

FORTY-FIVE

ROWAN

I go straight up after eating dinner, wanting to be alone. Despite the unplanned nap on the sofa, I still feel so tired – exhausted, even. I have a quick shower and get into bed, but I'm too wound up to sleep.

Why hasn't Theo messaged back? Maybe something is wrong – a car accident or some other disaster my imagination quickly fills in. I'm holding my phone, almost call him but manage to stop myself, put it back down. If anything has happened, I'll be notified. Calling would make me look both needy and neurotic.

The other thing preying on my mind is Ellie. I'd been so angry, sure she had set up the music and hidden my phone so I couldn't turn it off. But it couldn't have been her as far as the phone goes, not when Vera identified its location before she'd even made it across the room. Guilt made me make dinner but anger kept me silent while we ate it. I shouldn't let her get to me but knowing this isn't helping tonight.

When I finally drift off to sleep, I don't stay there for long. I keep waking up, as if there was a voice or some other sound interrupting my sleep, but when my eyes open wide, startled, the house is quiet. The sound of my breathing is all I can hear. I check the alarm, the doors, windows. The CCTV cameras on the drive and gate. Nothing.

FORTY-SIX

ELLIE

When I get home the next evening, Rowan has finally picked up all the cushions and the room is back as it should be, but she's not looking herself at all. Like she hasn't slept or isn't feeling well. Or both. She must catch me staring.

'What?' she says.

'Are you OK? You look terrible.'

'Gee, thanks.'

'Dad's going to be home soon. Shouldn't you, you know, put on a face or something?'

'Do you know when?'

'Didn't he tell you?' Interesting. 'I don't know the exact time, but he messaged and said he'd be home tonight.'

It's after midnight when I hear the car, the front door. I'm prepared. The override codes I found in Dad's locked files have let me get into the system and enable me to do all kinds of things, like that playlist for Rowan yesterday that she couldn't turn off with a voice command. Just now I have the sound from the front room routed to my headphones in my room.

'Hi Rowan. You didn't need to wait up.'

'We need to talk.'

'It's late. Tomorrow?'

'It can't wait.'

A sigh. 'I'll get a drink.' I hear the cabinet. The clink of a bottle. Scotch, probably.

'So, what's up?' he says.

'I didn't hear from you. I've been worried.'

'It was busy – back-to-back meetings.'

'Ellie knew you were coming back tonight. I didn't.'

'Seriously, Rowan? I told you when I'd be back.'

There's a pause. 'I'm sure you didn't.'

'I did, Rowan. The night before I left.'

Another pause. 'You didn't have time to message me when you were away, but you did to message Ellie.'

'Well, she said something that made me alarmed enough to answer.'

'Oh?'

'That I'd left her with a crazy woman. I gather you lost your phone?'

'Is that all she told you?'

'Is there more?'

She sighs and I wonder if she'll tell him about the playlist. 'It doesn't matter,' she says, instead.

'What does matter, then? What is it you want to talk about in the middle of the night?'

'Is something wrong, Theo? Tell me. You seem angry and I don't know why.'

'Don't you trust me, Rowan? Is that the problem?'

'No, of course not.'

'So why be worried over not hearing from me for not much more than a day when I'm in back-to-back meetings and long-haul flights?'

'It's just... it's not like you.'

'Maybe I've had a lot on my mind.' There is a clunk, like he's put his glass down on the table, hard. 'You didn't think you'd get away with that without me finding out?'

There's a pause. 'Get away with what?'

'Checking up on what I told you. Asking Maxine all those questions about Naomi.'

'I wasn't checking up on you—'

'Well, then, what would you call it?'

'You wouldn't talk about her. You left me with no choice.'

'No choice? How about this. You could accept what your husband tells you when he says the past has no bearing on our lives. Is that so unreasonable?'

Another pause. 'It is unreasonable,' Rowan says, her quiet voice in contrast to his angry words, 'because there was an important detail you never told me.'

'Oh?'

'You said Naomi left. You never said she was depressed, that she was missing – that the police were looking for her, too.'

I sit bolt upright, eyes open wide. My mum was missing – the police were involved? I'm so shocked I almost don't take in Dad's answer, his voice quiet again now:

'Why did you think you needed to know that my first wife likely killed herself? Does knowing make you feel better in some way?'

His words spin around in my head. They don't make any kind of sense. I must have misheard him; he couldn't have said what I think he did.

'Of course it doesn't make me feel better,' Rowan says. 'But it helps me understand you, and that's important.'

'Then understand this. It was the worst time of my life. The agony of losing Naomi, not knowing what happened to her. Wondering if there was anything I could have done to stop her from doing whatever she did. And having to care for Ellie, alone. *Don't* dredge up the past again. Please. I can't bear it.'

She's silent, doesn't answer. A moment later, 'Rowan, you need to start caring for yourself, caring for this baby,' he says, his voice soothing now. 'Bringing up distressing things from the past isn't going to help. Is it? And another thing. Maxine told me about that photo album she has, of Naomi. That she showed it to you.'

'She said she made it for Ellie.'

'I don't think Ellie has any interest in Naomi or her photos, so don't even think about upsetting her with it. I've told Maxine to get rid of it, too. Now, I don't know about you, but I'm exhausted. Goodnight, Rowan.'

Footsteps on the stairs.

Faint snuffling noises. Is Rowan crying?

I take off the headphones and sit there at my desk, eyes wide open, seeing nothing. The words I heard going back and forth in my head as if I'm trying to shake them into an order that will make any kind of sense.

Missing?

Depression?

Suicide.

It's not the story I thought I knew. Or is it? In one version, she left us behind. In this new version she did the same thing, but maybe in a different way and for different reasons.

I've heard of postnatal depression. I don't know much about it. But with what Dad said about Mum, doesn't it basically mean that having a baby depressed her so much that she killed herself?

That baby was me.

It's my fault. Is that why Dad never told me?

And tonight, the things Dad said and the way he said them – I've not heard him speak like that to Rowan before. As much as I want there to be problems between them, this felt, I don't know, *wrong*. Like there was more behind what they were both saying, and I'm not sure I want to know what it was.

And then there is this album of photos Auntie M has of my

mother, that she made for me. And Dad told her to get rid of. I'm not sure how I feel about that.

There had been a few photos of her here, years ago. I broke the glass, the frames, and tore them up. I can almost remember what she looks like from then, but not clearly – a generic pretty face, blue eyes and long blonde hair, like mine. Doubt I'd recognise her if she walked past me on the street. There is this chasm, inside me – an empty place that never goes. Now I'm crying, too.

Damn it, Rowan. I don't need this to deal with now, along with everything else.

It's later when it occurs to me that it was pretty rich for Dad to accuse Rowan of checking up on him. All she did was talk to his sister. He was the one who hired private investigators to snoop into every corner of her life.

FORTY-SEVEN

GRACE

When I get home from school, Mam's face is pinched, worried. She grabs me by the shoulders, holding them so hard it hurts.

'What have you done?' she says.

I can feel the colour draining from my face. Do they know?

How could they? At the clinic they said they couldn't tell my parents, they promised. It was confidential, that was the word they used. This must be about something else – the missing money?

Play dumb until I know for sure.

'Let go, you're hurting me. I don't know what you're talking about.'

She releases me and pushes me towards the door at the same time. 'Go to your father. He's waiting for you at church.' I stumble back out the door.

Run, a voice whispers inside. *Run, and don't look back.*

But where could I go? I only have a few friends and none of them could stop Father finding me – he'd know where to look. I'm shaking as I walk down the road and then across, through the doors of our church.

His face is thunder and this isn't just about the missing ten pounds; it can't be. He isn't alone, either. They're all here – the elders. Five men with faces of stone, Father at the centre. Gold crosses glint at their necks.

'Confess,' he says.

He comes closer. 'Confess your sins!' He shouts the words, standing over me. Pushes me to my knees. Slaps me so hard across the face that tears spring to my eyes. I'm shocked. Even though he's hit me many times before, it was always hidden, behind doors, at home.

He knows. Doesn't he? I don't know how, but he must know.

It might go better for me if I say what he wants me to say, but I'm struck dumb, terrified, and the words won't come.

Later he carries me home to the room I share with one of my sisters, throws me on the floor and slams the door. I manage to stir, to pull myself up enough to crawl into my bed.

I confessed, finally. He hit me enough times that I would have said anything to make it stop. They know I'm pregnant and the even worse sin, that I wanted rid of it, to have an abortion. He made it clear that can never happen.

Maybe he's beaten me enough that I'll miscarry. That never happened to Mam, though. I've got nine brothers and sisters, despite how much sin he beat out of her.

I'm beyond tears, empty. Maybe when I don't turn up for my clinic appointment next week, they'll come looking for me, to make sure I'm all right. Or maybe not. Maybe that nurse lied about even making the appointment for me and then told Father.

What is going to happen to me now?

FORTY-EIGHT

ROWAN

When I finally go upstairs, Theo is sound asleep. I've never seen him so angry before. He's never spoken to me like that, either. It took me out of myself, out of now. Back to other arguments I could never win. Back to a time when any hateful thing could be directed at me and I couldn't protest. All I could do was take it, try to close my ears and retreat inside. Switch off before the beating started.

I should have asked Maxine not to tell Theo, not that she would have necessarily listened to me. But why did knowing I spoke to Maxine about Naomi make Theo so angry? His reaction seemed over and above what it should be, and not just because he thought the subject was closed.

Why didn't I just leave it alone? I have it all, more than I ever thought possible: the successful, good-looking husband, the beautiful, perfect home. Baby on the way. Even with a stepdaughter as part of the deal, my life is enviable, and she'll be off to live her own life soon enough. I just have to always be the woman that Theo met and fell in love with, but I've slipped up. That Rowan would never have questioned anyone about her husband's first wife: why would she? She isn't insecure; she's

confident in her own attractiveness and her husband's undi-
vided love. It wouldn't have occurred to her that there was
anything to worry about. My focus has slipped. I need to stay
vigilant. On guard. Protect my family, my life.

It's being pregnant, isn't it? Taking me back to the girl I
never want to be again.

I can't let that happen.

FORTY-NINE

ELLIE

Not a great night. I kept waking up, mind busy with things I didn't want to think about. Now it's not quite six: way too early to be conscious. I punch my pillow, try to get comfortable, but it's a lost cause.

I finally get up, shrug on a dressing gown and stalk to the kitchen. Kettle on, teabag in cup. Cue footsteps, on the stairs – too heavy a tread to be Rowan. There is a split second where I almost bolt back up the hall, not sure I want to see or talk to Dad, not when everything feels so muddled inside.

But he'd notice my quick departure and wonder why. I stay put. The kettle clicks off and I'm pouring it just as he comes into the kitchen.

'Morning, Ellie. What are you doing up this early?'

'Making tea.'

'For two?' He grins and I find another cup and put the kettle back on. This all feels weirdly normal but it isn't, not at all, and not just because I never appear until well after seven.

Say something.

'Didn't you get back late? What are *you* doing up?' Pour another cup. Add milk, stir.

'Stuff to do.' He starts telling me about the meetings he had, contract details being negotiated and so on. And I'm listening – or pretending to – and thinking, did she, Dad? Did Mum kill herself? How can something as fundamental as that be a secret? I could ask him. Straight out. And he'd explain things in a way that makes everything all right, like he always does. But can he, this time?

'Ellie?' he prods.

'Sorry. Did you ask me something?'

He shakes his head, amused. 'You're not really awake, are you?'

I yawn, hide behind my hand while I do so, and pick up my mug. 'Sorry. I should go – coursework due soon,' I say. Which is true and an excuse for being up so early, though I'm unlikely to be working on it this morning.

'We'll talk later.'

I head down the hall to my room, relieved to shut the door with me on this side of it. I get back in bed, tea next to me.

If Mum was missing, and police were looking for her, there'd be stuff online. There'd have to be. Phone in my hand, wanting to do this and not wanting to at the same time.

I type *Naomi Blackwood* into the search engine. Hit enter.

And there it is. Links to news reports, all variations on a similar theme: concerns grow for missing woman. A photo, an article. Mention of the recent birth of a daughter – me. Pleas for anyone who may have information on her whereabouts to come forward.

Why is this a family secret when it can be so easily found? Last night, Dad said to Rowan that I wouldn't want to see Mum's photos or know anything about her. He was right. If someone had asked and I didn't know what I'd heard last night, I'd have said no, like he thought. Does he think he knows me so well that he can speak for me?

I'm thinking back to every conversation we've had that I can remember about Mum, and that's what I always said. I don't care, don't want to know. And Dad was proud of me, that I was so strong. That I went, *stuff her* – she left me and I don't care. Even though it wasn't really true, not completely. Was any of it real, or was I hiding my feelings and saying what he wanted to hear?

That's not fair. I'm just confused by what I heard last night, and how it fits in with everything else.

A Facebook page comes up on the search with my mother's name. Is it the same Naomi? I click on the link.

The profile photo – I recognise it. It was one of the framed photos I destroyed. Mum is holding me, a tiny baby. It was this photo that made me so angry: this woman I don't know, gazing at her baby with what can only be described as dopey eyes, full of love. How could that be true and then she just left?

There are public messages on her wall, from over seventeen years ago when she went missing, and more recently, too – family and friends pleading with her to get in touch. They don't think she killed herself or why the posts? Or maybe they just hope.

Her family... they're my family, too. Aren't they? Why don't I know them?

There are photos of her they've posted up, too, from when she was a child right up until she vanished, and I'm studying her face, committing it to memory. In every one of them, she has a big grin – even just looking at photos on a screen, I get the sense that she was the sort of person who brightened up a room just by walking into it. Not something I've ever been accused of.

What happened to change all that?

Me, that's what.

A girl from my school killed herself last year – took pills. I didn't really know her but the shock was huge just the same. They brought in someone to talk to all the students about depression. I get it – that if someone is depressed, they're not thinking right, they're in such a dark place that they're not thinking about what their actions will do to anyone else. If Mum had depression and killed herself, maybe it didn't mean she wanted to leave me.

But it doesn't *feel* that way. She still rejected me, in the most final way possible.

I go back to Naomi's Facebook page. Start to read through the public posts on her wall again. All these people, so desperate for word from her. Which means they never found a body, so, to these people, she's still missing. Maybe Dad is wrong and she really did just bugger off.

I have to know: did she leave me without a glance back and go and live another life? Or end her own?

One of those commenting is Pamela Baxter – Mum's maiden name was Baxter. Could she be related to Mum?

Before I can think too much about whether this is a good or bad idea, I send her a friend request. I'm still reading through the posts on Naomi's page when a message comes through from Pamela: *do I know you?*

She wouldn't guess who I am; on Facebook and other places, I've always been EllieRichmond. I answer. *Naomi was my mum.*

She instantly accepts my request. *Elliana? Is that really you?*

I've always gone by Ellie. It was a mouthful, that name. *Are you related to Naomi?*

She's my sister. Oh Ellie. I'm so glad to hear from you – it's an answer to a prayer. Guessing your dad doesn't know?

No. Why?

Long story but best to keep it that way.

I hesitate, looking at the words on the screen. Maybe I should talk to Dad about this, no matter what she says. I don't know.

Ellie? Are you still there?

Yes. A pause. *I want to ask you about my mum.*

Of course. Guessing from your username that you live in Richmond still – we could meet up in London?

An aunt I've never met. The sister to the mum who left me. Am I crazy? Maybe there are things I'd rather not find out.

I find myself saying *yes*.

FIFTY

ROWAN

I pretend to be asleep when Theo gets up, not sure I want to speak to him.

After I hear him leave, I have a shower, a cold one – hoping it will wake me up enough to be safe to drive. There is only one thing that will make me feel better today, and that is Sasha. She's been gaining some confidence but is still very wary. I've been back several times and she'll come to me now but hides from most of the other volunteers and trainers.

There are a few small, fenced training areas and one of the trainers brings her to me, unclips her lead.

'Sasha! Hello!' A hesitant almost wag, then she comes over. She sits next to me, leaning on my legs. Her head back, asking for strokes. I tell her what a good girl she is, get her to sit for a treat. Bring out a ball on a rope, let her sniff it, throw it up in the air a few times and then throw it away from us on the grass. She looks at me with a considering expression. You want me to chase after *that*? I run for it myself in comedy mode and throw it again. Repeat. Before long she's into the game – running to catch it – playing tug. Not so sure about letting it go so I can throw it again, but she's starting to get the idea and bouncing around like the young dog she is. Being silly, playing, and I'm thawing a little inside along with her.

I don't notice the video camera being pointed at us at first. It's Amanda, one of Charlie's assistants.

'Hey. What's with the camera?'

'Sorry, didn't you know? I assumed you did because Charlie suggested I get some footage of you and Sasha. It's part of our outreach to get new volunteers, to do what you've been doing: spending time with a dog, getting them to trust and play. That's OK, isn't it?'

'It's just – I'm such a mess. I'd have brushed my hair or something.'

'Honestly, you look fine.'

I'm uneasy but can't think of an acceptable reason to ask her to delete it.

I head home soon after and stay busy the rest of the day, trying not to think about last night and the things Theo said, the way he said them. It's a losing battle.

Dinner is nearly ready when Ellie gets in and looks in the fridge for a fizzy drink. She looks tired, too, and I am about to ask her if she is OK, even though I know she's unlikely to answer if she isn't. But before I can think what to say that is least likely to upset her, Theo comes in. He's a little earlier than usual – not quite seven.

'Hi Ellie, Rowan darling. How was your day?' he says to me, then kisses me on the cheek. Just his usual self, and I'm part relieved, part confused. Not sure if I should ask him about last night – though not in front of Ellie – or go along with pretending nothing happened.

'Ah, good, thanks. I helped out at Richmond Rescue for a few hours. Sorted out some shopping. Got dinner on the go.'

'Anything I can do?'

I shake my head. 'It'll be ready by eight.'

Ellie is quiet, looking back and forth between us with a

sceptical look, as if she is wondering what is going on, too. They both wander off in different directions soon after and I'm on my own again.

I know I'm sleep-deprived, but I don't understand how Theo can talk to me like he did last night and then pretend it never happened. Without an apology or any reference to it at all. Maybe I shouldn't let it go, but I'm tired and pregnant and could use the peace.

That night I'm tossing, turning. Feverish. Am I sick? I throw the covers off and sit up. Sweat is trickling between my breasts, down my back. I'm burning up. Theo isn't here. Where is he? I get up and go to the window, open it and a cool breeze flows in, revives me, and, exhausted, I stumble back to bed.

Later I'm shivering, pulling up the covers. Drifting in that place between awake and asleep, I can hear a faint voice calling my name, but it's wrong. The wrong name. It must be part of a dream. I wake myself, shift the blankets tight around me. Start to drift back to sleep.

Grace, Grace...

FIFTY-ONE

ELLIE

I'm early on purpose and get off the Tube near the Millennium Bridge, for a walk and a think. I head across the bridge, then along the river.

What am I going to say to Pamela – an aunt I didn't even know existed a day ago? *Where the hell have you been for the last seventeen years?* might be a good place to start.

I sigh. There is a mother-shaped hole inside me that has always been there. No matter how much I deny it, even to myself. But she can't change that. Is there any actual point to meeting her? And she told me not to tell Dad. That makes me curious, but also, nervous. If Dad wanted to keep Mum's family out of my life, he might have a good reason.

I walk automatically, eyes not really taking in the view. Blue sky and London skyline wasted on me today.

My steps get slower as I get closer to the Southbank café where we agreed to meet. Glance at my watch. Right on time. I hesitate in the doorway, then spot Pamela at a table in the corner, nearly empty glass of wine in front of her: in the morning? I recognise her from recent Facebook photos, though there were also a few of her on Naomi's page, the two of them next to each other. In the latter, she was a younger version of Naomi – beautiful, blonde hair, a wide smile. Now she has lines around anxious eyes, is more than a few kilos heavier and her hair is grey-streaked. She hasn't spotted me yet – last chance to walk away. But I go up to her.

'Hi, are you Pamela?'

She nods. Her eyes light up to see me. 'Call me Pam. Oh, Ellie. You're so like Naomi.' She's out of her seat and I can tell she wants to hug me but isn't sure if she should. I hold out a hand. Instead of a handshake she holds it between hers a moment. There are tears she's blinking back and so much pain – out there to see. Naked, in a way I almost never allow my emotions to be. It's pulling at something inside and now I'm blinking.

She gestures at the seat opposite hers and we sit down.

A waiter walks over.

'What would you like?' Pam says. This is the sort of awkward situation wine is made to ease. But wine at 11 a.m. seems wrong. Anyhow, she knows how old I am and I want a clear head. Caffeine might help, too.

'A flat white, please,' I say to the waiter when he reaches us.

She's staring at me like she can't believe that I'm here. 'I can't begin to tell you how happy I was that you got in touch.'

'So why didn't you? If that's how you feel. It's been seventeen years.'

'You don't know, do you?' She's thinking, choosing her words. 'After Naomi disappeared, your father wouldn't let us see you. We tried, again and again. Even went to court for access rights but they were refused.'

I'm shocked. But if access was barred by Dad and the courts agreed, there must be a reason. Stay on guard.

'Who is *us*, that wanted to see me?'

'Me. Your grandparents. Mum died a few years ago. I swear it was from a broken heart, losing Naomi, losing you. Her only grandchild. But I've never stopped hoping Naomi would come back. Even though reason says she's gone. And I was counting the days until you were eighteen, old enough to decide for yourself to let us into your life. But here you are, now.' The pain she still feels after so many years is etched on her face, part of who she is, like it was programmed into her DNA when Naomi first disappeared and she'll always carry it with her. Just like there has always been a void inside of me.

At least she knew Naomi, who she was. All I can remember about her is that she wasn't there. I'm not even sure if I want to hear about her, sketch her in. And I don't understand why Dad kept Naomi's family away from me – assuming she's telling the truth.

'I've got a million things about you and your life I want to know. But you said you wanted to ask me about Naomi?'

'It's about when she left. That's why I went looking for Naomi online, found her page. And then you. Anyhow, I only found out recently that she had postnatal depression. That Dad thinks she killed herself.'

She flinches at my words. 'He told you that?'

I shake my head. 'I overheard – he was arguing with Rowan. My stepmother. But it's Naomi I want to talk about. Was she depressed? Did she kill herself?'

'That's what the police thought, though no trace of her or a note was ever found. But I don't know about any depression. Your dad kept us from seeing her after you were born, with one excuse after another. But even before the birth, something wasn't right. She was half completely blissed out about having a baby, and half – I don't know. Troubled. She was normally really chatty and outgoing, but she retreated into herself more and more. I was sure that things weren't right between her and your dad before you were born, but when I asked her, she wouldn't tell me what the problem was.'

I'm uncomfortable, don't want to believe her. She's making

it sound like something else was wrong, beyond Mum's mental health. That Dad kept them away so they wouldn't know one way or the other. But maybe it wasn't Dad keeping visitors away; maybe it was what Naomi wanted. Maybe Pam is lying or stretching the truth to see things the way she wants to.

'You didn't like my dad, did you?'

'Not at all; I really did, at first. He was so charming and Naomi loved him so much. It looked like the perfect marriage. And then she got pregnant, and things started to go wrong.'

Maybe I shouldn't be talking about Dad behind his back, to someone who is critical of him. Without him here to defend himself. Or maybe I'm just afraid to hear what she has to say. Either way, I've had enough.

'I should go,' I say.

'Please, stay. Just one more minute. I knew Naomi inside and out. And I know that she loved you more than anything. She would never have left you, not voluntarily.' Pam's voice is steady and calm, her gaze direct. She either believes what she says or is a good liar, but why would she lie?

I blink back tears. No matter how much I want to believe her, she must be wrong. *Mum left me.* Both things can't be true at the same time.

I don't want to ask but can't stop the words. 'What do you think happened to her?'

'I don't know. But I do know these things: there were problems between your parents. She'd never have left you. So, what do you think? What options are left?'

My hands clench into fists and I stand up. 'Are you actually implying that my dad had something to do with her disappearance? How dare you!'

'I'm sorry if I've upset you,' she says. 'You asked, and I answered.'

I grab my bag off the back of the chair, turn to go.

'Please, Ellie. One more thing. There's a necklace your

mum was wearing at the wedding. It was my mother's – the sapphires were from her mother's engagement ring.' I'd started to walk away but paused at the word *necklace*. I'm getting an odd feeling, like I know the one she means: the one I found in Dad's locked drawer.

I turn back and she shows me a close-up of the pendant on her phone. It is. It's the same one. 'I asked Theo if he had it but he never answered. I know our mum wanted it to go to you. I'm hoping you already have it.'

Why would he keep it but hide it away?

I don't know what to say, what to do. 'I don't think I've seen it,' I lie, turn to leave.

'Take care of yourself.'

I head for the exit, half running. I breathe easier once I'm outside. I'm so angry I'm shaking. First she makes me hope my mum actually wanted me; then she hits me with that complete BS about Dad. I shouldn't have come. What did I think it could possibly achieve?

I march to the Tube. Despite my fury, I can still see the concern in Pam's eyes. The pain at the loss of her sister, and me, from her life.

She said Mum loved me. Would never have left me. I want to believe it, so much, but I can't. Because that isn't what *happened*. Pam is crazy if she really thinks Dad had something to do with my mum's disappearance – I'll never believe that. Anyhow, the police must have considered Dad and ruled him out. They had all the evidence and investigated, and from today I'm sure Pam wouldn't have hesitated to tell them what she thought. But the police thought she had depression, likely killed herself. End of story.

That must be why Dad wanted to keep Pam and her parents away from me – because they couldn't accept the truth.

FIFTY-TWO

GRACE

I open my eyes wide, suddenly awake. I need the loo, is that
what woke me? My sister Patience isn't in her bed. I'm alone.

If I leave and go to the police, tell them how Father has
beaten me, they might help. I hope this even though I don't
really believe it. God is the highest authority and Father says
God moves through him. How could the police stop God?

But I have to *try*.

I concentrate on listening, being still: the house is quiet.

Take the chance, take it now.

I slip out of bed, gasping with the pain of so many bruises.
Manage to stand almost upright, to move, slowly. Bare feet
across cold floor. Reach out my hand, find the doorknob. Carefully, quietly, turn it, pull and... nothing. Is it locked? Has he
locked me in my room? My mind, fuzzy from pain and sleep,
can't take it in or understand what it means. I try the door again,
sure I must be wrong.

No. It still won't open. Panic swirls inside me. Forgetting
about being quiet now I pull on the knob, rattle the door and
then hammer on it with my hands.

I don't hear the door down the hall or the footsteps, but I

both feel and hear it when a hand slams on the door on the other side. I step back.

'Be quiet.' A sharp command from a voice that can never be ignored. Fear lurches in my gut. 'Go back to sleep.'

'Why is my door locked?'

'Why do you think?'

'I – I need the loo.'

'There's a bucket. Use that. Do *not* make another sound.' The threat is clear in his words, the way he says them.

A bucket? I flick the light on, and yes, there is a bucket. It wasn't there when I finally went to sleep, exhausted from all that came before. His footsteps are retreating and my anger turns to fear, to tears. He can't keep me locked up in here, can he?

Even if he does, he can't be here all of the time. When he isn't, Mam will let me out – won't she? Or my brothers or sisters will tell someone, get help.

That is what I will pray for.

I use the bucket, then muffle my sobs with my pillow.

FIFTY-THREE

ROWAN

After another night of disturbed sleep, I stay in bed late. Theo and Ellie are both gone by the time I make it downstairs. I put the kettle on, then start to empty the dishwasher. A glass slips through my fingers, shatters on the floor. I just stand there, looking at shards glinting on the floor as if I don't know what they are or how they got there.

I finally stir myself to find a dustpan and brush under the sink. Bend down to sweep up the fragments but that makes my head spin so much that I have to grip on to the side of the cupboard. What is wrong with me? I sit on the floor, head in my hands. It's the lack of sleep, that's all it is. Last night I was staring at the ceiling, hour after hour. Every time I nearly fell asleep something jolted me awake. I've had problems with insomnia now and then for years, but never as bad as this. At least, not since—

No. Don't go back there.

My phone is ringing. I open my eyes. I'm on the floor? Glass. I sweep up the rest of it, pull myself to standing. My phone has stopped ringing by now. It rings again a moment later and this time I answer. It's Theo.

'Hi Rowan. Is everything all right?'

I remind myself who I am, who he thinks I am. 'Yes, I'm fine. Why?'

'Did you forget something?' I'm trying to think when he answers the question himself. 'Your GP just called me. They were worried as you didn't show up for your antenatal appointment. They called you and you didn't answer so they called me. What's going on?'

'Nothing. I just forgot, that's all. And missed their call.'

'They want you at one instead. Try to remember.' And he ends the call without saying goodbye.

I go to the calendar on my phone and there it is – nine thirty a.m. GP. It's eleven now? I must have dozed off on the floor for ages. How can I sleep on the floor like that when I can't in bed?

I set an alarm for the hour before the new appointment time; this way, awake or asleep, I can't forget. Noticing as I do so that also on my calendar is a reminder that the printer deadline for the charity dinner is today.

A warm shower gradually turned colder followed by eggs on toast, and I'm feeling a little better. I make the final tweaks Charlie had wanted and send them to the printer. I stay awake and remember to leave on time for my appointment.

FIFTY-FOUR

ELLIE

I head for the Tube after meeting Pam, meaning to go to school. But when I check the app and spot Rowan going out, I change my mind. In the midst of everything Pam said and all my other problems, I can't stop thinking about the necklace I found in Dad's office, the same one Pam showed me in a photo. It belonged to a grandmother I've never met, then my mother. Pam said it was meant to go to me. I want to retrieve it from where I hid it in Rowan's dressing room. Take it as mine, hold it in my hands, as if it will somehow make me understand who wore it last and what happened to her. Even if all I do with it afterwards is hide it away.

On the way, I remember that I haven't checked the drawer I unlocked in Dad's office, to see if he noticed and has either locked it again or moved the contents.

Once home I double check no one else is here. Then go to his office. The drawer opens easily... but it's empty.

Curious, I have a quick look through the other drawers to see if he's integrated the files that were in the locked drawer. But there is nothing under King, Grace, or anything else I can think of that was there. He must have moved them, maybe took them to work or hid them somewhere else. But why hasn't he said anything about it?

He should have been outraged when he discovered the drawer was unlocked and that the necklace was missing, wondering about the cleaners and anyone else who has been in the house, as well as both of us. But he has said nothing.

I go up to Rowan's dressing room and open the drawer of scarves, feel around for the little box at the back where I'd stashed it. Nothing. I take the scarves out in case I missed it but it most definitely isn't where I left it.

It's gone. The necklace Pam said her mother – a grandmother I never met – wanted me to have.

It hurts, and I'm not even sure why. It's not like having it was going to change anything. It's just something else I've lost without even knowing I wanted it.

I shove the scarves back in the drawer.

What's happened to the necklace? Two possibilities: Rowan found it. Or Dad went looking for it whenever he moved the files. Neither of them has mentioned it to me.

Dad kept it hidden away for so long. Maybe he was planning to give it to me one day; I don't know.

I should go to school now and not miss another physics tutorial. But how can I sit and think about quantum physics with all this mess in my head? The missing necklace. Pam. The things Dad kept from me. It's all itching inside and I can't just ignore it. Now that I've calmed down, I can't stop going over what Pam said. Despite how I reacted at the time, I don't think she was lying, but I can't accept that what she said – what she implied, about Dad – was true, either. Maybe she is so desperate to know what happened to her sister that she's made up an explanation, looking for someone to blame because she can't accept that it was suicide.

In the end I get the Tube to Auntie M's. I don't tell her I'm coming. Dad was right when he told Rowan that if he'd asked me if I wanted to see this photo album of my mum, I'd have said no. *But he didn't ask.* It's not his right to take this away from me. And there is this kernel of anger inside to think that is what he's tried to do, and – put together with some of the things Pam said – it's unsettling.

I get annoyed at Dad, regularly. In recent years usually for Rowan-shaped reasons. Angry, not so much. I'm uneasy, as if I'm siding with Rowan against Dad and that feels all wrong.

But that's not the only reason I'm going. Pam's story and Dad's are so different. Auntie M was around back then. She must know what was going on.

There is one problem. I'm not supposed to know this album exists, assuming that it still does. And Dad never told me anything about Naomi being depressed and suicidal. If I ask her not to tell Dad that I've come about these things, will she? I don't know. But I need a cover story, just in case.

FIFTY-FIVE

ROWAN

'Good morning, Rowan,' Dr Khan says. 'Please. Take a seat.'

'I'm sorry I missed my appointment this morning.' It's embarrassing that I forgot but this isn't the NHS – they'll charge me for the no-show.

'It's fine. How are you feeling?'

'Tired. I haven't been sleeping great.'

'Why do you think that is?'

'I don't know. I get insomnia now and then, so it's not unusual.'

'Has something been worrying you, or have you been feeling unwell?'

Lying is second nature – it's part of me, automatic. Like breathing. But for a fraction of a second I think about telling her – if not everything, then part of the truth. She is my doctor, it's not like she can tell Theo – there has to be some sort of confidentiality requirement.

Like that clinic told me all those years ago, but Father found out, somehow. And this morning, when I didn't answer my phone, what did they do? They called Theo.

No. I can't trust her.

'Nothing worth mentioning. The usual, I think – about being a parent, how I'll cope. That's all.'

She's nodding, waiting, wanting me to say more. The best form of defence? Ask questions.

'Is insomnia usual in pregnancy?'

'It is with some mothers. Things like needing to pee in the middle of the night or feeling nauseous can interfere with sleep. And as things progress, feeling uncomfortable, physically, can make restful sleep more difficult.' She's finding pamphlets to give me, a list of web links. Stuff about sleep hygiene; best positions to sleep in when pregnant.

Next is the usual checklist. Pee in a cup. Measure something with a tape measure. Weight. Blood pressure – it's still a little low, she says. 'Have you had any problems with feeling faint or fainting?'

I shake my head, then remember. 'Though I felt dizzy this morning when I bent over to sweep up something on the floor. Had to steady myself against the cupboard.' I don't mention the unplanned nap.

'Try to stay well hydrated; it'll help. Any other concerns?'

There is something else that maybe it is safe to ask her. 'I wondered if I'm coming down with something. I woke last night feeling really hot and flushed. Opened the window, went back to sleep, then woke up shivering. Could it be from hormones or something?'

'Hot flushes – especially at night – aren't unusual in pregnancy, and it is hormonal. Though not so much the shivering afterwards.'

She takes my temperature – says it is perfect.

'Rowan, are you sure there isn't anything else you'd like to talk about?' She's concerned. I see it in the set of her face, and wonder if it is just because I look tired or if there is something else behind it. Or even *someone* else. Was she the one who spoke to Theo? What did he say?

'I'm sure. Thank you.'

More appointments are arranged: another scan. A long list of things to do and not do, and I'm so weary.

I finally escape, head for the Tube. An alert pings on my phone – someone is at the gate at home. I check the camera: it's a grocery delivery. I must have forgotten to put it on the calendar. I connect to the camera, give them a temporary gate code, tell them to leave everything by the front door.

The Tube is packed. I must finally look pregnant enough for someone to offer me a seat. I thank them, sink into it gratefully. Lean my head against the window.

The train lurches and I open my eyes, sure they'd only been closed a moment, but then we pull into Ealing. I've missed my change. Off to the platform, go back the other way. Make myself stand so I can't fall asleep again. Change. Off at Richmond. The walk I always do seems endless. I'm so relieved to reach our gate that tears prick in my eyes.

Then I see the boxes of groceries I'd forgotten would be there and the tears won't blink away.

I lug them into the hall, collapse on the sofa and close my eyes.

FIFTY-SIX

ELLIE

'Darling, you should have told me you were coming by.' Auntie M sweeps me in for an almost kiss on each cheek. Missing by the correct fraction of an inch is an art.

'Sorry, are you busy?'

'Of course, but I'm always delighted to see you. Come in, in. Warning, things are a bit chaotic. I've got my grandson for the afternoon and it's Alison's day off.' Excellent. She'll be distracted. She's barely said the words when an ear-splitting screech hits my ears. I wince as I follow her into the back sitting room. There's a playpen set up on the floor and a toddler dictator inside it, screeching and pointing at a soft toy dog that I bet he just threw out where he couldn't reach it. She gives it back to him and he throws it out again, screeching once more but a happier sound this time.

'He could do this all day.' She says it with part exasperation, part, well, adoration. But I'm guessing an hour or two of this is easier to handle than the extended version.

'So, what brings you by?' she says, as she fetches the toy again. There is a hint of something else in her eye, some worry, as if she's guessed why I'm here.

'Rumour has it you have a photo album you've been keeping for me.'

'Rumour?'

'Well, OK. Rowan told me.'

'I see.' Now she looks very worried. I might even feel guilty if landing Rowan in trouble wasn't one of my favourite pastimes.

'Rumour also has it that Dad told you to get rid of it. Did you?'

She hesitates, like she's not sure what to say. 'Well, no, I didn't,' she finally answers. 'I didn't think it was something he should be able to mandate. But I haven't told him that.'

'I won't tell if you don't tell.'

'Does that mean you want to see it?'

'I think so,' I say. And even though I've seen so many photos of Naomi now on her Facebook page and other places online that it shouldn't bother me, I'm still feeling uncertain.

'Watch Ethan a moment?' She leaves the room and he shrieks again. She's back in a moment, an album in her hands. 'Do you want me to look with you?' I shake my head. 'Why not go to the conservatory, then. For some peace and quiet.'

'Thanks,' I say. Relieved she won't be next to me, watching my face. I go through to the conservatory, shut the door. Sit down with it on my knees. Dad was furious with Rowan for coming here, seeing this. Would he be as angry at me?

I don't care. For better or worse, she was *my* mum.

I have a quick look through. Turning pages at a regular rhythm, a second or two to scan what each page holds. Pretending I'm at a friend's and they're boring me with an album of their family.

It's the photo of baby me in her arms – the same one I saw on the Facebook page and that used to be framed and on the wall at home – that undoes me. The dopey look on her face. How could she feel that way and leave me? *How?*

A light tap on the door, and Auntie M peers in. 'He's gone down for a nap. Are you all right?' I shrug, don't look up and she comes and sits next to me.

'I look at this photo and think, how could she leave me? Why?'

'Oh darling. I'm so sorry.'

'Was she depressed? Was it suicide?'

She's shocked, trying to hide it. 'Who told you that?'

'Rowan.' She did – she doesn't know I was listening, but she did.

She sighs. Brushes hair from my cheek. 'That seems most likely.'

'But then why couldn't the police find her?'

'Sometimes, they can't. Theo thought she might have walked out into the sea.'

I'm trying not to picture that, push it away. And Pam's poison words are still whispering inside me.

'How was Dad back then? When she disappeared.'

'Heartbroken. I'd never seen him like that before. Even when our mother died. He did everything he could do to try to find her – hassled the police constantly and hired private investigators when they weren't getting anywhere. It was such a tragedy. You really should talk to your dad about this if you want to know.'

He'd think I was like Rowan – checking up on him. He'd be furious if he knew I'd spoken to Pam. I shake my head. 'Don't tell him I was here. Please?'

She hesitates. 'I still think you should talk to him about Naomi. But I won't mention it until you're ready.'

'Thank you.'

'What do you want me to do with this album?'

'Can you keep it here for me?'

She gives me a proper hug. 'Of course. I'll hide it away

somewhere safe, and if you want to come and see it again, just ask. Our little secret. Right?'

'Right.'

Ethan starts to screech again. The nap didn't last long. I make her a cup of tea and say goodbye.

What now?

It's too late to bother going to school. I check the app; Rowan is home. I can't deal with her now. Instead, I go for a walk, then a coffee shop. Try to make sense of how I'm feeling.

FIFTY-SEVEN

ROWAN

'Rowan...'

Oblivion so sweet, so close. But a voice is pulling me back from the edge.

'Rowan?'

I open my eyes, confused. Then remember – I'm on the sofa, I just meant to rest a moment but I must have fallen asleep. The voice – it's Maxine. Why is she here?

'Hello.' Groggy, I rub at my eyes, sit up.

'You must have been in a deep sleep. I had to get Theo to let me in with the app – you didn't answer.'

I see her concern, and the groceries. Boxes in the entranceway, right in sunshine streaming in from the windows next to the door.

'Are you all right?' she says.

'I'm fine. I just had an unplanned nap.'

'I'll help you get this in.' And I get up, too, but she's faster, gets most of it into the kitchen when I'm still bringing one box.

'Nothing is cold any more,' she says. 'How long has it all been sitting there?'

'I don't know. They were delivered when I was out.' I

glance at the clock and get a shock when I see it's after six. 'Three hours maybe.'

'You're going to have to throw some of this away.' She's efficiently going through what can stay and what should go. Tsk tsk-ing as she does so and I'm putting what passes muster in the fridge. We'll have to go vegetarian until I get more meat in. Ellie won't mind but Theo will hate that.

'Thank you for the help,' I say, and mean it. But why is she here? She's never just dropped in before. 'What brought you by today?' I say, trying to sound casual, not like I'm demanding an explanation.

'Didn't Theo tell you?'

I shake my head.

'He said he mentioned it. No matter. Really just wanted to see how you are. Have a chat.'

'OK. Sure.'

I need to take care what I say to her in case she reports back to him again. I put the kettle on. Keep things neutral. Get advice on morning sickness – which I'm blaming for the state of me – and getting better sleep at night.

She finally takes her leave and I see her to the door.

'Oh, I meant to say. I'm glad you and Ellie are getting along better.' I must look puzzled. 'Theo wanted me to get rid of Naomi's photo album, but Ellie came by to see it earlier this afternoon. She wants me to keep it for her.'

'Did she look at it?'

'She did. I wasn't sure if she would want to or not.' She pauses. 'I think it was because she found out about Naomi's depression. I won't tell Theo – either that I still have it, or that you told Ellie. Our secret.'

We say goodbye and I watch as she goes through the gate.

My sleep-deprived brain takes a moment to put all of that together. Ellie told Maxine that I told Ellie about the album, and about Naomi's depression. But I didn't. And I know Theo wouldn't have done, so how did Ellie find out?

There's only one answer: she was listening in on our argument. Either she was eavesdropping in the hall, or – more likely, knowing Ellie – she's found a higher tech way. If Maxine changes her mind and tells Theo I told Ellie about the album and the rest, he'll be absolutely furious with me.

I've been so distracted by Theo that I've taken my eye off the one I should be monitoring – Ellie. I have to be smarter than her.

I manage to get dinner together. Once it's in the oven, Theo messages to say he'll be late and not to wait. I wonder why I bothered.

It's ready by the time Ellie gets home, almost like she stayed away until the last possible moment. She slips in her seat opposite mine and ladles veg casserole onto her plate.

'Where's Dad?' she says.

'Working late.' I study her. She seems a bit subdued, off-balance. Despite her lies and everything else, there is a surge of sympathy. 'Ellie, is everything OK?'

Her eyes meet mine, narrowed – annoyed. 'Why wouldn't it be?'

'You don't seem yourself.'

'One thing I can promise you: I'll never change.' Those three words, the way she said them – with such venom. Unmistakably a threat.

FIFTY-EIGHT

ELLIE

What is up with her? The way she looked at me, as if she actually *cared.*

I flop on my bed, search my playlists for something loud and put it up, but it doesn't drown out my thoughts. Everything is just too much, piling on me at once, and who is behind it all? Rowan.

If it wasn't for her, I wouldn't know my mother hated me so much that she killed herself. I wouldn't have all these images of her engraved on my memory, so she is all I see when I close my eyes. I wouldn't have known that photo album even existed. And OK, it's Dad who kept things from me – but maybe he was right to do so. Knowing doesn't help. I wouldn't have contacted Pam, either, or heard the poisonous things she implied about Dad. But Auntie M confirmed Dad's version and as far as I'm concerned, that's the end of it.

Lurking underneath it all is the main thing I don't want to think about. I'd almost managed to put it out of my mind completely with everything else going on, but my period definitely should have come by now. Where the hell is it?

Another thing that is Rowan's fault. I'd never have gone out and got drunk like that if it wasn't for her.

I'm angry at Rowan. I'm angry at my mother. I'm angry at Stuart. Just plain *angry*.

I drag myself to school the next morning.

On the way my phone pings with a message: it's Pam. Both curious and uneasy, I open it.

> *Hi Ellie. Talking to you had me going back, remembering. I'd told you Naomi and Theo were having problems and she wouldn't tell me why, but there was something she did say that has come back to me now. I can't remember the exact words, but there was something she'd found out about Theo's mum that was troubling her. Don't know if that helps. Take care.*

Block. Unfriend. That's what I should do. But she's reminded me that Auntie M said that after Naomi disappeared, she'd never seen Dad that distraught, not even when their mother died. Of course he has told me his mum wasn't around much when he was growing up, so maybe that explains it. But now I'm remembering the file that Dad had locked away, with photos of his mum and press clippings about her accident. It was another mystery – there was an inquest. Open verdict. They didn't know if it was an accident.

Then it hits me: did she kill herself, too? Oh my God. Maybe that's part of the reason he lost it even more with my mum – because it wasn't the first time someone he loved took their own life.

I'm getting it, now, why he didn't tell me – didn't want Rowan looking into things. It was so painful that he couldn't bear it.

Dad was so angry that Rowan went to Maxine and asked her about Mum. It makes me wonder what he might do if he caught her nosing into his mum's death, too.

FIFTY-NINE
GRACE

Won't school miss me? Mam – the only one apart from Father allowed to speak to me – says not. They've been told I've gone to stay with cousins, which isn't unusual in our community, so why would they question it? I plead with her to help me get away, or even just leave the door unlocked, but she won't. I hate her, even though I know she's even more frightened of Father than I am.

I'm allowed out once a week, to shower. As I can't go to church, Dad prays with me every morning and evening. He hits me if I say anything other than *amen*. The only book I'm allowed is the bible and I'm so bored I'm reading it, but not finding it a comfort.

It's hard to keep track of the days with nothing to mark them. Spring blossom gives way to fruit on the trees and school is out – I can hear my brothers and sisters clattering up the stairs and in the garden. Silence falls when Father is home. Ball games I watch with my face against the window. I sweat through days of intense heat but my window won't open; Father nailed it shut soon after he locked me away.

I can feel something growing – moving – inside of me. It's

not part of me. I refuse to consider it so. A separate entity that wants to use me, take over, feed off me. Alien, foreign. It doesn't belong. TV is forbidden but I'm remembering a scene from some horror movie that I saw on a friend's TV last year; I had nightmares for months afterwards. In that movie something bursts out from someone's stomach, kills the host. That's all I am now – a host.

If I took a knife, slashed into my stomach, would it kill it or me? Maybe both of us. But sharp knives are never left where I can reach them so I'll never know.

SIXTY

ROWAN

I take precautions. Message Theo, asking what time he wants dinner. He says he probably won't be home until eight – hours from now. Message Ellie, asking if she'll be home for dinner. Get an abrupt *probably not* back – no doubt complete with a rolling of her eyes. Even if she ends up going out, she might still come home first. But if I ask too many questions, she'll either ignore me, wonder what I'm up to, or both. It's the best I can do.

Ellie's door is always closed. I haven't been over the threshold in ages and have this insane moment thinking I should wear gloves, not leave fingerprints behind. Then I remind myself that I'm the adult, she is the adolescent. If she catches me in person or any other way, tough.

I go through the door to her bedroom: double bed, built-in wardrobes, dressing table, bookshelves. It wouldn't pass Theo's tidiness test but it's better than I thought it'd be.

Not sure what I'm looking for, I quickly go through her bedside table, dressing table. Drawers and wardrobes. Bookshelves. There is nothing untoward. Next, through to her bathroom. It's a mess. I feel sorry for the cleaner. So many skin and hair products, make-up marks on the sink, the floor. Next door, another room with her desk. A widescreen TV and sofa. A quick search of her desk – nothing. I leaf through some of her folders and schoolwork, careful to put things back where I find them. Something loose in the back of one comes part way out – it doesn't look like it belongs, and I pull it out further. It's a detailed plan of our house. Why would she have that? Curious, I unfold it and have a quick look. This must be an early plan; a few things are different, especially downstairs. I put it back where I found it.

Time to go. I glance around her bedroom on the way to the door. Is there anything I missed? And I see the overflowing make-up bag on her dressing table.

I go through it quickly. There, at the bottom, are two small medicine pots, pills in each. Strange place to keep them. Ecstasy, maybe, or whatever is in these days?

I read the labels – Mifepristone and misoprostol. I've never heard of either and quickly search them on my phone. Then just stand there, numb, staring at the words on my screen. I feel physically sick. Surely Ellie would never... would she?

I check the names again, hoping I made a mistake. But I haven't. She's somehow got her hands on *abortion* pills. They are only meant to be used up to ten weeks but will still cause abortion much later.

I wrap my hands around my stomach, an automatic protective move. She was so angry about this baby. Is she planning to put these drugs in something I eat or drink, to kill our child, her sibling? I'm shaking with fear and fury. I'm remembering now that I'd thought something had been put in my champagne at Theo's birthday party, something that made me look drunk – and Ellie is the one who handed it to me. I'd dismissed that when I found out I was pregnant, assumed that's why I'd been feeling off that night, but now I'm questioning it again. Even if that is true, this is a huge step beyond one of Ellie's pranks. It would be murder.

What do I do now?

I could go to the police. But what would Theo say? There is too much risk to our relationship if she ends up in jail, even if she deserves it. Or I could confront her, show Theo. But if I do that, what is to stop her from getting more that I don't find, and trying again? I go to the front room and watch out the window for Ellie or Theo coming home while I think through what I should do.

Dr Khan prescribed vitamins, folic acid and so on. I take the pills out of Ellie's pots, flush them down the loo. Replace them with folic acid supplements, tuck them back where I found them in her make-up bag. One last check – everything looks as it did when I came in. Lights off, door shut and then I hear the front door. Footsteps.

I dive into the walk-in cupboard opposite Ellie's door just in time. Footsteps go past to her room. Her door opens and shuts. I wait a moment to make sure she doesn't come straight out again, then open the door quietly, step down the hall. Go back to the kitchen and I'm leaning on the counter, shaking, feeling sick, in shock, that Ellie would actually even think of doing that – killing her half-sister or -brother.

I wasn't serious when I thought about wearing gloves when I went into Ellie's room, but they are well and truly off now. If she thinks she could do something like that and get away with it – she's in for a surprise.

SIXTY-ONE

ELLIE

When I hear Rowan's footsteps heading upstairs a while after I get home, I slip into the kitchen. Her tablet is where it usually is, tucked down the side of the microwave. She has a laptop she uses for most things; the tablet is only for looking up recipes when she's cooking. Dinner is hours away so I should be safe.

Her password is ridiculous, I worked it out years ago; she uses Dad's birthday for everything. I've no doubt he knows that, too. Now to leave a trail of crumbs for him to follow.

First, a search: Vera Blackwood. Her death predates general use of the internet, so I'm not expecting to find much, but an in memoriam website comes up – it was founded on the tenth anniversary of her death. I read it and read it again, eyes wide. The page is run by someone named Christopher McAllister. He says that Vera was leaving her husband to be with him. He is sure she didn't kill herself; she'd been full of joy, plans. There is a photo of the two of them together. It was taken almost forty years ago but even with dodgy hair and fashion choices, he was gorgeous. They somehow look *right* together. I've seen photos of her with her husband; he must have been twenty years older than her and looked a right stuffed shirt. These two are smiling, arms around each other. Vera's face – it's lit up. It's not hard to believe that something was going on between the two of them.

Bloody hell. If she was having an affair, what if her husband – my grandfather – found out? He'd have been angry, hurt. Jealous. Maybe enough so that he did something to her car to make it crash. I'd thought if it wasn't an accident, it must have been suicide; it never occurred to me she might have been *murdered*.

Focus.

There's a contact link on the website. I click it, get diverted to send an email. What should Rowan say that would completely infuriate Dad? I think for a moment, then type this:

> I've found your page and I'm concerned. I'm married to Theo Blackwood. Do you think the accident that killed his mother might have been caused by his dad tampering with her car? Could Theo have known?

Hit send.

A bit later I call Dad.

'Hi Ellie. What's up?'

'It's Rowan. She's been really weird. Weirder than usual, I mean. She was on her tablet earlier and I heard her muttering to herself, something about how someone died. When I asked her what was up, she recoiled – actually held the screen up against her to hide it. Wouldn't answer. I'm worried about her.'

There is a pause. Then, 'Thanks for letting me know. It's probably nothing – she may have been talking about a book from her book group or something. Don't worry. I'll talk to her.'

'Thanks, Dad.'

I smile as I hang up the phone.

SIXTY-TWO

ROWAN

A door opens and I'm afraid. I want to stay hidden, in the dark.

Footsteps echo, sound hollow. Not the way they should with the carpet in my bedroom. They come closer and closer.

'Rowan?'

I stir, confused. My head is down on my arms on a hard surface. I'm sitting – on a chair. I open my eyes and reality rushes back: I'm at the breakfast bar. I made dinner, then sat here after it went into the oven. I must have dozed off.

'Interesting place to nap,' Theo says. 'I'd suggest the sofa, or even upstairs in bed.'

I'm stiff, roll my shoulders, stretch. Delay looking directly at him until I have more control of myself, my face. Meet his eyes and smile. 'In other news, dinner is in the oven and it's actually on.' I glance at it hastily to make sure, but it is. It had taken a while to get myself together enough to come downstairs and start dinner, nervous the whole time that Ellie would come in and I wouldn't know what to say, how to look at her. But she didn't.

'How was your day?' I say, before he has a chance to ask me the same.

He gives me a kiss on the cheek. 'Let's just say I'm glad to be home.' He looks tired, too.

Theo sets the table and calls Ellie. I fill plates, bring them out just as she comes in and sits down, and I don't know how I'm going to eat dinner across from her, pretend nothing has happened.

Years of experience, that's how: hide what I'm thinking. Pretend.

We eat, not saying much. As if all three of us are in our own thoughts. There is a moment when Ellie exchanges a glance with Theo – one that says they are sharing a secret. I'm uneasy.

I go up to bed early and lie there and stare at the ceiling as minutes and hours tick by, too tired to sleep, too many things rushing through my mind to let go. Theo comes up eventually and I close my eyes, pretend. He's soon snoring softly.

My thoughts are floating, random. Am I dreaming or awake? I can't tell the difference any more.

Pain makes me open my eyes. I'm standing in the kitchen in the dark. There is just enough light from the microwave and oven displays to see dark blood dripping down my left hand, the blade of a knife glinting in my right. I drop it and it clatters to the floor.

Was I sleepwalking? Down the stairs and to the kitchen, the knife block?

Not just any knife – the sharpest, most lethal blade. What if I'd done what I'd wanted to do all those years ago – stabbed myself in the stomach. Got rid of it.

No. I could *never* – surely not—

The lights come on. 'Are you all right?' It's Ellie, wide-eyed, staring as blood drips from my hand.

'Like you care.'

She grabs a clean cloth from the drawer, gets me to press it against my bleeding fingers. Fetches the first aid kit. It's not as bad as the amount of blood suggests, just a small slice in two fingers that hurts like paper cuts but bleeds rather more. Did I grip the blade of the knife in my left hand?

Almost as if... I was trying to stop the right hand, the one clenching the knife.

I feel dizzy, confused, caught between now and then, who I was and who I am.

'Do you want to tell me why you're lurking about in the kitchen with a knife in the middle of the night?'

I look at her. What reasonable explanation for this could there be? 'I thought I'd add some variety to my insomnia by sleepwalking.'

'I'll keep my door locked, then.'

'Probably a good idea.' I say it like it's a joke, but there isn't anything I wouldn't do to protect this baby – to her, or to me. Ellie holds up two hands as if saying, OK, I'm done with you. She goes back down the hall to her room.

The bleeding has mostly stopped. Two plasters – sorted.

I rinse the knife and put it in the dishwasher. See there are spots of blood on the floor and clean that as well.

It's 4 a.m. I should go back to bed, but I'm trembling, thinking about what I almost did. What if I fall asleep, and sleepwalk again? Who knows what I might do?

That was then, this is now. A completely different time and place. I'm not who I was all those years ago. Then, I was a terri-fied child. I'm a grown woman now. I've put that behind me.

If I tell myself that often enough, maybe I'll start to believe it.

SIXTY-THREE

GRACE

A dog lives in the house next to ours. Beware of Dog, says the sign on their gate. If he's in their front garden when we go by, he barks and throws himself at the fence. I don't know what kind of dog – he doesn't look like others I've seen – but he's big, and we're frightened whenever we see him.

There is only one place I can see into our neighbour's garden from my window – a back corner, far from their house. I don't know his name but this dog often stays in just this place, behind bushes, trees. Looking my way. Watchful, like he's been told to keep an eye on me. But after a while we seem to look for each other – me standing on the bed so I can see him, the dog likewise in the only place he can see me. His eyes on mine say he knows what I'm going through. We lead parallel lives. Both left alone, me in my room, him in his garden. Whenever someone remembers we exist it doesn't go well for either of us, prayers and beatings for me, angry shouts and smacks for him. He shrinks down and away from their fists, even though he looks big enough to fight back.

Together, we make a plan.

I wait for the only day and time no one is home but me –

Sunday morning. Take the mattress off the bed. There are wooden slats that support it underneath. I take one and hold it like a spear in my hand, then slam it as hard as I can into the glass window. Shards of glass go everywhere and I get splinters in my hands from the wood. I bash it against the jagged edges of the window again and again but there are still some fragments of glass in the frame. Duvet doubled up to cover it. Climb from the bed to the window frame, awkward, unbalanced with this different shape I have now. I look down, down. It's so far. I can taste fear, heavy and metallic, my bitten tongue. I look across, over the fence. Watchful eyes on mine. You can do this, he's saying.

He doesn't know I lied to him. I told him I'd escape, come get him and we could run away together. But that's just a dream for a child and I don't feel like a child any longer. It doesn't matter if I die on the concrete below – I'll have got away, and that is the best I can hope for. I step into space. Time seems to stop, to leave me suspended in the air. Then I hit the ground, hard, pain in my feet, legs, my head that smacks back against the concrete.

The last I know is barking next door – shouts – then silence.

SIXTY-FOUR

ELLIE

'What's wrong, babes?' Maisie says, sitting next to me in the sixth form common room.

Of course she knows something is up; no amount of foundation could cope with my face this morning. I feel sick, too, nauseous. Did Stuart tell the truth – could it actually be morning sickness? Maybe, or maybe it's because this morning I didn't want to face Rowan so didn't stop for breakfast. I feel unwell enough that I would have just stayed home today but, same problem – didn't want to be around Rowan. And I couldn't sleep. I kept thinking about Stuart, what he implied we did. It makes me want to cry and scream at the same time. And whenever I closed my eyes, I saw my mother's face. Part of me wants to tell Maisie *everything*, but more of me can't even think how to say the words out loud. But for now, at least, I've got something else I want to talk about.

'You'll never guess what Rowan did last night.'

'Tell.'

'I woke up hungry, went to the kitchen to get a snack. She walked in from the lounge, looked through me as if I wasn't there. Then she went to the knife block, picked up a knife, held it like she was going to stab herself. But then she grabbed the blade with her other hand, cut her fingers instead. It all happened so fast, I didn't call out, I didn't know what to do. And it was so eerie – the expression on her face. Completely blank.'

'Seriously?'

'Yeah. Then it was like she came back to herself. She said she'd been sleepwalking. Which makes sense, I guess, the way she was. Afterwards I thought, what if I'd gone over, tried to take the knife from her while she was still asleep? Would she have tried to stab me? I don't know.'

'That's really scary.'

'And then I was like helping her stop the bleeding, got the first aid kit out, and you wouldn't believe the completely filthy look she gave me. When all I was doing was trying to help her.'

'God. She is clearly unbalanced.'

'I know, right? Afterwards, I put a chair in front of my door so she couldn't get in if she did it again, but I still couldn't get back to sleep.' The sleeplessness wasn't all due to Rowan, but Maisie doesn't have to know that.

'Did you tell your dad?'

'He was gone when I got up this morning. I didn't see Rowan, either.'

'What are you going to do?'

'I don't know. What do you think I should do?'

'Tell your dad. Maybe Rowan told him already, but if she didn't, he needs to know. In case it happens again. She might hurt herself, or someone else.'

I sigh. 'I have a feeling if I tell him, she'll make it sound like I'm being a drama queen; it didn't happen the way I say; it was just an accident; I made it all up.'

'Is there someone else you could tell? Like her doctor or something?'

'I don't know who they are, though maybe I could find out.

She's got vitamins and stuff, maybe it says on the label. Or I could tell her friend, Alex. The one I told you about. And if that stirs things up between Dad and Rowan, all the better.'

'You say that, but you're not fooling me. You're worried about Rowan. You actually *care*, don't you?'

I deny it; of course I do. But is that part of the reason I'm so angry with her?

Despite setting her up with the searches on her tablet and what I told Dad, I realised late last night that if there was anyone I could tell about Stuart, it's Rowan. That after what she went through so many years ago, maybe she would understand in a way no one else could. But last night when she cut herself and I was trying to help her, she looked at me with such loathing. I was a fool to have thought I could trust her. We're on opposite sides. I just needed to be reminded.

SIXTY-FIVE

ROWAN

I stay in bed late, still unable to sleep. I'm so tired that when I finally do get up, I feel dizzy. My brain fog is even worse than yesterday, and I wouldn't have thought that possible. But I can't stay in bed all day. If nothing else, I need to eat. I'm not hungry but it's not just me I need to look after.

I can't face the shower, and instead just pull on some trackies and a T-shirt. I'm with it enough to know I look a complete mess but lack the will to even brush my hair.

When I get to the kitchen, I can't stop looking at the knife block, thinking about what happened – what I could have done. Ellie did a good job at pretending to be worried, helpful, but she can't fool me, not after I found those pills. She'll tell Theo, I'm sure. Make it sound worse than it was, though even as I say that to myself, my imagination can't come up with anything worse than what I almost did. I had a knife, in my hand. Poised and ready to stab myself, my baby. The shame that fills me threatens to take me back to bed. But not eating would be another thing to feel ashamed about.

I force myself to have some toast and Marmite, juice. Put

another slice on to toast when my phone pings with a message: it's Charlie.

Watch our new ad on TV. I think you're going to like it!

She gives the channel, the time – ten minutes from now. I find the remote, open the TV cabinet hidden in the wall, and wait.

It's the usual plea for sponsors, funding, volunteers. But then there is a before of Sasha, cowering in a corner. Then a video clip of Sasha playing. With me. On TV. There is actual video, of me, on *TV*? My breath is choking in my throat, heart beating too fast.

Don't they have to ask my permission to use that? Amanda thought Charlie had asked about videoing me, and I said she didn't. I didn't tell Amanda to delete it – did she take that as consent? But she didn't say anything about what they were going to do with it. Would they pull the ad – find some other volunteer to include – if I asked them to? Legally, they would probably have to. But what reason for insisting they take me out of the ad could I possibly give? And it's out there now, anyway – it's too late to close the door. The horse has already bolted.

This can't be happening. What if someone who knew me from before sees this? Would they be able to recognise me? I rewind, watch it again. You can see my face clearly, but there is nothing to identify me in any way beyond that I'm a volunteer. Though what if Father saw it, knew me, and asked the charity who I am, how to reach me? They shouldn't give my name or any details – privacy and all that – but what if he somehow persuaded them to do so? He could be charming when he wanted to be. Even if they didn't – he could go to Richmond Rescue, watch, wait. See me going in or coming out. Follow me home.

Tears rise in my eyes. I'm so sorry, Sasha. I won't be able to come and see you any more. I can't risk it. And the thought of never seeing her again hurts so much. It's not the first time I've broken a promise to a dog. That was the real reason I started volunteering there.

The rest doesn't sink in, not at first. The end of the ad. When it does I rewind, pause it so it's frozen on the screen. It's about the charity dinner, but it's not right. The date is wrong. I go to the website – it says the same as what was on TV. I check what I sent to the printers: the date is the week before. Whose mistake? I go through the email trail, and there it is. Charlie emailed me that the date was changed, but somehow I missed that. I didn't change it. All the stuff they've probably printed by now is wrong.

I was so tired when I was finishing it up. I should have double checked everything. I didn't.

I call the printer: the job has been done and is out for delivery. I explain what happened. What is the fastest they can redo? There's hesitation. They're really busy. I say I'll get back to them. Maybe I can find another printer who can do it faster.

As much as I want to, I can't put it off. I call Charlie. Tell her I'll pay to expedite the corrected version and find a printer who can do it quicker. She's nice about it, but admitting I messed up is excruciatingly embarrassing. And because of this screw-up, even if I could manage to find an acceptable reason for them to take me out of the TV ad, there is no way I could ask now.

I start trying to look up printers but I'm so tired it's hard to even focus on the screen.

An alert on my phone that someone is at the gate makes me sit upright. Did I fall asleep again, without meaning to? I check the camera; it's Charlie. I'm tempted to ignore her, pretend I'm not home. *I know you're in there,* she mouths at the camera. I buzz her in.

I go to the door as it opens and I can see in her eyes the

surprise at how I look, what I'm wearing. *This* isn't the Rowan she knows.

She sweeps me into her arms for a hug. It feels good and I want to collapse against her, cry it all out. But I have to be careful what I say. I'm not up to it. But I have to be.

Apology first. 'I'm so very sorry—'

'I know you are. Put it out of your mind. Mistakes happen, it's fine. But I also know, you rarely make them. I'm worried about you, Rowan.'

'No need to be. I know I look a mess; I still have morning sickness. It's making it hard to sleep. I'm just worn out, that's all.'

Charlie insists on making us both lunch, sits me at the breakfast bar. Sees the plasters on my fingers, asks what I've done. Cut myself chopping veg, I tell her. She chatters about a new dog that has come in; says I should come and meet him. That Sasha would love to see me, too. The trainer hasn't been having much luck engaging her when I'm not there. The guilt stirs in my gut and I tell her no, that I'm going to have a nap this afternoon – something she can't argue with; she can see how tired I am. But I know I'll have to keep making excuses and it's just going to get harder.

A clean break is for the best.

'The thing is, Charlie, I think I need to take a step back from the charity. Focus on looking after myself, on being a mum.'

She's surprised. It's months to go; she knows I'm not working. 'Is it because of the error with the printer? It really is fine.'

I hold firm. It's for the best, I know it is. I manage to keep the tears back until after she's gone.

I curl up in bed, trying to take the nap I promised Charlie I would. I'm drifting in and out of this world, to a dreamscape that fills me with dread. Like quicksand, it's pulling me down, down, no matter how hard I struggle. It nearly has me when my phone vibrates with a call – the sound it makes on the bedside table brings me back. I reach for it – number withheld. I don't answer, let it go to message. No voicemail is left.

I'm just starting to drift off when it rings again – still number withheld.

I hesitate, press answer call. 'Hello?' No reply. 'Hello, who is this?' The call ends.

My stomach lurches and I sit up, hold my knees in against me. I was on TV. Now I'm getting calls from a withheld number.

Father has found me, I know he has. I'm shaking, heart pounding. My throat is tightening. I can hardly breathe. I roll up in a ball on the bed. The walls closing in, all around me; soon I'll be crushed and I'm caught in panic.

There is nothing I can do to escape – I'm trapped.

SIXTY-SIX

ELLIE

I buy a pregnancy test on my way home. It might still be too soon to be sure, but I can't wait any longer. I get it out of my bag, rip it open to get the bits I need and go into my bathroom. Lock the door. Pee in the cup, dip the stick. Count down the minutes and seconds.

It turns out it isn't too early. There they are: two lines on the stick. I read the instructions again, make sure it is the same as the one I used the last time, that two lines means what I think it does. I had been hoping, so much, that we didn't – that he didn't. But here is the proof. I'm fucking *pregnant*.

I want to rip Stuart's face with my fingernails. That absolute bastard. I was so drunk I couldn't remember what happened, and he did *that*? I'm thinking more closely of what he did to me and then I'm running to the loo, throwing up. Did he notice I was a virgin? Was he surprised? Did he care? He obviously didn't use a condom. Forget tearing his face – kick him, as hard as I can, between the legs, until he screams in pain.

This doesn't happen to *me*. It can't.

He should be arrested, thrown in a cell where other inmates might show him what it feels like to be raped. But if I go to the police, everyone will know. Imagine what they would say. The look on Dad's face. I'm crying. I didn't want to have sex with Stuart, but I was drunk – what was it Rowan said? That I was *vulnerable* in that state. I hate to think she might have been right, but I refuse to think that it's my fault. If it is anyone's fault beyond Stuart's, it's Rowan's. It was completely because of her that I went out on my own, that it happened at all.

I find the pills in the bottom of my make-up bag. Check the instructions again. The first one I take now; most people have no symptoms afterwards. The second pill I am meant to take a day or two later. It's after the second one that I'll be unwell. Tomorrow night is Maisie's birthday party, so I'll take the second one the day after.

My mother couldn't handle being a parent. Neither can I. Like mother, like daughter, right?

At least I know the truth. I don't have to fuck up someone's life like she fucked up mine to find out.

I get a glass of water and swallow the first pill down.

SIXTY-SEVEN

ROWAN

I don't know how long the panic attack lasted this time. I must have either passed out or fallen asleep and come back to myself a while later.

I'm exhausted, shaky. My brain is struggling to reboot, to point out that even if Father saw the ad and recognised me, how could he have got my number? And silence and hanging up – no. He wouldn't do that. Unless... he was just making sure it was my number – just needed to hear my voice to confirm it was mine. I shouldn't have answered—

Just stop it. It wasn't him. It couldn't be.

I manage to drag myself to the shower, find something half decent to wear, try to look more normal, but when I study myself in the mirror I barely recognise the white face, the wild-eyed stare. I put on some foundation, blush, mascara – my hand is shaking and I have to take it off and do it again. It helps but there is still so much fear in my eyes. I need to get it together before Theo gets home. And is Ellie here? I ask Vera, who says she was home for a while and then went out again.

Just do normal things, I tell myself. Go to the kitchen. Try to think what to make for dinner. Something easy?

No. Something difficult, that will make me concentrate. I'm going through recipes on my tablet when the door opens, then Theo comes into the kitchen. I glance at the clock – it's only six.

'You're early,' I say.

'You forgot, didn't you?' he says, and I'm panicking, trying to think of what I've forgotten this time but coming up blank. He shakes his head. 'Well, *I* remembered. It's the twentieth of June. We met six years ago today.'

'Of course we did! Sorry.'

'I've got something for you.' He takes a small jewellery box out of his jacket pocket.

'Theo, thank you!' And I'm really touched that he's remembered this day. Despite all the weirdness lately, this is real, what is most important – Theo and me. A family, together; one that will soon be bigger. All I have to do is keep it together. I kiss him.

'Well go on, open it.' He hands it across.

It's a blue velvet box; something about it says vintage rather than shiny new. I open it. Inside, a gold chain and pendant. A beautiful pendant of sparkling blue sapphires. There is either something familiar about it or it reminds me of something, but I can't think what or why. Does it have some significance beyond just being a generous gift? I look into his eyes – they are watchful, waiting for my reaction.

'Don't you like it?'

'It's... it's beautiful.'

'Let me put it on you.' He takes it out of the box, stands behind me. The chain slithers against my skin, the cool weight of the pendant rests near my throat as he does up the catch, then drops lower, goosebumps from the light touch.

'Thank you.'

'Maxine messaged me earlier. She saw you on TV – sent it to me.'

'The ad for Richmond Rescue?'

He nods, an odd expression on his face. A pause.

'What did you think of it?' I ask.

'It was great. I'm sure very effective at drawing in more funding and volunteers.'

'But?'

'I'm a little surprised, that's all. That you'd want to be on TV.'

Why? is on the tip of my tongue, but I don't say it out loud. He doesn't know the reason I'd never have chosen to have my face on TV, or anywhere else I could be found. But the way he said it made me wonder.

It's the calls earlier, the panic attack. I'm feeling paranoid, that's all. Everything is fine.

Theo is off to the airport after dinner. Some complications, he says, in the US contracts. He'll be gone two days, maybe three. He asks me if I'll be all right without him. There is only one answer: of course I'll be all right. Why wouldn't I be? Or more accurately, why wouldn't *Rowan* be – and that is who I am, who he knows. Though I'm far from sure I'll be anything approaching all right, and again I get the sense there is something behind the words he is saying. As if he knows things he has no way of knowing. And no matter how often I tell myself I'm being needlessly paranoid, growing unease is making me fearful, nervous. So much so that when the door closes behind him, I'm not sure if I'm relieved to get away from his eyes that assess, judge, seem to find me wanting, or want to call him back so I'm not alone.

Ellie gets home soon after, almost as if she was waiting for him to leave. She stares at the necklace around my neck, an odd expression on her face.

'That's pretty. Is it new?'

'Your dad gave it to me.'

She looks like she's going to say something else, then changes her mind. Says she's already eaten and goes to her room.

I check and recheck the alarm system is set; the gates and doors are locked. Get ready for bed.

I'm so desperate for sleep, even thinking of not being able to makes me want to cry. But I'm still scared, uneasy, and afraid to let go, as if sleeping would make me lose all control, make everything go wrong.

My mind is tumbling, drifting. Out-of-order images float in and out. Playing with Sasha. The ad – TV. Sapphires, sparkling, like Theo's eyes. Ellie's, too. My phone ringing – an unknown caller.

Someone saying my name...

I'm burning, hot. Drenched in sweat. Manage to sit up, stand, open the window. Accidentally knock a houseplant that sits on the wide window ledge. It smashes on the ground below. *Sorry*, I say to the plant. Stand in the cool breeze a moment, breathing in, out, in, out.

Stumble back to bed. Drift away.

Grace, Grace...

SIXTY-EIGHT

ELLIE

What was that? A loud noise – a crash. I think it was outside, but I'm not sure. I check the security cameras, alarm. Nothing. Could Rowan be sleepwalking again? I *really* can't be bothered getting up to check on her, but now that I've thought it, I'm going to have to. Dad's away; what if she fell down the stairs or something?

I sigh. Pull on a dressing gown, grab my phone. I set the lights to dim illumination that comes on automatically as I go, follows me as I have a quick look around downstairs. All the knives in the knife block are thankfully present in their slots. Next, the stairs – no one is lying at the bottom. I go up, quickly check in guest rooms, bathrooms. Dad and Rowan's door is closed. She's probably sound asleep. Should I make sure? If so, do I knock, or just open it quietly and have a look?

I could really do without a 3 a.m. heart-to-heart with my stepmother. I override Vera on my phone app so the lights won't come on in their bedroom when I open the door, then do so, carefully, quietly. Her room is dark. Window wide open. She's in bed, eyes closed, breathing evenly. The covers are thrown off and it is absolutely sweltering. I close the door as quietly as I can.

Why is it so hot? I go to climate control in the app on my phone. Their bedroom is set at thirty-five degrees. She's pretty clueless with tech so maybe she did it by accident, but it's hard to see how. I set it back to the usual twenty, then head back downstairs.

Changing the room temperature sounds like the kind of thing I might have done to muck Rowan around, but I didn't think of it and most emphatically did not do it. If she didn't do it accidentally, then who? Dad is the only other one signed into Vera on our app, but that's ridiculous. Why would he? She must have done it herself.

I get back into bed, but now I'm wide awake and it's her fault. What the hell is going on?

And I keep thinking about the necklace, too. She said Dad gave it to her. Did he search for the missing necklace, find it in her drawer and then give it to her to see her reaction? But she wouldn't react – she's not the one who put it where he must have found it. Then I remember that the Grace King file was in that locked file drawer alongside the necklace. He'll think she's seen that, too; that she knows he had her investigated and knows her past. Of course, that all assumes he *did* give her the necklace – I only have Rowan's word on that. Maybe she found it and decided to wear it, to see how *I* reacted – maybe she's on to me. I don't see how, though.

None of this makes any sense. I try to put it out of my mind. Wait for morning to come.

SIXTY-NINE

GRACE

I open my eyes. It's almost dark; quiet. I'm disorientated, the ceiling seems too far away but I know every inch of it. I'm in my bedroom, but on the mattress on the floor. I try to sit up but pain in my head, my leg, makes me gasp and stay still. My head is bandaged. There is a splint on one leg. As if deliberate, to tell me I failed, I feel it – a sharp kick in my stomach.

It didn't work. I'm still alive. Even worse, *it* is, too.

Across the room there are slivers of light where the window should be, between pieces of wood nailed across it. I won't be able to see my only friend any more. I'm sorry I lied, I tell him, but I know he can't hear me any more than he can see me.

There are voices in the hall, the scrape of a key in the lock. I close my eyes, pretend I'm asleep. They talk about me, Father and a church elder. To jump from the window like that, I must be possessed. It's the only explanation. They can't do a proper exorcism until the baby is born. The door shuts and locks again and their voices fade away. I'm alone.

They've got it wrong. If anything needs to be exorcised, it's this thing inside of me.

SEVENTY

ROWAN

I open my eyes. It takes a moment to know where I am, to see the open window and remember last night. I get up, cross to the window. See the smashed houseplant below. I was so hot. I still feel sticky, sweaty, but I did sleep, at least a little, thankfully. But not enough to make me feel anything like alert. I have a shower in our en suite, gradually turn the water colder at the end until I can only just stand it. Get dressed.

I walk across the room to the door and turn the knob, pull. Frown. Is it stuck? I do so again, pull harder, rattle the door. It's locked.

Blood is racing through my veins, pulsing so loud I can hear it. I can't breathe. Try the door again but it won't open and I'm pounding on the door. Screaming. This *can't* be happening, not again. It can't—

The door opens. Ellie is standing on the other side. 'What the fuck is going on?'

'It was locked, I couldn't open it.' I'm collapsing against the wall, sinking to the floor. My head in my hands. Rocking myself back and forth. Dimly aware Ellie is there, dropping down next to me. A hand on my shoulder, and then I remember the pills, the poison, and pull away.

'Leave me alone!'

She stands, looks back at me. Walks down the stairs. Soon after I hear the front door slam. She's gone.

Eventually I manage to get up, go downstairs. Make tea and toast. Try to think logically. What happened with the door? I didn't lock it. I was in too much of a panic to think to check my app or ask Vera to open it. Then Ellie was there, and the door opened. She must have locked it and then unlocked it – it's the only explanation that makes sense. It's embarrassing how freaked out I got, that she saw me having a panic attack. It's also given her way too many hints on how to get to me.

I must remember: the next time I can't open a door or do anything else that Vera controls, don't panic. Use the app. Or say, Vera, unlock the door. Simple, and it is, but the panic was so immediate that I couldn't think.

After a while I go outside, clean up the broken pot and plant, put the plant and dirt into compost. See the postman putting post in our mailbox and wave, empty it. Take it inside.

I'm bleary eyed, so much so that when I skim through the post, I almost miss it. Then think, no. I imagined it. This can't be. My hands are shaking as I go back through it all. There it is. A postcard – Wigan on the front. A place I haven't been in a long time and never want to go to again. I turn it over.

It's addressed to... Grace King. At this address. A scrawl on the other side:

We miss you, come home for a visit. If you don't, we'll come to you.

It's unsigned.

It's a threat. We know where you are. We're coming...

My vision is blurring and I'm breathing too shallowly, too fast. I put it down, walk away, focus on breathing in, out, in, out, more slowly. Try to quell the panic. It can't be what I thought I saw. It must have been some sort of waking dream – nightmare, that is – because I've had so little sleep.

But when I go back and look again, it's still there: addressed to a name I'd banished, almost forgotten. Both the name and the life that I left behind.

I'm not sure I recognise the handwriting, but would I after so long? There are so many things I've buried, compartmentalised away as Grace's life. Not a part of mine, not any longer.

How could Father possibly have found me here? With the name changes, first to Rowan Jones, then to Rowan Blackwood when I married Theo; several changes of address, too, along the way, and so many years – decades – have gone by. Yes, I was on an ad on TV recently, and he might have guessed Richmond from the name of the charity. But even so – how could he possibly have found my address?

Never mind how, because he did. And the writing on the card ends with a threat:

If you don't, we'll come to you.

SEVENTY-ONE

ELLIE

She's a freak. But she's a pregnant freak with my half-sibling inside of her, and no matter how much I don't want to be in that state myself, I'm worried about her.

Dad is away. I could still call him, ask him what to do, but given that he gave her the necklace – assuming Rowan was telling the truth – I'm not sure I want to talk to him until I figure out what that means.

Then who?

I get the number for the company where Rowan worked from a search. Ask to speak to Alex.

'Hello?'

'Alex. Hi. It's Ellie. Rowan's stepdaughter.'

'Ah, hi.' A note of surprise, swiftly followed by worry. 'Is everything OK with Rowan?'

'Yes, well, no. I mean, I'm not sure. I think she needs a friend just now. She won't talk to me and something is definitely wrong, and Dad's away for a few days. I'm not going to be there tonight and I'm worried about her.' I tell him about the sleepwalking, her panicking when she couldn't open the door.

That she's not sleeping in general. That I don't know what to do.

'Thanks for letting me know. I'll give her a call. And I'll give you my mobile number too, OK? If anything else happens that worries you, call me.' He says the numbers and I note them down.

'I will. Alex – I'm not one of her favourite people. It might go better if you don't mention I called, that's all.'

We say goodbye.

I feel relieved. She's back on the not-my-problem list – I've got enough of my own. It's Maisie's eighteenth birthday party followed by a sleepover tonight, and that might be just enough to distract me from the things I desperately don't want to think about.

SEVENTY-TWO

ROWAN

I'm in my car and going out through our gate before I've even decided where I am going. I just needed to leave, to be somewhere else. But my destination is obvious a moment later. If he already knows where I live, I don't need to keep away from Richmond Rescue.

I'm in luck; Charlie's car isn't in the car park today. I couldn't take a well-meaning third degree just now.

I get the key from one of the assistants, go to Sasha's kennel. Progress: instead of the back corner she's curled up in her bed with a toy. When I unlock the door she stays still, looks at me for a moment, like she's deciding if she forgives me for not visiting recently. I go in, sit down, and she launches herself at me, wildly licks my face, jumps up and down and makes squeaky excited noises. I wrap my arms around her, breathe in her doggy smell. She settles against me and I can't hold the tears back any longer. I'm crying, hiccupping sobs against her fur. As if she knows what I need, she leans in even closer, solid and warm in my arms.

There is a tap on the door, and I look up. It's Anna, one of the trainers. When she sees my face, she apologises, starts to back away.

I wipe my face and wave her forward. 'It's OK.'

'Anything I can do?'

'No. Just a bad day and pregnancy hormones messing with me.'

She hesitates. 'If you're feeling up to it...' She explains and we go to one of the fenced training areas. Sasha has only bonded with me; when I'm not with her, she retreats into herself. With me there, the trainer makes all kinds of progress. I wish I could take Sasha home. I promise to come again tomorrow.

By the time I get back in my car, I'm feeling better. Partly Sasha and having a cry, but then also focusing on her problems, her needs, instead of my own, took me out of myself. But I can't avoid it forever. It's time to head for home.

So tired, I drive with exaggerated care. Stopped in traffic a moment. Move forward again and I'm not falling asleep, I'm not, but it's like I'm caught in treacle – me, the car. The world is slowing down around me. Someone must be impatient behind. They pull out to overtake. A car comes around a bend the other way. I slam on my brakes so the overtaking car can get in front of me but they bump into the side of my car. Now I'm spinning – screaming – slamming into a tree. There is a loud bang and the airbag jams me into my seat. It smells like smoke and I can't breathe, panicking, struggling to get free.

Someone is at my door, tries it but it won't open. He goes to the passenger side and opens that one.

'Are you OK?' he says.

I'm shaking, crying.

'Rowan?' Another voice. It's Margaret, our neighbour. 'I was just coming by the other way, I saw what happened.'

Paramedics arrive, they get me out of the car on the passenger side. I hear her telling them that I'm pregnant and I'm filled with panic and fear for my baby, and guilt, too – that should have been my first thought. I should have stayed home. Why didn't I? Margaret asks for Theo's number. I say no, wait. He's in the States.

She comes with me in the ambulance to hospital. Waits with me, holds my hand. They do a scan. My baby is fine, they tell me over and again, but I'm struggling to believe it. I'm unscathed except for some bruising on my chest from the airbag, that's all – though it's enough. I feel stiff, sore. They say I'm fine to go home.

Margaret left her car behind when she came with me in the ambulance. She gets her grandson to collect us – he's in the police, I remember now. She introduces him as Timmy.

He rolls his eyes. 'It's Tim,' he says. He's solid, reassuring. There's something about him I feel comfortable with immediately.

I ask him what I've been afraid to ask. He calls someone. No one else was hurt. A witness says my eyes were closed, that I was slumped over the wheel, but I remember what happened – that I braked – how could I have done that if I was asleep?

Either way, I shouldn't have been driving, not when I was as tired as I was. Logically I knew this but did it anyway. Was it just that I had to get out of the house, away from feeling trapped inside four walls, the same walls that card to Grace was delivered to? Or maybe there is part of me that still doesn't want to carry a child. Memory that I can't access consciously, deep in the very core of me – muscles, bones – that takes me back to the last time. An evil core that lurks, hiding, inside. Waiting for its chance. The exorcism that would have torn it away from me never took place. It's been dormant and waiting, all these years.

Tim takes us to where Margaret parked her car; she follows us to my house, and soon after Tim says goodbye. After Vera opens the door for my face, Margaret comes in with me. I insist I'm OK on my own, even though *OK* seems a distant concept.

It's only after I'm settled with a cup of tea and she's left that I realise. My phone – I don't have my phone. Did I leave it in the car? Which must have been towed away, as it wasn't there when we stopped for Margaret to get her car. No phone, no app. If Vera won't do as I say, I'll be trapped. No way to control the lights or open doors, and fear is spiralling inside.

Just stop it. Vera is not sentient. She is not out to get me. I mean *it*, not she. *It* isn't out to get me. I'm in control.

'Vera, what time is it?'

'It is seven thirty-four p.m.'

'Vera, dim the lights to half illumination.'

The lights dip appropriately.

See – I'm in control. Everything will be fine. And then I remember my tablet – it's got the app, too. I find it in the kitchen. Open the app. Adjust the lighting up a little.

Everything is fine.

The more times I say those three words the less I believe it.

Tim told me a witness said my eyes were closed, but I didn't close them – I didn't go to sleep – I know I didn't. But I've been so tired. Could I have been asleep and not know it?

I do a search: *sleep deprivation.* Link after link comes up and all of it disturbing.

I read about microsleeps – when the sufferer falls asleep for short periods of time with no awareness of it. And it gets worse. Visual hallucinations are common. Even psychotic episodes if the sleep deprivation is severe enough. There is a correlation with conditions like schizophrenia, paranoia.

I need to sleep tonight. Reading this isn't helping – it's making me feel more and more anxious.

Do something normal. I check my emails. There are a few about deliveries that are coming, junk about shopping. And one from someone I've never heard of before – Christopher McAllister. The subject line is *Re: your email.*

It must be spam. I send it there.

SEVENTY-THREE

ELLIE

Finally, after a long, boring day at school – it's party time. I get ready at Amy's – didn't want to go home so planned ahead – and we've just arrived at Maisie's. There are balloons all over the fence at the front of her house, a giant pink eighteen full of helium attached to the front door, but before we get to it, my phone rings.

I glance at the screen, intending to let it go to voicemail, but it's Auntie M. That's unusual and there is a lurch of something like fear in my gut – has something happened? I wave Amy into the house without me. I step back from the door and answer.

'Hi Auntie, what's up?'

'Hello, Ellie. Just calling to say hello, check things are OK.'

'Why wouldn't they be?'

'I know your dad is away just now, that's all.' He goes away all the time but she doesn't call to check in. 'So. Is everything good at home?'

Not sure *good* is a word I'd apply. 'As far as I know. It's Maisie's eighteenth party today. Just arrived.'

She chats without saying much else. Makes me promise to call her if I'm concerned about anything, anything at all, and finally says goodbye. I stand there a moment, puzzled. Does she know some of what has been going on with Rowan? If she does, how? Or maybe she was fishing with no inkling. If so, *why*?

Should I check that Rowan is OK?

No. I am not her keeper. Besides, I called Alex. He'll make sure she's all right.

I have no actual idea what that call from Auntie M was even about. It feels like every adult in my life says one thing and means another. I shake my head, go through the door to my friends.

Time to switch off.

SEVENTY-FOUR

ROWAN

It's eleven now and Ellie still hasn't come home. As much as I tell myself I don't care, not after what I found hidden in her room, what would Theo say if something happened to her on my watch? I start to hunt for my phone to message her and then remember – it's missing. I reach for my tablet, instead.

Where are you?

She sends an eye-rolling emoji almost immediately.

It's Maisie's birthday sleepover, remember?!

She did say about the party – I forgot. I keep forgetting things, like my brain can only hold a few thoughts or emotions at a time and lately there has been too much panic and fear to admit anything else.

I check the security cameras and that the alarm is on, all the doors are locked, even though I know I don't need to do this. Vera locks everything automatically when the alarm is set. Then I do it again and again until I make myself stop.

It's midnight now. I should go to bed but somehow, even though I know I need sleep, I don't want to, as if something will happen as soon as I close my eyes. Even just thinking of doing so makes me feel more panicky.

One thing at a time.

I take my tablet with me. With each step up the fatigue is all encompassing, as if every movement is underwater, limbs heavy, awkward. I pause at the top of the stairs. I can't face going to bed, not yet. I'm afraid of where I will go when I'm asleep and, despite how tired I am, part of me is wired, awake, every sense hyper-alert. Sleep feels impossible. All this focusing on my senses makes the soreness and bruising from the airbag even worse; my fingers are throbbing where I cut them the other night, too. Can I have painkillers? I don't know what I'm allowed. What I'd like is a very large glass of wine. I sigh.

Or a bath? Yes. A bath, to soak and ease the bruises, and make me relax.

I put the water on, add some calming bath oil that fills the room with a lovely scent, breathe in, out, deeply. I peel off my clothes and get in once it's a few inches deep, keep it running. The level slowly rises. A sharp kick inside, an echo of pain from bruises on my skin above it. A ripple in the water. My belly is getting bigger now, last to be submerged. The heat soaks in, soothing...

I cough. Choking, struggling. I'm underwater. He's found me, he's holding me under – I'll drown. I struggle, kick, almost slip over but manage to sit up and breathe in deep.

I'm in the bath. At home. No one is here. No one was holding me underwater. The bath – it's full, it's over-flowing. I turn the taps sharply to off, turn the plug to let the water drain. I stand up, step out of the bath into inches of water on the floor, almost slip but grab the towel rail. Get towels out of the cupboard and put them on the bathroom floor but it's too much to soak up, it's everywhere. I hurriedly dry myself, then get my dressing gown from the back of the door and pull it on. I open the bathroom door, and it gets worse. Water has come out under the door to our bedroom carpet. It's saturated, reaching half across the room, and I'm standing here, stunned. I can't believe what I've done.

Put it on the list, Rowan. Things not to do when tired: drive. Take a bath. I'll get spare blankets to put on the carpet, and—

The lights go out. Panic surges through my body, my gut. I crouch down on the soggy carpet, hold my arms around myself, try to make myself small. He's found me. He's here and turned the power off, the alarm won't work—

Even as I panic, a corner of my mind fights for control: I'm hyperventilating. I'll pass out if I don't stop. If anyone is here, I won't be able to defend myself or do anything. I force myself to breathe slower, to think what to do.

Ask Vera.

'Vera, why are the lights out?'

'The power has gone out. I've switched to battery power.'

'Vera, does the alarm system still work?'

'It will work for up to twelve hours on battery backup.' I breathe a little easier, stand up.

'Vera, why has the power gone out?'

'Insufficient information. There could be a blackout in the area, or a fault in the house.'

Then it dawns on me – maybe water has seeped through the floor and got into the electrics somewhere, and that caused the fuse panel to trip?

Theo is going to completely flip out. And our bedroom carpet is probably ruined, too, and anywhere else the water has seeped.

I feel my way to the bedside table and my tablet. The screen lights up enough to provide a little light, but no power means no Wi-Fi. I go to the window – through the trees to next door there are lights. It's just us.

What now?

The fuse panel is downstairs, in the walk-in cupboard opposite Ellie's room. I think there is a torch in there also. But I'm shaking, afraid, tempted to ask Vera to lock my bedroom door and then just huddle on the bed until dawn.

But the woman I am supposed to be wouldn't do that, would she? She'd handle things. So that is what I am going to do.

Using the tablet as a light, I open my door. The hall carpet is dry at least. It's not much of a light, enough to move around but not enough to see all the dark corners, and there is a creeping feeling on my skin, as if hidden eyes are watching me. I make myself go down the stairs. To the hall. Open the cupboard door. Angle the tablet at the fuse box for light before I remember the torch. Find that on a shelf and put it on. Yes, it's tripped. I try the main one and the power comes on for a split second and it trips again. How about just one? I find the switch labelled upstairs lights and sockets. Flick the switch up – it stays. I try the one labelled kitchen but it trips again. OK, just upstairs will do for now.

The torch has a powerful beam and I sweep it all around the downstairs, into every corner; reassure myself no one is here. Go up the stairs – the lights are working upstairs now. I check each room. All empty. Get spare blankets, spread them out on the wet carpet in our room in case it helps.

It's after 4 a.m. now. My hair is still wet from the bath but I don't care. I get into bed, covers pulled up all around. Arms around a pillow tight against me. It's not much of a barricade against the world but it makes me feel a little better. Leave the lights on low; I don't want to be in the dark. I'll try to sleep for a few hours, then find an electrician in the morning.

Everything is in such a mess. *I'm* a mess. So tired I'm shaking, but I still can't make myself shut my eyes. The pain of the bruises on my chest is coming back, my head aches, my fingers throb where I cut them, too, but there is something far more serious wrong with me. I keep doing things that are self-destructive. Wrecking the car. Nearly drowning in the bath. I'm glad Theo is away, hope I can get everything fixed before he gets back, but even as I think this I'm scared to be alone, afraid of what I might do next. Theo never said anything about me sleepwalking and cutting myself with the knife the other night – I'm surprised if Ellie didn't tell him – but put that together with all this? I *should* be locked up. I'm dangerous, to me, people around me. My baby, most of all.

I'm sorry, so sorry. I'm crying now. I don't deserve what I have... I don't deserve anything. They were right, all those years ago. There is a wrongness inside of me that will never go.

Darkness is settling all around. I can't fight it any longer. As I drift away, a name is whispered over and over again, the name I don't answer to any more.

Grace... Grace...

SEVENTY-FIVE

GRACE

I've stopped talking. To Mam or Father or even myself. It's not the silent treatment. I just have nothing left to say to anyone.

Even as I retreat inside, there is no way to avoid what is happening to me. My belly is more and more exposed between T-shirts that won't cover it, trackies below. Ripples of movement underneath my skin like a shark about to break the surface. Horrified at the changes in my body, the *thing* moving inside of me. I'd cut it out if I could, be rid of it, no matter what that might do to me.

If jumping from a window didn't hurt it, nothing will. No matter what I want, what I do, it will survive. And I will survive long enough for it to leave me, then what it leaves behind will be expendable. Disposable. Subject to exorcism or whatever else Father and the church want to inflict on me, until the end.

It takes a while, but I find an electrician who can come this morning. I thank him and his assistant for coming so quickly, explain about the flooded bath. They soon trace the problem to a light fitting that caused the short – it's in the utility room, directly under our en suite upstairs. Damp in the ceiling seems to be limited to that one point. They ask me about the fuse panel – something is puzzling them, there's an unlabelled switch. I didn't notice when I was looking last night. I don't know what it is for.

They isolate the light in the utility room and change the fitting. Power is restored everywhere else while it dries out. They suggest heaters. I put the heat right up in the relevant rooms, then lug all the towels and blankets that I used to sop up water to the utility room to deal with later. There are no signs of damage downstairs, other than in the utility room – the light that has been pulled down and replaced has left a bit of a mess of the ceiling. The only other visible sign is the water-marked carpet upstairs in our bedroom.

Not long after they leave, an alert on my tablet tells me that someone is at the gate. I check the camera. It's Alex. What is he doing here?

I unlock the gate and open the front door. He reaches it as I do. Seeing him is like a link to another time, before I stopped sleeping, before everything started to unravel. I'm so happy to see him and wanting to cry at the same time. I pull myself together, smile.

'Hello. This is unexpected.'

'I've been calling and messaging since yesterday – why didn't you answer? I've been worried.'

'I'm so sorry; I misplaced my phone. It's a bit of a long story. Shouldn't you be at work?'

He shrugs. 'Took a half day.'

'To come and see me?'

'Yes. I would have come by last night but had the boys.'

'Come in, I'll make tea.' He follows me into the kitchen. I wince as I pick up the kettle.

'Are you all right?'

I hesitate. 'I had a minor car accident yesterday. Air bag gave me bruises.'

'Oh my God. Are you sure you're all right? Baby, too?'

'Yes. Margaret – our neighbour – happened by just after it happened. She came to the hospital with me. I had a scan and everything. I'm fine – we're fine.'

'You must have been so scared.' And with his words, it's coming back, along with everything that happened last night. My hands are shaking and I put the kettle down. 'Let me,' he says, fills the kettle. He's close, putting his arms around me and I nestle against his chest. His heart, beating so fast against me, and then mine is as well.

I pull away enough to look in his eyes. 'We said we wouldn't do this again,' I say.

'I know.' He leans down, kisses me, so sweetly, so gently, as if I'd break if he wasn't careful. Then two things happen at once. The kettle whistles and the front door opens.

We spring apart. Alex is sitting at the breakfast bar and I'm getting milk out of the fridge for tea when Theo comes into the kitchen. I try to banish guilt from my face, school it to a normal expression. But I can feel the flush on my cheeks.

'Theo! Hello. I thought you were coming home tomorrow or the next day.'

'Obviously,' he says, his eyes on Alex.

'Alex just dropped by to see if I was OK. Since I wasn't answering my phone.'

'This phone?' Theo holds it out.

I take it, confused. 'I thought I'd left it in the car.'

'You did. It was found at the garage it was towed to and they called me as registered owner. Apparently, the car was in an accident.'

'A minor one.'

'I stopped there on my way home to get your phone and there is enough damage to the car.' Theo had painstakingly restored that Jag for me; it must hurt to see it like that. 'Why didn't you call me?'

I waggle my phone. 'I couldn't.'

'Last night, then. When you got home.'

'I didn't want to worry you while you were away.'

Theo turns to Alex. 'I think now would be a good moment for you to leave.'

Alex is looking even more worried than he did before. He doesn't instantly jump on the chance to escape an awkward situation. 'Rowan?' he says. One word that asks so many questions.

I should stay, have it out with Theo. Tell him about the accident and flooding the house last night. I could go with Alex, instead, and part of me wants to – to run as far and as fast as I can. But this is my family. I can't risk it, not after working so hard to be where I am today.

'It's fine. I'm fine. Go.'

'If you ever need help – call me. Take care.'

'I will. Thanks for coming by.' Theo waits for the sound of the door closing behind him.

'I tried the landline last night, too, again early this morning. It was out of order. Know anything about that?'

'Oh. That must be because the power was out.'

'And why was the power out?'

'Long story.' He raises an eyebrow, waiting. 'I had a bath and it overfilled a little, some water got into a light fitting down-stairs. Electrician sorted it out this morning.'

'An electrician was here? You should have called me.'

I'm looking back at him – his narrowed eyes, aggressive stance. He's gone past annoyed to angry, more than I'd have expected him to be. About the possible mess or damage, or that I didn't get him to sort it out? But he wasn't *here*. This is ridiculous. 'I'm perfectly capable of sorting out a tradesperson by myself.'

'What light fitting?'

I explain, show him in the utility room. 'To get down here that must have been a lot of water. How did you manage to do that? Did you turn the taps on and just forget about it?'

'No, of course not. I was in the bath, and...' I hesitate, not wanting to admit it.

'You fell asleep. Didn't you?'

'Just for a moment.'

'Something is seriously wrong with you. What the hell is going on?'

Tears are rising in my eyes. If he'd asked the same question in a different way, I might have found a way to answer. To ask for help.

He's shaking his head. 'And can you explain what Alex was

doing here? When we got married, I thought, this is a woman I can trust. What is going on between you two?'

'He's a friend. I've told you that before,' I say. Alex *is* a friend. The most believable lies have an element of truth, and I'm a good liar, usually. Just now I'm so far off the edge that I have no idea if I'm convincing him at all.

'There are a few reasons I'm having trouble believing you.'

There is something he isn't saying. Was he watching us with one of Vera's cameras – did he see that kiss before he came in?

He's walking away. Back to the front door, into his car and out the gate. He's gone.

SEVENTY-SEVEN

ELLIE

Throwing up this morning at Maisie's had a good party-related reason: how much I had to drink last night. My vow to keep off it after I threw a glass of wine in Stuart's face didn't last. But I had much less than everyone thought. I was afraid if I got drunk that I'd cry, tell my friends what happened with Stuart. I don't want anyone to know.

I cut my afternoon class and go home. Rowan's car isn't here, she must be out. I'm relieved to have the house to myself, even as there is an edge of worry. Where has she gone? Given the state she was in the last time I saw her, she probably shouldn't be driving.

Not. My. Problem.

I take the second lot of pills. Hide in my room and wait for the pain and cramps that are supposed to come soon after, but nothing happens.

Minutes, then hours, tick slowly by – still nothing. From everything I can find online, this isn't right.

I can't wait any longer.

I head out. Walk to a chemist. Check there is no one who knows me and buy another pregnancy test.

What am I going to do if the pills didn't work?

SEVENTY-EIGHT

ROWAN

Theo won't answer messages or take calls. I don't know where he is and I don't know what this means. I'm unable to think things through clearly, to come up with a plan like I usually would. I'm too scattered, too tired.

I can't stop thinking about that kiss, either. Alex has never appeared unannounced like that before. Why did he come, really? He said he was worried when I didn't answer calls, but somehow it feels like I'm missing something.

Despite how tired I am, every sense is on overdrive. I can't even sit down for more than a moment. Instead, I'm pacing.

When I hear the gate below, I rush to the window, hoping it's Theo – instead, it's Ellie again. Maybe she knows where he is? Do I want her to know that I don't? I think a moment. It's probably a bad idea, but not knowing what's going on is making me crazy. I'll see if I can find out without asking directly. I head downstairs. She's not in the kitchen. I hesitate, then go down the hall to her room. Surprised to see the door open – she never leaves it open.

I look in through the door, and there, on her bed, is something I recognise, and really didn't expect: the box for a pregnancy test. Same kind I used recently. I'm staring at it when she comes out of the bathroom. There are tears on a face that turns to fury when she sees me. She stands between me and her bed as if hoping I hadn't seen what was there.

'What the fuck are you doing here?'

'The door was open – I wanted to ask you something, but – I saw the test, Ellie. Are you pregnant?'

She's still furious that I'm in her room, in her space – even just standing in the doorway – but it's warring with some other strong emotions. She doesn't deny it. My mind that couldn't think or reason or anything a moment ago is brought back online, as if it needed an emergency to reboot.

'We can deal with this. OK? However you want to. Everything will be all right.'

'Dad...' And she's shaking her head, her face a misery. Whatever she was going to say falls away.

'I won't tell him, Ellie. I promise.'

'I thought I dealt with it already, but it didn't work.' And before she finishes the sentence it slots into place. The pills – the abortion pills. They didn't work because I replaced them with vitamins. And I thought they were for me. How did I get things so wrong?

'Tell me what you did.' As I listen, I'm part horrified that she'd risk her health that way, part in an agony of guilt. It's eased knowing that they might have been dangerous if she'd taken them.

'You bought pills online, without a prescription? That's crazy, Ellie. They could have been anything.'

'I want rid of it. I want an abortion.' The set of her face – as if I'm going to try to talk her out of it.

'We'll book you an appointment. At a clinic, where they know what they're doing. Are you sure you're pregnant?'

She nods. 'I tested positive twice – once before I took those pills. And just now. Though maybe it would take longer to test negative even if the pills did work?'

'They can check you're still pregnant at the clinic. Do you know how many weeks?'

'Not much more than a month.'

'There'll be no problem, if you're sure that's what you want to do.'

'You really won't tell Dad?' The child that hides inside her most of the time is looking out through her eyes.

'No. I swear it. Unless you want to tell him, he'll never know.'

'Thank you.' And she moves towards me, she's crying, on my shoulder. Poor Ellie. I've been horrible to her because of what I thought she was planning and all the time she was hiding this away and trying to deal with it alone. I'm a terrible step-mother, so far beyond the worst I could be.

'I'm sorry I've been such a bitch to you lately,' I say.

'You have.'

Should I tell her the truth about the pills that I found and substituted? Maybe. But not now. She only trusts me a little, and that might only be because she feels she has no choice. I don't want to destroy this now, not when she really needs somebody.

I pull away and look at Ellie, her tear-stained face, and I feel her fear, her pain, as if it was my own. As if it was yesterday, not so many years ago.

'I'm sorry,' I say. 'I've just been dealing with my own stuff. I shouldn't have taken it out on you.'

'OK.'

'Friends?' I hold out my hand.

She hesitates, shakes my hand.

Friends will do. A huge improvement on whatever our rela-tionship has been before.

I do some searches, make some calls. There is a clinic in

Richmond and I make her an appointment next week. Go to tell her – her door is still open, and somehow that feels important. But she is sound asleep. And now I realise I never did ask if she knew where Theo was.

I was exhausted to start with and the emotions of the day – it's all too much to deal with. There is one thing that would get Theo back instantly – knowing about Ellie. I consider it for a moment, even though I know that after what I went through all those years ago, this is one promise I shouldn't even think about breaking. Though it's not the same situation, not at all. There's a world of difference between Theo and my father.

Maybe it would be better to keep this our secret – that way, Ellie will always owe me something.

I'm in the kitchen when Ellie emerges a few hours later, looking better for having slept. I envy her. I tell her about the appointment I've booked for her next week.

She's awkward. 'Thank you,' she says, like it's hard to say. It's far from the way we usually interact. She admits she's hungry and I start making pasta – her favourite, with home-made pesto.

'Have you heard from your dad?'

She shakes her head. 'Not since yesterday. He said he'd be away another day or two, didn't he?'

'He was home earlier today.' She's surprised, a little alarmed. 'Could you check if he wants dinner?'

Phone out, she messages. It vibrates a moment later. 'Yes to dinner, and he's on his way.' She leaves for her room a moment later.

Is this how we'll be communicating from now on – through a teenage intermediary? There is the worry and all the rest, but also anger. I'm his wife, not someone he can choose to ignore. He needs to learn that lesson, too.

I've been doing the wrong thing today, I realise now, in calling and messaging repeatedly. Being needy. I've been losing touch with who I'm supposed to be. Everything feels out of kilter, like the floor is at an angle and if I don't keep one hand on the worktop I'll fall over. Things I normally know and trust about the world are full of doubt. This is a test, the most difficult one yet, and I *can't* fail.

The gate; the door opens. Footsteps. He stands in the doorway to the kitchen, comes in a moment later.

'Let's talk,' he says. I stop stirring the pesto into the pasta and face him. He's observing me like I'm an exhibit at a museum, or a portrait in a gallery – by an artist he's not sure of. 'I've made you an appointment for tomorrow morning. I'll take you.'

'An appointment? What sort of appointment?'

'Someone you can talk to about things. You need some help, Rowan.'

The kind of help I'm sure he means – psychologist, psychiatrist? – can't help me. They've tried before. But he doesn't know that and I can't really argue, not after the car accident and everything else. I'll do what Theo wants and go and talk to them. Be a model of stability and admit to problems sleeping, probably get some advice on that, and that'll be it.

'OK,' I say. I hold out a hand. He hesitates, takes it, pulls me towards him. His arms go around me. I lean into his chest, close my eyes. Everything will be fine. Won't it? He kisses my forehead, then lets go a moment later and starts to set the table.

Ellie reappears. She's changed, brushed her hair; careful make-up hides the ravages of earlier tears. Something I should have thought to have done also. Having slept on wet hair last night and no make-up, I must look the mess that Theo thinks I am.

We have dinner. All three of us seem a little subdued. Ellie asks about the US trip, why he came home early.

He glances at me. 'There were some things I needed to take care of at home. But I'm afraid I'll have to head back tomorrow to finish up there.'

Theo suggests I go up to sleep early. It isn't the sort of suggestion a sensible sleep-deprived pregnant wife can argue against. In our bathroom mirror, the face looking back at me is going to need work to convince whoever I'm talking to tomorrow that everything is fine. Some sleep would definitely help. But everything still feels wrong, off-balance. Even with Theo home, I have to check everything to make sure it's OK. The alarm system. Doors, windows. Still-damp carpet. I'm pacing around our room. Twenty steps by thirty steps. Pace, count. Listening for footsteps on the stairs as I go. Pace, count.

I finally convince myself to get into bed, to get as comfortable as I can. Arms again around a pillow, held tight to my chest. Deep breathing. Consciously trying to relax each part of me in turn, until I drift away.

Grace...

The turn of a key in my door. The nightmare that never ends. I know I'm asleep, I'm fighting to leave this dream behind, to claw my way back to consciousness, but it's like I'm being held down, can't move, can't breathe, can't scream...

I open my eyes. I'm sweating, throw the covers off. Open the window wide and breathe in. Theo's side of the bed, tidy, not slept in, though it's still early. I pace the room, count. Pace again and again. Trying to make myself tired enough to go back to sleep.

SEVENTY-NINE

ELLIE

There is a tap at my door.

'Yeah?'

Dad peeks in. 'Can we have a chat?' His face is serious. I can't remember the last time he's tapped on my door in the evening like this and I'm instantly flooded with alarm. She didn't tell him – she wouldn't – no. Of course not.

'Sure, what's up?'

'I'm worried about Rowan. The car accident, and—'

'Car accident? What car accident?'

'She didn't say?'

I shake my head.

'Sounds like she fell asleep at the wheel. She's just lucky she wasn't hurt and no one else was, either.'

I'd assumed she was out when her car wasn't here – that explains why she was here without it.

'The car?'

He flinches. He was so proud of that car. Despite having the money to get whatever new car any of us want, he loves nothing better than doing up an old classic. He started young –

the first one he rebuilt was a twenty-first birthday gift for Auntie M.

'It's fixable,' he says. 'That's not all, though. There was the flood upstairs last night.' He must read the surprise. 'You didn't know?'

'I was at Maisie's sleepover.'

'Of course. I think she fell asleep in the bath.'

I'm remembering now how pale she was, all the things I wasn't noticing because of my own stuff. How she apologised for being distracted, but maybe I need to make the same apology.

'I'm getting her some help,' Dad says. 'Booked her in to see a psychologist tomorrow. But I've been away a lot, so can you help fill in the picture? Any problems or anything Rowan has said or done out of the ordinary?'

I'm looking in his eyes and thinking, he knows she was Grace and all she went through, but he's not saying anything about it. Of course, he doesn't know that I know. Should I raise it? I'm uneasy, as if bringing Rowan's secrets out into the open might do the same to mine – that he'd realise it was me who went through his locked drawer. But will the psychologist know about Rowan's past? How can they help her if they don't?

'What kind of problems?' I hedge.

'So, for example, you told me she was turning the house over to find her missing phone when it was next to her the whole time.'

'Um, yes. And she's been, I guess, distracted. Not really present sometimes. I thought that was being pregnant.'

'Anything else?'

'She couldn't get the bedroom door open the other morning; thought it was locked. And kind of freaked out.'

'There's something else that you're not telling me. What is it?'

The knife; sleepwalking. That's the kind of thing he wants

to know. But I'm not sure if I should tell him. After how good she was to me earlier, it feels wrong, as if I'm telling on her. But maybe it would help if psychologist knows?

'Ellie?' he prompts.

'A few nights ago, she was sleepwalking. I went to the kitchen for a snack, she was there, couldn't see me.'

'And?'

'She woke up. That's all.'

He's looking at me quizzically, like he knows there is more to the story. I'm not even sure why I didn't tell him about the knife – it could be dangerous if she does that again. Is it because I owe her and know she'd rather I didn't, or some other reason I haven't quite worked out? I don't even know.

Change the subject: to the other thing I'm feeling guilty about now. The way I set her up about looking into Grandma Vera's death. 'Did you ask her about what she was doing on her tablet? That I told you about the other day?'

Something shifts across his face. 'It was nothing important,' he says.

Nothing important? I expected him to be completely furious. If he is, he's hiding it well.

'Is something else wrong?' he says. 'You don't seem yourself.' Now he's the one changing the subject.

'I'm fine,' I say, casting for a reason, finding one and it is even the truth. 'Just stupid maths coursework due tomorrow.'

'Not finished?'

'Almost. Not quite. Best get back to it.' If he notices the lack of books and coursework spread around, he doesn't say.

'Goodnight, Ellie.' A kiss on the cheek. For a moment – seconds, no more – I think, I could tell him everything. Fall to pieces, like I want to. Have him be there for me and look after me like he always has before.

No. He wouldn't accept the fact that I'm pregnant and

move on from it to what needs to be done, like Rowan did. He'd want to know who, all the details. I just *can't*.

After he's gone, I push away the tears. Get my books out. Make myself finish the coursework, as much for distraction value as anything else. Amy is in my class and helps – surprised at the last-minute call as it is usually the other way around. Not my best work, maybe, but in the circumstances handing it in on time tomorrow will be a bloody miracle.

When I'm finally done, it's late. The house is silent. I'm thinking back to that weird call from Auntie M; Dad's questions earlier tonight. The odd way he reacted when I asked him about Rowan's tablet. Something feels wrong in the midst of all the other things that are wrong, though maybe I'm just focusing outwards to avoid thinking about my own stuff. Either way, I slip out to the kitchen, take Rowan's tablet to my room.

If Christopher didn't answer and Dad didn't look in her sent items, maybe he missed that exchange.

Maybe he's answered since then? There's nothing from Christopher in her inbox, read or unread.

Next, I check deleted items; it's not there. Check spam and – there it is. An unread reply. She must have thought it was spam and sent it there. Dad didn't find it, did he, or surely, he'd have deleted it?

I click on the email.

Hi Rowan,

I had an almost identical message quite a few years ago now, from someone named Naomi – his first wife. I know she disappeared. I tried to talk to the police, tell them the whole family was rotten. They didn't want to know. As far as Theo goes, I'll say the same thing I said to Naomi. I don't know if he knew, but it's unlikely, he was only a kid at the time and by all accounts he worshipped his mum. But there was something not quite right about his sister afterwards. Wouldn't surprise me at all if she knew somehow that her mother's death wasn't an accident.

Take care of yourself. Get away from that family. Let me know if there is anything I can do to help.

I stare at the words a moment longer. He thinks Auntie M may have known about a murder, and not just any murder, but her own mother? *Get real.* This guy is probably a complete nutcase, some kind of stalker or someone with a grudge. Maybe Vera dumped him and he's the one behind the accident.

Not even quite sure why, I forward the email to myself, then delete both that sent email and the email from him. Slip Rowan's tablet back into its usual place.

I head for bed, try to sleep, but there's something about all of this that is bothering me. If I try to focus on it too closely it slides out of view. Maybe it's like a particularly thorny calculus question that makes no sense: leave it alone for a while, come back to it another time, and the answer will present itself. But physics and maths have rules, laws. I love both for being consistent and knowable.

People, on the other hand, are messy. If their emotions and actions obey any basic laws of motion or thermodynamics, I've yet to work out the code.

EIGHTY

GRACE

When the pains start, I don't say a word, or cry out for help. By the time Mam realises and sends for the midwife it has gone on half the night and into the next day.

She's in our church, of course – the midwife. I'm detached, switched off, inside myself and not part of what is happening to me, my body. It's a while before I notice that she is worried. Something isn't right. There are hurried conversations but I don't listen. I'm in another place, away from here, in my mind. A place without pain or church or Father.

Later there are voices, footsteps. A man and a woman come into my room, and I stare at them – the first faces I've seen other than Father, Mam and the midwife for so long. They're talking, asking questions, but they're too distant. I can't speak.

Then I'm being moved onto a stretcher, out of my room. I stare in wonder around me as I'm carried down the stairs, through the front door. A cool breeze against my skin. There are stars in the sky above. I haven't seen them for so long. They're beautiful.

I'm taken across to a waiting ambulance. The stars disappear when I'm put inside on the stretcher and I drift away.

Next thing I know we're in the hospital.

There are bright lights, noise, confusion. People saying things to me that I don't understand. Telling me what I have to do and I want to ignore them, go back inside of myself. But then I realise – they'll take it out of me, take it away, if I do what they say.

I thought I knew what pain was, but this is so much more than any pain I've felt before that I'll surely die from it.

It's a boy. They try to hold him to me afterwards, but I close my eyes and turn away.

EIGHTY-ONE

ROWAN

'Dr Wilson will see you now.' I'm shown to an open door, go in. A large room, tasteful art and framed certificates on the wall. Books on shelves. A desk and chair opposite it as well as the inevitable sofa.

'Hello Rowan. Lovely to meet you.' A handshake.

According to the degrees behind him, he is a doctor of psychology, not medicine. Dark hair, eyes too close together and there is something about the way he's looking at me. If I wasn't already on my guard I would have been so now. But I remind myself: don't be contrary. Keep him onside. Do it to reassure Theo.

'Have a seat. Why don't you begin? Tell me what's been going on that brought you here today.'

'My husband brought me here today.'

'I understand he's been concerned about you.' He's not as good at hiding secrets as I am. Understand? Bull. He's spoken to him, at length. Hasn't he?

'Oh?'

I have an automatic reaction to doctors with questions, one that started many years ago: say as little as possible. I know that shouldn't be my strategy today, not if the goal is to reassure Theo. But I don't know what I should do or say, instead; the woman I'm supposed to be would never have been brought here. That I'm here at all shows how badly wrong I've let things go.

He's allowing the silence to stretch. Don't fear silence; don't rush to fill it. That's the way to let things slip. Say as little as you can without coming across as difficult.

Finally, he looks at his tablet.

'I gather there have been a few... incidents.' His eyes on me, waiting. 'A car accident? A flood, at home. Anything you can tell me about these...'

'Incidents?'

He nods.

'The car accident was caused by a car behind me overtaking when it wasn't safe to do so. Flood is overstating it, but I left the bath running.' I shrug.

'It's been suggested you might have been asleep at the wheel. In the bath, also.'

Another moment of silence.

'Anything else?' I say.

'Groceries left in the sun to spoil. Panic at an unlocked door you thought was locked. And then there was the sleepwalking.'

Ellie told Theo. Didn't she? About my sleepwalking. And about the panic attack I had when I couldn't open the bedroom door, though she conveniently left out the fact that she was the one who'd locked and unlocked it. Though – be fair – that was before we were officially *friends*. If she even meant that. And Maxine, another telltale – about the groceries. All of them are against me. I'm hurt, upset. Don't show it. A whip cord of anger stings inside and with the pain, I find myself.

'I'm afraid Ellie has an overactive imagination. As for the rest, I've been having trouble sleeping – nausea and hot flushes at night have been disturbing my sleep. Nothing too unusual there.' I try to project poise, confidence, when everything is such a mess inside.

'Are there any other reasons for sleeplessness? Something worrying you, perhaps?'

I shake my head, half smile in place. 'Theo is the one who likes to worry; I'm here to reassure him. But there aren't any problems I'm lying awake thinking about, if that is what you mean.'

'Anything to do with the new arrival? The baby.'

There is a small slip in my composure with the B word. I'm sure it wasn't missed. Try to cover – give a reason.

'I never thought it would happen, after so many years of trying. And I'm so happy that it has now. It will be a huge change in our lives, but one I'm confident we'll navigate together.'

He carries on trying to chip away at my defences. Normally I'd be more than a match for him, but it's taking so much concentration, focus, when I have so little energy. It's exhausting and I'm not sure how much he can see past the front I've put up.

Finally, the hour is up. A card given, with his number. An after-hours number, too. Another appointment has already been made for next week. Out of his hearing, I cancel it with the receptionist. I'm not going back, not even to reassure Theo. I can't risk it.

Once out in front of the building, in fresh air and sunshine, the pressure eases a little. I breathe in deeply.

Instead of calling a taxi as Theo suggested, I wait at a bus stop. He did bring me this morning as he said he would, but then was on to work, and after that, the airport. I'd been surprised initially that he didn't come in with me – but he didn't have to, because he'd obviously told this Dr Wilson everything he could think of already.

After the bus comes, I go to the upper deck, tear the card

into tiny pieces. As if letting them go all at once would risk reassembly, I release them from the window one by one.

I'm uneasy, struggling not to cry. It felt like a trap being set, as if the point of the appointment wasn't to help me, but rather to trip me up, make me reveal things I want to keep to myself. Trick me into saying things I didn't want to say.

Why?

And he knew about the sleepwalking. I'm sure if Ellie had told Theo soon after it happened that he'd have mentioned it by now. Though he didn't mention the knife and I'm sure he would have if he knew. Did she just tell part of the story?

And then there is the way Theo was looking at me last night. At other moments, too. Watchful, and with something in his eyes that made me wonder what he was thinking. If he noticed me looking back at him, his expression changed so quickly to something more normal that I thought I'd imagined it. But maybe I was wrong. I wanted the love he had for me to always be there. I wanted it so much, maybe I imagined it was still in his eyes.

Maybe Theo doesn't love me any more. Even thinking the words cuts through me, a sharp knife that finds my heart. I can't push the tears away. I lean my forehead against the cold window, try to pull myself together.

Last night felt a little different, almost like... he wasn't sure who I was, and saw me as some kind of threat. I'm turning things over in my mind, going through everything I can think of. Things haven't felt quite right between us for a while, but it only really started to go wrong when I told him I was pregnant.

Then there was how angry he was that I spoke to Maxine about Naomi. What was it he said – that I was sneaking around? He made out that he was angry because it showed I didn't trust him, but his reaction seemed over what it should have been. At the time I thought it was because talking or even thinking about Naomi upset him too much. Maxine backed that up, said he just needed reassurance and everything would be fine.

But none of this *feels* quite right. Like I'm missing something, something obvious. I can't concentrate, can't focus any more. I look out the window, realise I haven't been watching where the bus is going. We've gone past the stop I need to get the Tube.

I get off at the next stop, walk back. Go down all the stairs and find my platform. When the train comes a moment later, it's not busy but I'm so tired that I stand so I can't fall asleep.

When I'm finally home I bring in the post. I feel uneasy as I flip through it, remembering the other day, the card addressed to Grace. I'm trying to put it out of my mind, but as if my thoughts have summoned it, there it is. Another postcard.

I stare at the front of it, numb. Not *that* image, *no no no*... My stomach contracts and I run to the bathroom, vomit again and again. Wash my hands, splash water on my face. Make myself go back. Pick it up from the floor where I dropped it.

The image on the front is Father's church. Down the road from us, it dominated both our street and our lives in all ways. Hands shaking, I turn it over. It's addressed to Grace King again, but this time there is no address, no stamp. It must have been hand delivered. He was *here*? Slipped it into our mailbox, right outside the house?

But that's not the worst of it. Written next to my name are three words:

See you soon.

EIGHTY-TWO

ELLIE

I have a message from Maisie after maths.

Meet me out front in five.

Why?

Just do it! followed by a string of happy emojis.

She pulls in front of the school and has a wide smile.

I get in. 'What's up?'

'I love your dad. Have I ever told you how much I love your dad?'

'Hmmm... I don't think so. Why, what's he done?'

'He arranged it with my mum last night, and she told me this morning – you and me, babes, are going on a surprise spa weekend.'

'What?'

'You heard me. Your dad apparently told her you looked stressed about coursework and thought a weekend away was what you needed. We'll stop at yours for your stuff – I've already packed a bag – and then we're off. Massages, treatments, all sorted.'

Here was me thinking it'd be good to spend the weekend in bed, counting down the minutes to the clinic appointment on Monday. Of course, Dad doesn't know about that and Maisie doesn't, either. She's chatting and excited as we drive and it's starting to rub off on me. Maybe this is just what I need to get through the weekend.

'Where is it?'

'Champneys Forest Mere. It's on a lake! It looks amazing. Mum was jealous when we had a look online this morning.'

We're approaching home now and I open our gate. Maisie comes in to help me pack.

'Hi Mrs B,' she says to Rowan as we pass through. She's white-faced, on the sofa, knees drawn up, doesn't acknowledge us.

I motion Maisie to go through to my room.

'Don't know if Dad told you, but I'm going away for the weekend with Maisie. He arranged it – a spa thing.'

An almost imperceptible movement – a nod.

'Rowan, are you all right?'

She stays still but her eyes turn to mine, slowly. 'You told Theo last night, didn't you? About me sleepwalking.'

She must see the guilt on my face. 'I was just trying to help—'

'Save it. Don't forget that I know your little secret. You better take care.'

I stare back at her, shocked. 'Is that a threat?'

She shrugs, the slightest movement. 'Just go.'

I can't believe she said that. Surely she wouldn't tell Dad just because of the sleepwalking thing. But beyond that, something is so obviously wrong with her – again. What is it this time?

Dad had it right when he sent her to see a psychologist. She told me to go and that is exactly what I'm going to do: get the hell out of here and not think about it until the weekend is over.

I find Maisie in my room, merrily going through my clothes and tossing things in a bag. 'This is going to be such a blast,' she says.

She's right. A weekend timeout – away from Rowan, my problems. And Dad, too – though he's gone back to the States. Just me and Maisie. What could be better? I take a quick look through my bag, take some things out, add some others. Grab some toiletries.

'Ready?' she says.

'Think so.'

'Let's go.'

'Car snacks?' I suggest. Go into the kitchen, grab some cans of fizzy drink, crisps. Walk past the dining table and then I spot the post. The card on the top, the name it is addressed to. And what it says:

See you soon.

What the fuck?

'Come *on*,' Maisie says. I look back at Rowan. Her eyes are open but staring, unfocused, like she can't see anything around her. Then Maisie links her arm in mine and pulls me to the door.

EIGHTY-THREE

ROWAN

How long I sit there, still, unaware of anything beyond that postcard and the words written on it, I don't know. The outside world has vanished but then, something in my inside world triggers my attention: a kick. Then another. A little one inside me reminding me that to look after them, I need to look after myself. When I move, my legs are stiff, pins and needles, and it's a moment before I can stand.

Was Ellie here? I frown, uncertain of my memory. Maybe I made that up and if I did, the postcard might be from my imagination, too—

No. It's still there, on the dining table. I can't look at it any more and if I put it in the bin or somewhere out of sight I'll know where it lurks. I tear it into tiny pieces, then don't want to put them in the recycling. You hear of people going through bins and taping together pieces of documents for identity theft. What if someone put this together, found out who I was? Instead, I go to the loo, flush the pieces away.

It's early evening. As much as I'm uninterested in food, I feel shaky; maybe food would help – and help my brain sift through things, too. I look in the fridge, mind blank. Something simple. Eggs? Fried eggs. Toast. Put the pan on to warm up, bread in the toaster. Sit a moment at the breakfast bar.

I'm startled by an insistent alarm – the fire alarm. Smoke. The toast is burning. I wave a towel at the fire alarm, the shrill sound pounding into my skull. Did I fall asleep again?

A sound – a voice – almost penetrates and when it repeats, a louder echo, I half scream, spin around. It's Maxine, saying *Rowan*. My name.

Smoke is still pouring out of the toaster. Maxine unplugs it and opens a window. The fire alarm finally stops. The frying pan is blackening, burning, too. I go to move it off the heat and yelp in pain when I touch the handle. Maxine takes my hand, holds it under running cold water.

She's been sent to check on me. Hasn't she? Theo must have sent her. Let her in. What good are locked doors that can be unlocked so easily?

Maxine is chattering, her words not penetrating beyond me checking for meaning to see if I need to respond. She finds another pan. Makes an omelette, toast, puts it in front of me. Prods me to eat and it's good.

I can finally speak. 'Thank you. Sorry about all that. I must have fallen asleep.'

Add to the list of things not to do when tired: drive. Take a bath. Cook.

'Are you feeling a little better now?'

I nod.

'What's wrong? Is there anything I can help with?'

I shake my head. 'Nothing is wrong. I'm just tired. Morning sickness has been keeping me awake at night.' The lies come out automatically, same as I told the GP days ago and the psychologist earlier.

'I'm worried about you, Rowan. I know Theo is, too. Is there anything I can do to help?' I'm looking at her closely, to something in her eyes that has always been there, papered over with concern and poorly hidden under the niceties of correct manners. She doesn't like me. She never has. She doesn't want to help. There is something she is fishing for, that she wants to know.

'Why don't you tell me why you're really here?'

Her mask shifts. 'A warning, Rowan. Stop meddling and looking into the past. It will only hurt you.'

EIGHTY-FOUR

ELLIE

Maisie is on form, singing along to her chosen playlist – one she has called Songs to Belt. Usually I'd be doing the same – though more in tune – but the further away from home we get, the more uncertain I am about this weekend. I turn down the music.

'Driver's rules, turn it back up,' she says.

'I need you to be able to hear me without shouting.'

'What's up?'

'I'm not sure I should be away this weekend.'

'Why? Got a hot date you haven't told me about?'

'Last thing on my mind, trust me.' I sigh. 'It's family stuff. I think I need to be at home. Or near to it.'

'Family stuff, yet your dad set up this weekend. And didn't you say he's going away anyhow? What's going on?'

I try to explain, but I can't, not without telling her about Grace and Rowan. Despite her threat earlier, I won't tell her secrets. I insist we stop at a services. I call Amy, sort out a swap. And we turn around and head back to Richmond.

EIGHTY-FIVE

ROWAN

I don't want to sleep until I figure things out and I can't stay awake if I sit down. I pace back and forth downstairs but all I can hear is *tick, tick* following me, as if that blasted clock is counting my steps. I go into the kitchen to get away from it. I need to think, work out how to manage the situation with Maxine. Why did she really come? What did her warning mean? The only thing it could have to do with is Naomi. But she already told Theo I spoke to her and I haven't done a thing since then. I don't understand.

Unless... she's trying to undermine me with Theo. Maybe she's been telling him tales, making him doubt me. What can I do about it?

I need a plausible way to discredit anything she might say, but it's eluding me just now. And apart from that, I may have destroyed the card to Grace, but it is still making it hard to think of anything else.

I check the alarm system is on. Again. That all the doors are locked. The windows both shut and locked. No one can get in. I'm safe.

It's twilight, almost dark. I'm hungry again but I can't risk cooking. I can manage cheese sandwiches. Juice. An apple. I can't sit still to eat, instead I'm up, walking, pacing, back and forth in our kitchen.

The landline rings and it so rarely does in these days of mobile phones that I'm uneasy, let it go to answerphone. No message is left.

It rings again a moment later and this time I answer. 'Hello?'

No response.

'Hello? Is anyone there?'

No answer. I hang up.

It rings again. I stare at it, telling myself to ignore it, to let it ring until they give up, but I can't stop myself from answering. 'Who is this?'

'Grace?' a voice whispers.

One word, that is all, but the fear is immediate. I feel sick, I'm shaking.

'You've got the wrong number.' I hang up.

A moment later it rings again. I'm flooded with adrenalin and rip the phone line out of the wall, with such force that the wall is damaged.

The card. The call. Father knows where I am. The urge to leave, to run, is strong, but maybe that is what he wants me to do. If I open the front door, he might be there.

Call the police? And say what, exactly? I can't.

Go and stay in a hotel? No car. Taxi? But that'd mean unlocking the front door, then the gate, and what if he's waiting outside?

I can't make sense of anything or work out what to do because I haven't slept. Sleep isn't optional. Humans need sleep to live. My baby needs me to sleep. Even just the thought of the word *baby* makes my heart rate speed up again with a lurch of fear, whether for them, of me, or both.

The house is secure. We have a top-of-the-range alarm

system. The best thing to do is to stay inside, not risk opening the door. And I have to sleep, at least a little. I'll go upstairs and try.

Should I take a weapon? I glance at the knife block, but after what happened when I was sleepwalking, the thought of touching a knife fills me with dread. Instead I go to the walk-in storage cupboard in the hall, look in the toolbox and take out a claw hammer. I hesitate. There's something odd about this cupboard. It's maybe five paces deep, shelves along both sides, stuff piled up at the back. It's on the opposite side of the kitchen from the utility room, but the latter is deeper. It runs the full width of the kitchen. This doesn't go as far back, but I'm pretty sure the house is square on the outside. I don't understand. Though maybe I'm wrong and it isn't square; there are plants and trees that obscure the house in the corresponding part of the garden.

I shake my head. There is no point to thinking about this. What does it matter? I'm just trying to avoid thinking about *him*. About trying to sleep.

I take the hammer with me, go down the hall, through the dining room. Now I can hear the clock: *tick... tick...* like a bomb, boring deep into my skull. Louder and louder.

Tick... tick...

Ignore it, leave it – this is what I should do.

Tick... tick...

I swing my whole body to slam the hammer into the glass front of the grandfather clock. Shards of glass fly everywhere, some in my hair, on my clothes, and I'm breathing hard, shocked at what I've done.

Tick... tick...

I hit it again and again, smash through the face and into the mechanism behind. Has it stopped? I stand there, panting, listening to blissful silence. No more ticking.

The clock is completely ruined. I've gone so far beyond

anything reasonable that I can't even believe what I've done, and now I'm laughing. Hysterical – I'm hysterical.

Sleep. I need sleep. Up the stairs, to a guest room, somewhere I wouldn't normally be. The smallest room so I can more easily check every corner. I pull a chair in front of the door. I want to pace, check the windows and doors, do anything, not be still.

Instead, I make myself take off my shoes. Shake my hair out over the bath and there are little tinkles of glass fragments. Take off my jumper and try to pick out more of it. A sharp pain in a finger, blood. I give up and leave it off. There are spare clothes in a wardrobe. I find a nightgown, pull it on. Get into bed, pull the covers up. By sheer strength of will, I force myself to stay still, breathe in and out a little slower, then a little slower again.

Strength of will – willpower. Wilful. I was a wilful child, they said. They tried to beat it out of me, break me, but there was always a part of me inside they couldn't reach. A dark place. The exorcism I should have had, that I deserved, never came. I got away but the darkness still lurks inside of me, doesn't it?

Focus: on breathing, relaxing each part of my body in sequence. Make sleep come. But there is a battle raging inside of me. I'm caught in the middle, between me-now and me-then, and *now* isn't winning.

There is distant music. 'Amazing Grace' – the song I was named for.

But the sound of my name isn't sweet, and it never stops.

EIGHTY-SIX

ELLIE

I should be blissed out after an amazing hot stone massage and dinner. Instead, I'm at Amy's – her parents are away – and she took my place at the spa with Maisie.

I'm completely certifiable. What is Dad going to say if he finds out I gave away this treat he's paying for? But I'm worried about Rowan – I admit it. That postcard I saw was real. Whether it was from someone from her past or, instead, someone from her life now who is trying to get to her, pushing her buttons – I don't know. But either way, I had to come back. I have to figure out what is going on.

I'm on the app. With these override codes I copied from Dad's files I can do just about anything. I can follow Rowan's movements around the house, tap into cameras in each room. Earlier she was on the move for ages, pacing around the downstairs mostly. I couldn't believe my eyes when she smashed the clock with a hammer. I mean, what the fuck? I know she didn't like the ticking, but that is a bit extreme.

She finally went upstairs to one of the guest rooms, an hour or so ago. Why not her own room? I don't know. Now she's probably asleep. I connect to the camera and sound in the guest room, thinking as I do how incredibly creepy it is that this system has been set up to let anyone with the right code look in any room of the house. I check: even my bathroom, bedroom. I'll be disabling that before I go home.

She gets into the bed, closes her eyes, and I watch her sleep.

EIGHTY-SEVEN

ROWAN

As hot as the sun. Burning, melting. I have to get away...

Grace...

I open my eyes and everything spins, as if gravity is pulling me the wrong way. I only just manage to hang on, not fall. The window is wide open and I'm sitting on the window ledge, both legs swung over. Was I going to jump?

If I hadn't woken up...

Ceiling heights are much higher here; it's a bigger drop than the one years ago. An image of my body, broken, on the concrete below rushes through my mind. My head spins again. I pull my legs back over and half fall to the floor. Crawl away from the window. My nightgown is plastered to my skin. Fear is a knife, cutting a jagged opening in my consciousness. It will never let go.

I was wrong to stay. I have to get out of here. *Now*.

EIGHTY-EIGHT

ELLIE

I must have dozed off and when I look back at the camera on the app, Rowan is sitting on the floor in the bedroom, leaning against the wall. She looks completely freaked out.

I check all the room settings. There have been spikes in the room temperature. I'm remembering now that time I went to her room at night and it was set really high. I check all the settings for the room she is in; scheduled sounds have played, too.

Rowan always looks so exhausted lately. Has someone deliberately been waking her up all the time – by changing the temperature, playing sounds at night – so she can't sleep?

I'll check what the recorded sounds were. Before I can do so, the history vanishes. Everything is usually stored for a week. Has it been set to delete sooner? I can get in to check with an access code: it's been changed from weekly to hourly. No record, no traces.

Rowan gets up, goes to the hall. I can follow her around the house with cameras but switching from one to the other takes long enough that I could lose her if I guess wrong which way she is going.

Then there is a screen notification from the app: the house is in lockdown. What does that even *mean*?

The level of weird has gone up way too many notches. I'm pretty sure that only someone with the access codes can do these things. As far as I know, apart from me, Dad is the only other one with the codes. But he's not even in this country, and anyhow, *why* would he torment Rowan like this? It doesn't make sense.

What am I going to do?

I could call the police. And say what, exactly? That the climate control and sound system are keeping my stepmother awake?

I could call Dad. But he's too far away to do anything.

There's really only one answer: Alex. He gave me his mobile number, said to call if I was worried about Rowan. Though maybe he didn't mean in the middle of the night.

I find his number. Hesitate, then hit call.

EIGHTY-NINE

ROWAN

That was then, this is now. That was then, this is now. I'm not Grace. I'm Rowan. I can handle this situation – I can handle any situation – so long as I stay calm.

I was wrong to stay in the house. I need to get out of here. I go down the stairs and run to the front door.

'Vera, open the front door.'

It doesn't open.

'Vera, why didn't you open the door?'

'Command function override.'

What the hell does that mean? At least Vera is speaking to me.

'Vera, can you open the garden door?'

'No.'

'Vera, why can't you open the garden door?'

'Command function override.'

I'm locked in. Panic and terror rise inside, threatening to overwhelm me again.

Windows. I try one of the dining room windows, but it's locked, won't open. They are never locked from the inside.

'Vera, why won't the window open?'

'Lockdown has been triggered.'

'Vera, can you unlock the window?'

'Command function override.'

I'm locked in, I can't get out. I'm crouched on the floor, arms around me, around my baby. I have to get through this, for her – or even him – but I'm struggling to hold on, to hold back the panic, my thin will against a rising flood.

Grace...

A voice whispers the name I tried so hard to leave behind, the same voice that I hear in my dreams. Who is there? Who is saying that?

Maybe it's a hallucination. A psychotic episode, from sleep deprivation. I tell myself it's not real. Ignore it.

Grace...

But it *sounds* so real – so like my nightmares.

Think. All those links I read about insomnia. It can cause hallucinations, yes, but visual ones – seeing things that aren't there. Not hearing things.

Someone is in the house. It's him, it must be. He's found me. I can never get away. Panic is returning and it can't, I need to stay calm. Focused. I need to get out of this house. Vera won't open the door so I need my phone to use the app. It's upstairs. Why didn't I bring it with me? I'm so pathetic, weak—

Don't go there. Get the phone.

Every sense on overdrive, I move as quietly as I can towards the stairs. I step on some glass and almost cry out. Glass from the broken clock. I ignore the pain, go up the stairs one by one to the guest room, to the bedside table, and—

It's not there – my phone. It isn't there. That's when I notice: the window. It's shut. I left it open. I'm sure I did.

He's here, in the house. He must be. The blankness of panic is coming for me. I fight for control.

Does he have my phone? If he does, there is no way to get out. Even if I hide, he'll find me eventually.

Though if he has my phone, there is a way to find out where *he* is.

'Vera, where is my phone?'

'Your phone is in the storage cupboard downstairs.'

Think.

That seems an odd place for him to be, as if he is the one who is hiding. Maybe he doesn't have my phone. Maybe there is no one in this house but me and I've been imagining it all. I did go to the cupboard to get the hammer; maybe I put my phone down, forgot to pick it up again. And the window – I could have shut it without thinking about it. I'm in such a state that it's as likely as not. But I pick up the claw hammer from next to the bed where I left it, hold it ready. Move quietly, stealthily, down the stairs. Avoid the glass this time and go to the hall at the back of the house. Ellie's room on one side, the cupboard door on the other. Turn the knob slowly.

I peer into the cupboard, then sag with relief – no one is there. But the room looks different somehow, like things have been moved around.

Then the lights go out.

NINETY

ELLIE

Hanging out on a street corner on my own in the dark in the middle of the night is probably on the list of things I shouldn't do. But when has that stopped me? I'm staring at my phone – the time – willing Alex to hurry.

Then our house lights go out. The streetlights and a few other neighbourhood lights are still on, but ours is in darkness.

Why? What's happening?

I thought he'd be here by now. I hesitate. Should I go in on my own?

Instead, I go to the app. It's still got this lockdown alert; I can't access any of the cameras. I go to my photos, copy a master code. It lets me in. I hunt for Rowan, room by room, using the cameras, but it's too dark to find her.

Something is very wrong.

NINETY-ONE

ROWAN

There are footsteps in the hall. Getting closer. I'm not imagining this; someone *is* in the house. Shaking, I grip the hammer tight and back away from the cupboard door. Maybe they don't know I'm in here. I can hide behind the hoover and things at the back. I'm feeling my way, as quietly as I can. Then there is a sound – a clunk and a whoosh. A change in the air. I reach back with my hand for the wall I should have got to by now but nothing is there. I step back, trip on something, and fall to the floor. Stale, horrible air – it tastes and smells *wrong*. I cough and struggle to my feet. Then the door opens and the lights come back on.

He's here. Framed in light from the hall. He found me. He was right. I could never get away. He's come to do what he threatened all those years ago.

Retreat inside – disappear – switch off. Then whatever happens, he can't hurt me where I hide. But even as I start to withdraw, I know that I can't. Not this time. My baby – I have to protect her.

I force myself to meet his eyes. Focus on his face. But then confusion and relief flood through me.

It's not Father. It's Theo.

'Theo? Thank God it's you, I thought there was an intruder...'

His face: it's wrong. Grim and angry. And he's supposed to be away. I glance back at what I tripped over. Ragged clothes, with something, some shape, inside them. I want to look away but I'm frozen, staring. Round and white, eye sockets – it's a *skull*. And a bony arm, reaching out of a sleeve, as if towards me. I'm choking, coughing, a scream fighting its way out even as I'm telling myself my eyes are wrong, it's another hallucination, like seeing Father in the doorway instead of Theo. But it doesn't change. It's still there.

And it was hidden. There was a small room, behind the cupboard. Open now. A body, on the floor. I can't make sense of any of this.

'You're all the same. Hiding, sneaking. Can't be trusted. First my mother. Then Naomi. Now you can join her.'

Join her – join Naomi? I'm trembling, acid rising up into my mouth. Coughing, choking. This is *real*. Her body was never found because it was hidden here, in this house, all along.

I can't understand, I don't want to. But a single word escapes. 'How?'

'How what – did she get here? The house was complete, signed off. We'd delayed moving in because of Ellie's birth. It wasn't difficult to alter the door, the mechanism. Lure her to the house and trap her inside.'

'You k-killed Naomi?'

'I didn't want to. I had no choice. She kept digging. She found out there was doubt over whether it was an accident; that my mother's car may have been tampered with. But she worked out that it couldn't have been Dad, you see. He was an idiot with anything mechanical. It was me who tampered with our mother's car. Mum was leaving us and Maxine said if I could make her car go off the road, she'd have to come back home. I didn't mean for her to die. But Maxine was right with what she said afterwards – she deserved it. No one suspected me, a twelve-year-old. And so many years later, Naomi worked it out and was going to leave me, take Ellie with her. I couldn't let her do that. I couldn't be sure that she wouldn't talk, either.'

I'm horrified, frozen. Staring at his face as he talks about killing his mum and his first wife as if it was all perfectly reasonable. How could he do these things?

'But what you've done is even worse, Rowan. Or should I say Grace? I was going to have you sectioned, take the child you thought you so desperately wanted away from you. You weren't fit to be a mother then and you aren't now.'

Stunned, unable to process what is happening – what has happened. I want it to be another nightmare. But my eyes are open.

And then I realise – he called me *Grace*.

'You knew about Grace? How?'

'You saw the file.'

'The file? What are you talking about?'

He's nonplussed a moment, then shakes his head. 'More lies, *Grace*? I saw the lock pick on your credit card. I know it was you. And I knew all of it years ago, and I married you anyway. I thought, here is a woman with a past she wants to keep hidden, like me. I thought we were a perfect match. But I was wrong. You started digging, just like Naomi did.'

'I didn't! I don't know what you're talking about.'

'Stop lying.' He's shaking his head. He doesn't believe me.

Something else he said is coming through. He wanted to have me *sectioned*? Everything that's been going on – has he been behind it all?

'The cards to Grace, the calls. Sounds and voices at night stopping me from sleeping. You've been trying to make me look like I'm losing it?'

'Sleep deprivation is a classic way to induce psychosis. And you made it so easy, Rowan. The way you've been acting lately was more than enough to get you locked up for your own safety as soon as the baby was born. But that's not enough any more. Not after I saw your browsing history. And your emails.' I'm shaking my head. What on earth does he mean? 'And then there is the icing on the cake – what started this all off. Whose baby is it, Rowan? Alex's?'

'There's never been anyone but you, I swear—'

'I had you followed, Rowan. I know you met Alex for lunch recently. Why did you lie about it if there wasn't something going on?'

I didn't imagine it. I *was* followed – but not by my father or anyone from church. Theo was behind it.

'And you know what?' he says. 'I'd still like to believe you. But given that I had a vasectomy after Ellie was born, I decline.' That shock on top of all the others almost undoes me. If it was just me, I might collapse to the ground, accept my fate. It's no more than I deserve. But it isn't just me. Whoever their father, I promised: this time, it'd be different. *I'd* be different. I'd look after this baby, care for them, always.

Theo – bigger, stronger – is advancing towards me, pushing me back. The hammer hangs by my side in one hand – unnoticed, disregarded? I swing it as fast and as hard as I can at his head. He must catch the movement, pulls away so there is a glancing blow only, on his shoulder, but he staggers, and I almost dare to hope that I'll – *we'll* – get away. But he pushes me so hard against the wall my head slams against it. The pain undoes me. I'm crumpling, almost losing consciousness. Then he shoves me back. I fall to the floor, on what is left of Naomi, and I'm horrified, trying to scramble up, get away.

'I'm sorry it has to be this way, Rowan. I really did love you, once.'

There is another whoosh – the secret door closing, trapping

me inside. It's pitch black and I'm screaming, banging against the door. Is that what Naomi did all those years ago?

Stop. Think. Just this once: master the fear. Control the panic.

What is this place? I run my hands over the walls: they are covered with wooden shelves with round supports – built-in wine racks. It was meant to be a wine cellar, until Theo found another use for it.

Put it all together.

Theo and Ellie moved in after Naomi disappeared. The half-remembered house plans, different downstairs. The unknown switch on the fuse board. Wine needs constant temperature, humidity, doesn't it? Maybe even a sealed, controlled climate?

He either killed her and then put her in here, or pushed her in, alive. Like me. Hid all traces of the entrance to this room. Closed it off completely. The horror of it – that Ellie grew up in the room across the hall from her mother's tomb.

There *must* be a way to open this room from the inside – or maybe I just want that to be so, because I can't find a release, a button, anything. Theo would have made sure I couldn't let myself out, wouldn't he? And Naomi, too, if she was still alive when he trapped her here all those years ago. I'm crying, sinking to the floor, as far away from her as I can get in this small room. It's getting harder and harder to breathe – the panic or the air, I don't know. I'm cold, shaking. Light-headed. Shutting down.

In the foetal position, I cradle my unborn child close, hugging my arms around my belly and rocking back and forth.

I'm sorry, I'm so sorry. I failed again.

NINETY-TWO

ELLIE

The lights came back on but I still couldn't find Rowan on any of the cameras. I unlocked the gate and went through to the front of our house, not sure what to do – whether to wait for Alex, or go in. I decide to wait a bit longer and try each camera again with the sound turned all the way up. Alex arrives just as the camera in my room picks up Dad's voice. He must be nearby, maybe in the hall. But he's supposed to be away. What is he doing here? We can hear Rowan's voice, too, though fainter and difficult to make out.

But every word Dad says is clear. Even hearing his words – his voice – I can't believe what he's saying.

Alex is saying something now also, but it isn't coming through the disbelief, shock. Though I knew at least part of this already, didn't I? It was what Christopher said. That Dad probably didn't know anything about his mother's death because he was so young. But Dad was already working on a car for Maxine. He'd had this knack with mechanical things since he was a child. And he'd said he didn't know where it came from – that it wasn't from his father who was useless with cars. Some part of me had put this together but couldn't believe it, didn't acknowledge it consciously, even though it stopped me from calling Dad for help.

Alex grabs me by the shoulders, shakes me and I look in his eyes.

'Ellie, I need your help. Can you unlock the front door?'

The door?

I change screens in the app. Use an access code to override lockdown and then slide the front door to open.

Alex tears down the hall; I follow behind. He takes a swing at Dad. Element of surprise – he connects, but Dad shakes it off and gives him one back. Alex falls to the floor and pulls Dad with him. They're fighting, grappling on the floor in the hall.

I'm numb. What we heard about my mum? I'm shaking my head, backing away. Not really seeing what is happening in front of me. Trying to make sense of it all.

Dad killed her. His own mother, too.

My mum didn't leave me?

He took her away from me.

I focus back on here, now. Alex doesn't look to be winning this fight. Dad is on top of Alex, his hands around his neck.

There's a heavy ceramic vase on a shelf in the dining room. I grab it and swing the vase, crash it into the back of Dad's head. He crumples to the ground.

Alex struggles to push him away. He gets up, gasping, coughing. Then he's on his phone, calling emergency services. He goes into the cupboard, tries to work out how to open the hidden room at the back. Calling out to Rowan, saying help is on the way. She doesn't answer.

Sirens – I can hear them in the distance, getting closer.

Dad groans. Looks up at me from the floor. 'You betrayed me too, Ellie?'

I kick him again and again until Alex pulls me away.

NINETY-THREE

ROWAN

I'm curled in on myself, not here any more. Switched off. I disappear to a dream land. Not the usual nightmare. In this dream I'm safe, well, cocooned with my beautiful daughter. No one can find or hurt us, ever again.

A change of air brings me back. Then a voice, one I don't recognise.

'Rowan, can you hear me? We'll have you out of there very soon.' More noise, then light. The wall pulled to pieces to get me out. I'm coughing, gasping, breaths in and out.

Paramedics are here, they're worried about the blow I had to my head; stabilise my head and neck in a brace, ease me onto a stretcher. Then I see Alex. Ellie, too. Alex takes my hand. He's a mess – a swollen, split lip, a cut over one eye.

'How...? Why...?' is all I can manage to say.

'Ellie called me.'

My eyes, filling with tears, find Ellie's. We don't say anything but sometimes there is a world in a glance. Everything she knows about her family has turned upside down. I want to say that it'll be all right. But it won't be, at least not for a long while.

I'm taken to the hospital in the back of an ambulance and I'm remembering the other ambulance ride, all those years ago. There was pain and fear then, but the fear today eclipses anything I've ever felt before. It anchors me in the here and now. *Please, please, let my baby be OK.* I'm bargaining with the universe, even God, and it's a long time since I've asked him for anything. *Give me this and I swear I'll love her and look after her forever. I'll get things right, and not just with her. With Ellie, too.*

At the hospital I'm checked over. I've got a concussion but my neck and spine are OK. My baby is scanned and they promise she is fine – *she* for definite, because I asked them to tell me while they were at it – and I'm crying, thankful. Terrified and determined in equal measure. I'm told I'll be staying for a few days. Besides the concussion, I'm dehydrated, exhausted, and they want to keep an eye on me.

I'm settled into a private room. Not long after, there is a light tap and Alex stands in the doorway. The bruising on his face looks even worse and there is a bandage over one eye. His neck is bruised, red, too. He's hesitating, unsure, and now the things that Theo said – that Alex may have overheard – are slotting into place.

'Did you hear everything Theo said to me?'

He walks across the room, sits in the chair by my bed.

'I think so. Even hearing him say it, I can't believe the things he's done.' But there is something else Alex is thinking of, isn't there?

'He also said that he'd had a vasectomy,' I say.

'Maybe he was lying.'

'Maybe.'

'The dates work out, though.'

'Don't, Alex. She's not yours.'

'How can you be sure?'

'You used a condom. And you weren't the only one besides

Theo,' I lie. 'And we weren't as careful, so if Theo actually did have a vasectomy, that is the likely answer.'

He's shocked. Hurt. But if there was anyone else, my husband was the injured party – not Alex.

'No matter what – it's not your responsibility, Alex. Friends?'

He nods. 'Friends.'

I thank him for coming when Ellie called and all that they did. Then he says goodbye.

He was relieved. Wasn't he? And so was I. Even though he came to my rescue tonight, I know it will be a good long time before I can trust anyone again.

After he's gone, I try to sleep but I still can't, even though I know Theo has been arrested, that it was him behind the cards, the calls. The voice saying *Grace* over and over again. It wasn't Father. He hasn't found me. It should be safe to sleep now, but everything is spinning around in my mind.

Theo had the wrong wife at the wrong time. If I'd been first, I'd never have said anything or left him for killing his mother. I wanted to kill my parents so many times – I'd have done it if I could – so how could I begrudge that?

But taking Naomi away from Ellie? I'll never forgive him for that, or what he tried to do to me, my baby.

Finally, my eyes close and I slip to dreamless, healing sleep.

NINETY-FOUR

GRACE

I scream when my parents come to take me home. After being silent for so long, my voice is finally back. I can't stop telling anyone who will listen – doctors, nurses, social workers, the police – that Father beat me, kept me locked in a room for months.

My baby is being put up for adoption. I still refuse to see it – him. Even thinking of doing so makes me shake, panic, lose connection with the world around me.

After a while in the hospital, I'm put in a foster home with three other foster kids. There is fighting and problems but it's better than anywhere I've ever been, and I start at a new school. Best of all, I can read anything I want. I lose myself in books.

The day for the trial gets closer. I'm told Father said I'd wanted to have the baby, that I could never have agreed to have an abortion, against the teachings of our church. That it was the clinic that confused me, booked an appointment. That I'd cried and asked to be kept safe from them.

I have to testify – tell everyone that Father lied, that he beat me and locked me in my room for months. They use a screen so I don't have to look at him, but my voice falters, shakes, just knowing he is there, and the words I said so clearly before about what he's done won't come.

Without useful testimony from me, the sentence he receives doesn't seem much for what he did. I don't much care until Father finds me in my foster home a year later. He couldn't have if he was still in jail. He is dragging me by my hair out to the street when the police come. He'll find me, he says. Kill me, to save me from the devil. And I know he means it, every word. I'll never be safe.

They tell me to pick a different name at my next foster home, to make it harder for him to find me. And I think for a while. There was a tree I used to climb and hide in when I was small – hoping it would protect me. It was a rowan.

NINETY-FIVE

ELLIE

I've spent seventeen years hating my mother for abandoning me. Like it's programmed into me, it's going to be a while before I *know* the truth, feel it in my gut. That Dad was the villain. That he took her away from me, lied to me my whole life. It's all tinged with unreality, like I've stepped from one world to another where all the rules are different, and the only constant I have left – if she wants me, that is – is Rowan.

I see her before she sees me. It's been two days since she was freed from that room where my mum died. She's lying down in a hospital bed, a private room. Her face is so pale, eyes dark-rimmed. A bruise purpling on her forehead but no other marks that can be seen. I know they said the baby is OK, but is she? I had to come and see her, even though I'm not sure how she feels about me. If she's worked out yet that it was me who set her up. I had no idea what it would lead to, but it was me who put her and her child's life in danger. How can she forgive that?

'Hi,' I say. She turns towards me, holds out a hand and I'm across the room at once without thought. Holding on to it tight, like a lifeline.

'Look at us,' she says, glancing at our hands, and smiles a moment.

'I know, right?' I sit on the chair next to her and don't let go.

We talk. Halting, at first. About what Dad did, what he tried to do. He was seriously fucked up, but neither of us could see it. Even going as far as naming his virtual system after the mother he killed, so every day he could tell her what to do – how twisted is that? I tell Rowan about the locked file drawer and what I found. What I did on her tablet. We talk about the police interviews we've both had, too. We've been told Dad has been charged with my mum's murder as well as attempted murder for what he did to Rowan. They're also looking into what happened to his mum. And Dad is in prison on remand. I can't imagine him in a place like that even as I hope they never let him out.

'I feel so stupid,' I say. 'I've spent my entire life hating my mother for abandoning me – but she didn't. He took her away. And then he tried to take you away from me, too. He had me so mixed up that I didn't even understand how much you meant to me.'

There are tears in Rowan's eyes. 'If there is one thing you most definitely are not, it's stupid. You're the one who figured out what was going on and called Alex, aren't you? If it wasn't for you – well, I wouldn't be here.'

'What now? Where do I live? Who with?' I've been with Maisie's family these past few days, but I can't stay there forever.

'I don't know the legal stuff, but you're almost eighteen. I think what you want will be important. You've got your mum's family, now. And you've got me.'

I swallow, struggling to say the words I want – *need* – to say. 'I want to live with you – but not in that house. Somewhere else. But after all the things I've done, maybe you've had enough of me.' I'm looking down, afraid what she might say, what I might see on her face. I wouldn't blame her if she wants nothing to do with me.

She touches my chin, tilts my face up and looks in my eyes. 'Don't be daft. It's you and me – and your sister-to-be – against the world. Right?'

Tears are running down my face now. 'Right. But just to be clear, I'm still not babysitting.'

She pulls me in close for a hug.

NINETY-SIX

ROWAN

After a few days of decent sleep, my brain is almost functioning again, but all it has are questions. Who am I: Grace, Rowan, or some hybrid between the two? What will happen next? Everything is confused, my thoughts a chaos of the known and unknown. Will everyone know that Theo tried to kill me? Will my other name and life be all over the news? If it is, Father might find out where I am. But I'm not as scared of him as I used to be. I'd thought marrying Theo would make me safe. Despite appearances, he was by far the bigger threat.

And then there is the other question that I can't ignore. Who is the father of my baby? Despite what I said to Alex, if Theo really did have a vasectomy – and I can't see why he'd lie, considering he wasn't expecting me to survive our last conversation – then it has to be Alex. There are no other options.

The automatic urge is to run and hide, to escape the whole mess. Go somewhere nobody knows me; start over. Become someone else. But I'm done with running. And this time I want to be there, in court; I want to stand up and say every word of what Theo did and tried to do.

I call Charlie.

She seems unfazed by Theo's arrest, my almost murder. The press don't seem to have tracked down my previous name and so on yet, but I tell Charlie anyway. If she wants to stay my friend, she'll know what she's getting into. She says she does, asks me to come and stay with her as long as I like.

When I leave the hospital, that first day when she opens her front door, there is a surprise: Sasha bounds out and jumps all over me. I kneel down and put my arms around her, cry into her fur.

Not long after, I rent a house and Ellie and Sasha come to live with me. Ellie is technically underage but she's so close to being eighteen that social services agreed her wishes should be followed, despite Theo's objections – who would listen to him in the circumstances?

Our new house doesn't have any fancy smart features: it has keys and light switches and doesn't talk back. Sasha never leaves my side. When I have bad moments, if I panic and I'm scared, she rests her head on my bump, looks at me with eyes of love that say, you can do this. And Charlie has fixed me up with a psychologist – a woman – one I like, that I can talk to and not hold back. It is helping this time. But there is no better cure for a panic attack than having Sasha with me, and gradually they're decreasing.

Soon after we move into our new place, Ellie and I make a deal: no more secrets. There have been so many for so long, and not just mine. We can see now that a good portion of the problems we had with each other over the years were engineered by Theo. So many lies he told to each of us. When Ellie tells me he'd said I wanted her sent away to boarding school, I couldn't believe it. Whether he did it to keep all of our attention on him, or if it was to stop us from seeing more clearly who he really was and what he had done, I don't know.

When Ellie tells me about Stuart and what he did to her, I'm beyond furious. I convince her to talk to Tim, Margaret's grandson in the police. I think it was what she wanted to do all along; she just needed the support. As for people finding out, she doesn't care what her father thinks any more, and with her mum and grandmother's murders at her father's hands being all over the news, she says it doesn't matter what anyone else thinks, either.

There were witnesses to how drunk Ellie was when Stuart took her home. Her pregnancy at his hands the other nail in his coffin, with a DNA test showing that he was the father. Stuart is arrested, charged. Awaiting trial, as is Theo.

As for Maxine, she has been interviewed by the police about her mother's death, and whether she knew anything about what Theo did to Naomi. Our police liaison officer said she has denied any knowledge on both counts. Unless Theo implicates her, she is unlikely to be charged.

I went with Ellie when she had her abortion. I held her when she cried, because no matter how sure she was that it was the right thing for her to do, this moment will never leave her, any more than when my first baby was born will ever leave me. I try to let go of the guilt that I didn't want him. I would have had an abortion – I should have – but with all the things that happened to me that year, far more guilt belonged on other shoulders. I can see that more clearly now.

Ellie wanted to know about Grace – me, I mean. Me as I was. How I got pregnant when I was fifteen. It was just a boy, from school. Someone who was nice to me. I was stupid but someone nice who said nice things? I'd never heard them before. I had no defences against that.

We've lived in our new place for a few months now. I still have problems sleeping sometimes so I'm awake when contractions start early one morning. I tell Ellie I'll let her off – that it's OK if she isn't sure she can cope. I'll be fine. But she knows how terrified I am to be a mother. And she goes with me and stays – my birth partner to the end.

My daughter is perfect and beautiful. Something in her eyes that only had to look at mine once for me to be completely, totally head over heels in love, for the first time in my life. Ellie cries when I tell her I've decided to call her Naomi. I'd already checked with Pam and her family that they were OK with Theo's child – assuming she is – having the name of the sister and daughter that they lost. Now that they've got to know and love Ellie, they welcomed the idea.

Holding Naomi, I start to believe that I can do this. Be a mother. Not just any mother, but a good one. Love my child, care for her and raise her to be happy, healthy and secure. Other than Ellie and Sasha, nothing and no one else matters. Certainly not Theo or my past and all its ghosts.

A paternity test is requested by Theo via his lawyers. If it isn't his child, the prenup is in place. He could begin divorce proceedings, leave me virtually penniless, though it seems unlikely in the circumstances that the courts would allow that. But the truth is, I don't know. Is my miracle daughter's father Theo, who had a vasectomy, or Alex, who used a condom?

Turns out the last laugh is mine. She is Theo's – DNA proves it. Happens sometimes, a vasectomy can fail. Everything that he did to me and all that flowed on from it – including finding out that he killed Naomi and his mother – was for nothing.

I couldn't even look at my first child. Being put up for adoption was the best thing for him. I left that life behind, then became someone else – to be someone no one could hurt as badly as I was before. But denying who I was and all that I lived through kept it locked inside. Unacknowledged, it lurked; it didn't go away. It poisoned me. I didn't know who I was, what I wanted – it was all refracted through a prism of *shoulds*: who I should be, what I should want. Who I should marry.

I've got to figure out who I am, all over again. But before I can do that, there is one more thing I must do.

NINETY-SEVEN

I take a train, then a bus. Charlie has Naomi for the day but Sasha comes with me, my constant shadow. She'll keep me safe. Be there if I start to panic. Ellie offered to come along also, but I'm coming here to close this chapter of my life. I want to keep it as far away from my life now as I can.

We walk streets that seem familiar and foreign at once. I go the long way around so I don't have to walk past the church. When we get to our house, I'm not sure I can do this. I almost keep walking. I might have done, but the door opens as I stand there, dithering on the pavement. It's Mam. Isn't it? Her hair is completely grey now, and she's dressed differently. In normal clothes, I mean. Not a long skirt and her hair isn't covered. But it's her.

She's bringing stuff out to the bin, only glances at me at first, then turns back again.

Her eyes widen. 'Grace? Is it our Grace?' There are tears in her eyes and she holds out her hands. I walk closer but don't take her hands and they drop down again.

We go inside.

Sasha growls low and deep in her throat when she sees

Father. He isn't the man I feared all my life. He's broken. His face is in a permanent half scowl, his body twisted and in a wheelchair. Unable to speak, trapped in silence.

'A stroke,' Mam says. 'Almost twenty years ago now.'

Divine judgement, maybe?

She's changed, too. Older – obviously, and not just her hair – but she seems less weighed down. The constant fear that was always in her eyes has gone. She tells me how Father beat her for calling the ambulance, for saving my life. She shows me photos, too, of my sisters, brothers – tells me where they live, who has married, their children. Sisters and brothers who could have told somebody, anybody, what my parents did to me. Got help. But they never did. She tells me that she and Father had tried to adopt my baby but were refused, given the charges against Father. I'm glad.

I've been terrified of him my whole life. Would he actually have killed me if he'd had the chance? I don't know. I like to think he wouldn't, that he couldn't look me in the eye and end my life. But one thing I do know is that Mam was a victim as much as I was. Knowing this and forgiving are two different things, though.

I've exorcised my past now. I see, at last, that that was the only exorcism I ever really needed.

I leave and know I'll never go back.

A LETTER FROM TERI

Dear lovely reader,

Thank you so much for choosing to spend time with Rowan, Ellie and Grace in *The Stepdaughter's Lie*. If you'd like to keep up to date with all my news and latest releases, it's easy to do: just sign up at the following link. Your email address will never be shared and you can unsubscribe at any time.

www.bookouture.com/teri-terry

I hope you enjoyed reading *The Stepdaughter's Lie*. Reviews make so much difference! If you can spare the time to write a review, I'd love to hear what you think. It makes such a difference helping new readers discover one of my books for the first time.

I also love hearing from my readers – you can get in touch on social media or my website.

Thanks very much,

Teri Terry

KEEP IN TOUCH WITH TERI

teriterry.com

facebook.com/TeriTerryAuthor
x.com/TeriTerryWrites
instagram.com/TeriTerryWrites
threads.net/TeriTerryWrites

ACKNOWLEDGEMENTS

Thank you to editor Jayne Osborne, who championed this story from fragile beginnings to what it became, as well as everyone at Bookouture – a formidable and dedicated team to have on my side.

To all my writing buddies – the Furies, the Slushies and the Harries – thanks for being there, with tea/wine/chocolate/motivation/sympathy as needed at just the right moments.

I couldn't do this without the support of my family. Graham and Scooby hold down the fort and remind me when I need reminding that there is more to me than words on a page.

I've spent a lot of time and thought debating what, if anything, to say next. Most of the time, I like my story and characters to speak for themselves. But here goes.

In part, I write to exorcise my own demons – things that worry or scare me, keep me awake at night. Sometimes they sneak into what I'm writing without plan and that is what happened with this story. At some level I was still processing Roe v. Wade being reversed by the US Supreme Court, and Grace and Ellie appeared on the page and demanded to be heard.

Many US states banned abortion almost completely after this decision. I live in the UK and the prevailing view is that this could never happen here, but abortion is still a crime under UK law. It is only legal if authorised by two doctors, acting in good faith, within specified exceptions. There is a postcode lottery as to what services are available where you live. There have also been a number of recent cases of women having criminal charges brought for having an abortion outside the exceptions to the law. Apart from their tragic stories, if women who suffer miscarriage are afraid to seek medical care in case they are accused of ending their pregnancy deliberately, their health is at risk.

Banning or restricting access to abortion increases unsafe abortions, avoidable injuries and preventable deaths. Desperation can lead to horrific consequences. Given the chance, Grace would have had an unsafe abortion or killed herself. Even Ellie, a girl with resources and opportunities, was willing to risk taking abortion medication bought online – something she could have been charged with in the UK, if Rowan hadn't found it first.

If you are affected by issues raised, in the UK we have the free and confidential National Sexual Health Helpline. There is also BPAS, the British Pregnancy Advisory Service. In Canada there is the Access Line, a confidential helpline provided by Action Canada.

In the US, the Guttmacher Institute – a pro-choice research group – has extensive information about the volatile legal situation, including an interactive map by state of US abortion policies and access after the Roe v. Wade reversal.

Finally – no matter your stance in all of this, thank you for coming along and reading Rowan, Ellie and Grace's stories. As for what I think, Eva Burch, a senator in Arizona, said it so well in her floor speech on 18th March 2024. Heartbreaking, brave and powerful. You'll find it in a search if you want to listen.

PUBLISHING TEAM

Turning a manuscript into a book requires the efforts of many people. The publishing team at Bookouture would like to acknowledge everyone who contributed to this publication.

Audio
Alba Proko
Sinead O'Connor
Melissa Tran

Commercial
Lauren Morrissette
Hannah Richmond
Imogen Allport

Cover design
Lisa Horton

Data and analysis
Mark Alder
Mohamed Bussuri

Editorial
Jayne Osborne
Imogen Allport

51259470R00203